To my dear friend Jay;
we owe it to the
future to make it
bright!

Sylvia
Brand

RICHIE ETWARU

DEDICATION

To my wife Vashti, and our two children, Aarjun and Aakash
Etwaru.

AFTER READING THIS NOVEL,
YOU MAY NEVER CLICK "I ACCEPT"
EVER AGAIN.

When Sylvia Brand reports for work on Monday morning, she discovers her lascivious, sexist manager has been abruptly transferred, and Sun Motors has replaced him with a genderless robot. At first, Sylvia and her co-workers are overjoyed to discover that Carin, the robot, is very nearly the perfect boss: unfailingly polite, eager to help solve problems, and dedicated to making the office a better team. As the days pass, Sylvia readily agrees to an increasingly invasive series of company policies - after all, she reasons, Sun Motors is a good place to work. But little by little, Sylvia is pulled into a totalitarian nightmare. After being sent to a secret facility to serve as a captive source of medical data, she embarks on a life-or-death journey to freedom to save both herself and her unborn child.

ACKNOWLEDGMENTS

This book would not have come to life without the support and encouragement of thousands of individuals in over seventy-five countries that continue to support the 31st Human Right: "everyone has the right to legal ownership of their inherent human data as property."

Specific thanks to Jim MacLeod for the cover design and illustrations, and Thomas Hauck for the editing.

PREFACE

I was probably about seven years old, and from my memory I lived on the veranda. My parents lived in a modest house in a poor village surrounding a sugarcane factor in the countryside of Guyana, an ex-British colony in South America. The veranda was the place to be, it gives you the best panorama of the village, the roads and the farmlands, and it was painted in blue and white, my favorite colors. It had all the ingredients for a super cool child's hangout, there was danger – you could fall down, there was privilege – it was a precious part of the house, and for me, there was freedom – it was the closest I could get to the birds, the electrical wires that ran near the house, and the sky, all of the things and places that helped me dream.

My father, a part time electrician and a full-time schoolteacher had already taught me about capacitors, transformers, and the ability to manufacture electricity. I'd experimented with hydroelectricity, and magnets, and all shapes and sizes of batteries from watch batteries to car batteries. Batteries were my quest. Most of my toys needed batteries, and the battle to get my parents to purchase more batteries for me to play with my toys was getting more and more difficult. I needed rechargeable batteries. I needed to find a way to capture and store energy, and redirect it to my battery-operated toy cars, trucks, and airplane.

I was never successful, and I suffered the pain of having to beg for new batteries, but I came close once. I was convinced that I could turn a paper pinwheel into a wind-powered electricity capture-source to power my toys. And the best place to mount these paper pin wheels was my veranda. I was seven. This is where the wind was. For days I experimented, weeks I dreamed, never catching a breakthrough. Lots of paper, lots of pins and glue, wood, wires, my father's soldering iron, his multi-tester to test voltage, and the ruin of several toys whose circuits I had fried.

My last hoorah was "Project Boost", I would mount four pin wheels in the front grill of my father's car and hope for a mega capture of electricity to be stored in a capacitor which I had learned how to strap to the toys with rubber bands. But Project Boost was quickly cancelled by both my parents, unanimously as it was above a danger threshold. I'd failed. And by eight, a brand called Eveready batteries distributed rechargeable AA batteries to my country, and my childhood took a turn for the better.

I'd forgotten all about Project Boost until October 10th, 2017. I was in an Uber which was a Tesla Model S, an electric car, and I was being driven over the Øresund Bridge which was one of the longest bridges in Europe connecting Sweden and Denmark. The Øresund Bridge is the longest combined road and rail bridge in Europe and connects two major metropolitan areas: Copenhagen, the Danish capital city, and the Swedish city of Malmö. If you're in an electric car, you want to check to make sure you don't need a recharge of your battery when going over one of the longest combined road and rail bridges in Europe. The Uber driver was a tall lean Anglo-Saxon man, he was in his 50s and dressed is a semi distinguished manner. His grey hair was crafted, he looked like Nordic intellectual royalty, and he spoke English with a distain only the French can top. He said to me "I will need a recharge on land."

I knew what he meant instantly. He was low on battery, and we were on a very long bridge. I figured I would talk to him to reduce any nervousness he might feel, and any embarrassment he might embrace. Right, I was talking to him to distract myself from nervousness that could build as a foreigner who knew no one in Denmark other than my co-workers who I was heading to meet with, and was about to be stuck in a car with dead battery on a long bridge in the middle of what definitely looked like nowhere. He met my chit chat with very stoic remarks. The one that stood out was "you can relax, we have very good wind on the Lillgrund." The Lillgrund is the largest offshore wind farm in Sweden, and as I looked out to the right of the car from the back seat of a Tesla, I saw the most beautiful sea of towering white wind turbines I had ever seen. From afar, it looks like a pasture of grey-white beautiful paper pin wheels, spinning magnanimously, on a beautiful blue ocean. And we, my seemingly pleasant but stoic driver were going to stop and re-charge the battery of a Tesla on land, with electric power that came from wind turbines, large paper pin wheels.

A little over thirty years after the cancellation of Project Boost unanimously by both of my parents, my entire mind went back to the veranda, with vivid imagery and deep emotional tug. Paper pin wheels. Nikola Tesla, Elon Musk, my Uber driver, and me.

It had happened again.

Something which I imagined, had come to reality and happened a few decades after. It drains you. You ask yourself if you are special, lazy, stupid, blessed, or cursed. You feel a mix of emotions, you feel anger, regret, and you feel a sense of responsibility. Responsibility for not having the courage to follow through.

Today I still dream.

I no longer have my parent's veranda. I live in the mountains of Northern New Jersey in the United States. I look out my windows of my home office at the trees, birds, wild turkeys, deer and squirrels. My two toddler sons chatter in the aftermath of my thoughts, and only my wife has veto power on any of my projects.

I am sharing this story with you the reader so that you can see what I see, and you might be motivated to act. Unlike the bright abundant energy future for humans I saw on the veranda with paper pin wheels, today I see a dark future for humans. We became the energy source. Action will not bring anything new to life, instead it stops something terrible from happening. I present to you Sylvia Brand, a fictitious character in my dreams, and her story to regain her data dignity.

CHAPTER ONE

Sylvia peered over the top of her cubicle. From her desk she had a clear view of the doorway leading to the executive offices. No one was coming or going. She glanced at her computer screen. The time was fifteen minutes after nine. She looked back at the door. Her stomach tightened and the familiar tension crawled up the back of her neck.

Through the door a man entered the room of cubicles. It was Joe, the regional logistics manager. A harmless guy. Actually rather nice, but in his own little world. He was eating a bagel while looking at his phone. He stopped to speak to one of the employees before quickly moving on. He was like that—friendly and thankfully not pushy.

Sylvia could feel her hands becoming clammy. She wiped them on her skirt. Damn! Why did this have to happen? All she ever wanted was to enjoy her job, be a good company person, get regular promotions, and look forward to well deserved retirement when she turned sixty. That's the way it was supposed to be at Sun Motors. The company's mission statement said, "We value equity, equal opportunity, and employee empowerment." The slogan was emblazoned all over the website and on every company report. But what did it mean in real life? As far as Sylvia was concerned, it meant that Randolph Meekin was empowered to put his hands on her, make lascivious comments, and generally act like an oversexed creep, all without facing any consequences.

She glanced again at the digital time display on her screen. Nine eighteen. On a Monday morning it was unusual for Meekin to have not yet made an appearance in the office. He wanted to be seen so his employees would know he was present and observant. You could call it "controlling." He was a control freak.

She picked up her phone and punched a number.

"Judy?" she said. "Have you seen him yet? No? Hey, maybe it's our lucky day, and he's got the flu. It's going around. Let his wife take care of him for a week and give us girls a break. See you at the meeting at ten."

Sylvia took a deep breath and slowly exhaled. The pain in the back of her head intensified. Relax, she told herself. Stay loose and maybe it will go away. Don't want to take a painkiller so early in the day. She checked her screen. No reply yet from human resources. Last week she had lost her patience with Meekin and had filed a formal complaint—her first.

He had come into the office at the end of the day, when people were going home. Sylvia had been at her desk trying to track down a shipment of battery current sensors due from the supplier in Mexico. The existing inventory was down to just one day, and shutting down the assembly line of the highly profitable Comanche truck because of one part was not what anyone wanted. Meekin had circled the room, and while she was on the phone speaking to the trucking company dispatcher she had forgotten to track Meekin's location.

Suddenly she felt hands gently grasp each of her shoulders. Without seeing, she knew to whom they belonged. She stiffened, put her hand over the phone mouthpiece, and turned her head.

"Mr. Meekin—I'm talking to a dispatcher," she hissed.

"And I'm sure you're doing a fine job," he said with a smile. With his fingers he gave her shoulders a tender squeeze.

"Julio, just tell me the truck has cleared customs," Sylvia said into the phone. "I can't tell from the RFID tag. Yes? Okay. Gracias. Buenas tardes." She hung up.

"See?" said Meekin. "It all worked out. Everything will be fine." He eased his hands down the outsides of her arms nearly to her elbows before sliding back towards her neck. "You seem tense. Relax—it's almost quitting time." He leaned down so that Sylvia could feel his warm breath against her ear. "You look especially nice today. Got a date tonight?"

"No."

"We should go out for a drink," he said. He paused and Sylvia could sense him peering intently down at her chest from his position just above her right shoulder. "Is that a black bra you're wearing? Wow, that is so hot. Do you realize how hot you are?"

Instinctively Sylvia reached for the top button of her blouse, which—how foolishly!—she had left open that morning, revealing the slightest glimpse of skin and lace. With fumbling fingers she quickly buttoned it.

"Mr. Meekin, this is extremely inappropriate," she said. She could feel the muscles of her jaw begin to twitch.

"The only thing inappropriate is how unfriendly you're being," he replied. His hands continued their clumsy massage. "Especially considering there's an opening in logistics for a regional manager. Rob Jones is retiring. You could be in the running for that job. But I need team players. You're a team player, aren't you, sweetheart?"

A drop of sweat tickled her forehead. With her hand she quickly wiped it away. "Yes, Mr. Meekin. I'm a team player. But really, this is not appropriate."

Removing his hands from her shoulders, he pivoted to lean against her desk. "I'll tell you something." By this time the workers in the immediate vicinity had left for the day and he was speaking more openly, less furtively. "I like you. You might be able to handle the job. But not yet. Not on your own. I can help you. Show you the ins and outs, so to speak. What do you say?"

"Say about what?" she replied, stalling for time.

He smiled. "You know what I'm talking about. Imagine what that job could mean to you. Bigger salary, more vacation time. But we need the right person. Let's chat about it over dinner tonight."

"Tonight?" Her mind was racing.

Reaching into the neighboring cubicle, Meekin pulled out the empty chair and sat down. He scooched up until his knees were nearly touching Sylvia's chair. She remained as she was, facing her desk.

"Yes, tonight," he said to the side of her head. "Table for two at the Beaujolais Bistro. We can talk about your future. Get to know each other better." His hand slid onto her knee.

Twisting in her chair to face him, she pushed away, leaving his hand hanging in midair. He showed a humorless smile as with feigned nonchalance he clasped both hands together with one elbow resting lightly on her desk. His greedy eyes slid down to her legs.

"I'm so sorry," she said. "Tonight I have a board meeting. At the church. I've got to grab dinner there."

His eyes narrowed into reptilian slits. "That's too bad. I want to talk about your future. It could be very bright." His eyebrows came together in a frown. "You're not saying no, are you? That would be a big mistake. I could do a lot for you. I have influence not only at Sun Motors but at the upper levels of the Industrial Council."

"I understand that. I'm not ungrateful. But tonight is not going to work. Why don't we talk in your office tomorrow?"

"My office?" he shrugged. "Maybe. We'll see." He stood up and leaned closer, with one hand on her desk. "You really are super hot. I hope you know that. I wouldn't waste my time on just anybody. Do you understand?"

"Yes, Mr. Meekin."

With one last appraising look up and down, he sauntered away.

When he had left the room, Sylvia began shaking and her stomach churned as if she were going to throw up. She could not hold back her tears. Without bothering to shut off her computer, she grabbed her purse and ran to the door.

After a sleepless night, the next day she had gone to human resources and filed a complaint.

"Do you really want to do this?" said the assistant manager, a woman named Estelle. "Of course you have very right, but it's going to be rough. Mr. Meekin will attack you. Call you a liar. He's been with the company for over a decade. People respect him. You could be destroying your career. Is there anybody who can corroborate your story?"

In fury Sylvia had said to Estelle, "Corroborate my story? Are you kidding? All you have to do is get off your ass and talk to any woman in the logistics office. He does it to all of us."

"Excuse me?" Estelle's eyes flamed. "Do you know to whom you're speaking?"

"I'm sorry—forgive me. Don't take it personally. But do you know why the turnover rate in our department is off the charts? I can name you three girls who have left in just the past six months. All for the same reason—Randolph Meekin. You should know—it's your office that hires them and puts them there, and then takes their separation papers. It's a horrible environment."

"As long as the Industrial Council approves, there are no violations," Estelle had replied. Grudgingly—so it seemed to Sylvia—she took the form Sylvia had filled out. "After we process this," she had told Sylvia, "we'll call you in for a formal interview. Up until that time, you can withdraw your complaint. But after the interview, the wheels will start turning. Mr. Meekin will be notified and will have the right to respond. Do you understand?"

Sylvia had nodded yes.

For the remainder of the week her interactions with Meekin had been tense—or at least she had been tense, while he had seemed maddeningly relaxed and confident. Together they had reviewed the contracts for the new supplier of Comanche ignition relays. And the center link contract was put out for bidding—a company in Ireland was the frontrunner, and Sylvia was hoping to wrangle a visit to inspect the factory. It was always nice to get out of Detroit for a few days, especially to get away from Randolph Meekin.

In his pursuit of the women in the office he was relentless, and if one evaded his snare, another might be caught. A few months earlier Sylvia and Meekin had been slated to fly together to visit the Sun Motors assembly plant in Hermosillo, Sonora, Mexico. They would have stayed overnight at the Hermosillo Marriott. The plan had filled her heart with terror and disgust. In panic, she had concocted a story about needing surgery that same week. Nothing serious, she took pains to say, but it simply had to be done, and that was the only week the hospital could fit her in.

Oh—what hospital? Meekin had asked.

A clinic in Canada, she had said. I'd really rather not discuss it.

Sylvia was not surprised to learn that Meekin had then recruited a young assistant manager named Pamela to go with him to Hermosillo. Sylvia didn't know whether to feel sorry for Pamela (if she were simply naïve) or to condemn her for selling herself to gain favor with Meekin. But the following week, after Sylvia's "surgery" and the trip to Mexico, Pamela seemed edgy and tense. A few days after that, she was transferred to the Sun assembly plant in Kansas City, Missouri. That was the last Sylvia heard of her.

And now it was Monday morning. Sylvia knew that Meekin wouldn't give up. That was his pattern. He'd hit on you hard for a few days and then back off when he sensed he wasn't getting anywhere. He'd be nice for a while before circling around, like a wolf, for another run at his prey.

Sylvia checked her personal email on her phone. There was a message from the executive placement agency. They had reviewed her resume and wanted her to come in for an interview. With the automobile industry having rebounded after the devastating Global Depression, Sylvia knew that other companies were hiring. There was no reason for her to live in misery under the leering eye of Randolph Meekin. Despite having worked at Sun for her entire adult life—the summer after high school graduation she had started as an intern—she felt she had no choice. It was time for her to join the other women who, seeking professional respect and a collegial work environment, had fled the Sun Motors Detroit Assembly Plant logistics office.

At ten o'clock, with still no sign of Meekin, Sylvia went to the contracts team meeting. He would attend because as the director of plant logistics, vendor contracts were an important part of his portfolio. As Sylvia approached the door to the conference room she steeled herself for a bad experience. Oh, he'd probably be all right during the meeting itself—there were usually three men and four women present, and Meekin knew enough to behave himself in public situations—but it was likely he'd ask one of the girls to stay behind, or meet him in his office. It was like a twisted game of Russian roulette—you never knew if the chamber with the bullet would be aimed at you.

She walked in and sat next to Judy. Soon Mei Lien, Edouardo, Roger, Maxwell, and Lauren came in and took their seats.

After a few minutes, Roger asked, "Has anyone seen Mr. Meekin this morning?"

The answer was no.

"I'll give him a call," said Lauren. She picked up his phone. After a moment she said, "Strange—his voicemail went to a generic box."

"I'll go to his office," said Maxwell.

The members of the contracts team sat around the table and waited. After a few minutes Maxwell returned. "He's not in his office," he said. "His desk is clean. I mean all the papers are gone. No family photos. His football signed by Joe Montana is gone. His diplomas are off the wall. All that's left is the phone and the computer."

"That's bizarre," replied Mei Lien. "I saw him here on Friday. We were among the last to leave at closing time. He seemed perfectly normal. He said that he wanted to be sure to go over the quarterly report this morning. Then he said, 'Have a good weekend.'"

"What are we supposed to do?" asked Judy. "We need him to sign off on a bunch of proposals and approve the production numbers for the next quarter."

At that moment a man appeared at the door. Sylvia had never seen him before. Middle-aged, dressed in a gray suit, white shirt, and narrow necktie. His hair was close cropped, like a member of the military. Very old school.

"Pardon me," he said. "This is the contracts team, is it not?"

They replied it was.

The man entered the room. "My name is Howard Starling. I'm the vice president of human resources for the company. I normally work in the Sun Motors building downtown. I know this is a bit unexpected, but I hope to have a few minutes of your time." He took the seat at the head of the table, where Meekin usually sat. "I'm sure you're wondering where Randolph is. He's been transferred to corporate. He'll be working downtown. As for your team, the Detroit Assembly Plant has been selected for an innovative new pilot program named Bright Horizon. Starting today, the combined positions of director of logistics and director of operations will be performed by Carin."

"Carin," repeated Maxwell. "Is that someone's name?"

"In a sense, yes," replied Starling with a smile. "Carin is an autonomous humanoid operator."

"You mean like a robot?" asked Sylvia.

"We don't like to use that term because it conjures up all sorts of outdated images—you know, clumsy clanking machines with blinking lights. Carin is something quite different. However, 'robot' is a familiar label and I'll admit to using it out of a sense of convenience." He glanced at his phone. "Ah— instead of us sitting here and talking about Carin, let's go meet him."

"Him?" asked Judy.

Starling stood up. "To be honest, Carin has no gender. That was a deliberate design decision. But because of the limitations of the English language, the only gender-free pronoun we have is the word 'it.' But no one wants to call Carin 'it.' To do so would seem heartless and rude. But to call Carin 'he' or 'she' would be equally inaccurate. So we're stuck. Some linguists have proposed a gender-free human-like pronoun in the form of 'dee.' The object form would be 'deem.' So if you were to say, "She gave the assignment to her," then the gender-free version would be, 'Dee gave the assignment to deem.'" Starling shrugged. "I don't know how it's going to be resolved. So for now, you can call Carin either 'he' or 'she.' It doesn't matter. Carin doesn't care."

"What does Carin look like?" asked Mei Lien.

"You'll see for yourself in just a few minutes," replied Starling. "But so that we will not be tempted to talk about Carin in front of him, I'll take this opportunity to say a few things about the design approach. The key thing is that the project executives and builders agreed it would be a mistake to produce an entity that appears exactly human, or which at first glance could be mistaken for a human. We're fully aware of the principle of the 'uncanny valley,' and have made every effort to avoid that problem."

"What's the uncanny valley?" asked Roger.

"As a robot becomes increasingly human in appearance, real people—you and I—are more likely to be able to relate to it and to form an emotional attachment to it," said Starling. "We're more likely to empathize with it, as we would a pet dog or cat. The field is called social robotics, which is related to anthropomorphism. This common human tendency is used to facilitate social interactions between humans and social robots. The objective is to give robots social behaviors that are sufficiently credible for human users to engage in comfortable and productive relations with them.

"If you were to plot it on a graph, the level of empathy would continue to rise as the robot became increasingly human in appearance and behavior.

"The problem is that when a social robot looks very nearly human but still retains some subtle mechanical qualities, people who interact with it feel not attraction but revulsion. The almost-human robot suddenly seems creepy and disturbing. On the graph, the level of human attraction suddenly dips. This is called the uncanny valley—the 'valley' referring to the dip in the graph. The concept was first identified in 1970 by the robotics professor Masahiro Mori as 'bukimi no tani genshō,' which was first translated by Jasia Reichardt as 'uncanny valley' in her 1978 book Robots: Fact, Fiction, and Prediction.

"Then, as the robot's appearance continues to be more and more human-like, the emotional response again becomes positive and can approach human-to-human empathy levels.

"The zone of repulsive response aroused by a robot with appearance and motion between a 'barely human' and 'fully human' entity is the uncanny valley. In the design of Carin, instead of trying to cross the uncanny valley, we stopped short, and aimed for an appearance that we call 'humanesque.'"

He went to the door. "Carin will be working out of Mr. Meekin's old office. He doesn't really need a personal space—he could work from anywhere—but from time to time he'll need to speak privately with a team member, just like any other supervisor. So we gave him an office."

CHAPTER TWO

Starling led the group down the hall to Room 320. They went inside. Sitting behind the desk was a humanoid figure of average proportions, dressed in a plain, one-piece jumpsuit. The hair was short and dark. The mouth was closed, with the pinkish lips turned up in a vaguely friendly smile. The skin was a pale brown, suggesting no particular race. The ears resembled those you would see on a department store mannequin—ear-shaped but nonfunctional.

Carin was clearly not human. Sylvia noted that the entire structure seemed to be simplified, without any of the idiosyncratic details that distinguish one person from another. If there were one word that Sylvia would have used to describe Carin's appearance, it would be "generic." Carin was a generic humanoid entity, as if you had taken photos of thousands of people of different ages, genders, and races, and had combined them into one.

This was comforting. Suddenly Sylvia knew what Mr. Starling had been talking about in his discussion of the uncanny valley: Carin appeared human enough to relate to, but not exactly human enough to provoke feelings of revulsion. He was a perfectly likeable robot.

"Why don't we introduce ourselves?" said Starling.

Carin stood up. His height was average for a man. His eyes—or rather his two eye-like cameras that were obscured, Sylvia noted, behind a pair of what looked like sleek, form-fitting tinted glasses, giving him a vaguely athletic look—scanned the room.

"Pleased to meet you," said Carin, his mouth and lips moving effectively enough so that Sylvia could believe the sounds were being formed not by a hidden speaker but by air passing through a pharynx and over tongue and teeth. The timbre of the voice was somewhere between masculine and feminine—Sylvia couldn't decide if it was a man with a high voice or a woman with a low voice.

After the five members of the contracts team had given their names and job titles, Carin smiled with the corners of his mouth and said, "Throughout the day today, I'll be meeting with each of you individually. The goal is to get to know you better and learn more about how I can help you succeed at your jobs. I strongly believe in team cooperation. As a leader, my policy is to share the credit for our successes while taking responsibility for our shortcomings. There is an old saying by the Chinese philosopher Lao Tzu: 'A leader is best when people barely know he exists. When his work is done, his aim fulfilled, they will say: we did it ourselves.' This I believe. I also believe in the words of Woodrow Wilson: 'You are not here merely to make a living. You are here in order to enable the world to live more amply, with greater vision, with a finer spirit of hope and achievement. You are here to enrich the world, and you impoverish yourself if you forget the errand.' At Sun Motors, our job is to help people and their possessions get from one place to another safely, reliably, and pleasurably. This is our mission and our goal.

"You are aware that I'm not a human being. I will tell you that I'm aware of this also. While human beings have many remarkable qualities of which I can claim to possess only a very few, I will promise you that I care not for material gain and do not seek personal power. My role is to do the very best in the position to which I've been assigned. As you may have been told, I'm assuming the dual roles of director of operations and director of logistics for this facility. Traditionally these roles have been performed by two people, but my data processing and decision making capabilities allow me to identify and exploit untapped efficiencies, and my designers believe it's advantageous that I perform both." Carin paused. "Are there any questions so far?"

"If you don't mind me asking a personal question," said Sylvia, "who exactly are—or were—your designers? From where have you come?"

"I was designed and built by Morta Laboratories in San Mateo, California. Technically, I'm a Morta AHO 6-C. That means autonomous humanoid operator, model 6, version C. While some of my components have been functioning independently for almost a year—being tested and so forth—I came online as Carin exactly four months, three days, and six hours ago. Since then I've been in training. I arrived in Detroit on Saturday afternoon. This is my first day on the job at this facility."

Sylvia had heard about Morta Laboratories. It was a privately held company that did a lot of classified defense work in advanced robotics. This was the first time she had heard of a Morta product being used in a civilian setting.

"As far as your day-to-day jobs are concerned," continued Carin, "nothing will change. I'll function the same way as my predecessor. As I said before, my goal is to help you succeed. I'm what they call a 'servant leader.' If you have a problem you cannot solve, my first priority is to ensure you have the appropriate training to find the solution. I may then actively step in to assist you. I believe you're all highly qualified and we're going to make a great team. Now then, I see it's already twenty minutes past ten. We need to move ahead with our contracts meeting. Let's adjourn to the conference room, where everyone can sit at the table."

The group, without Starling, who had excused himself, went down the hall to the conference room. Sylvia noted that Carin walked with confidence, albeit a bit stiffly, like an older person with a mild case of arthritis.

To Sylvia's pleasant surprise, the meeting was efficient and businesslike, with none of the little psychological games in which Meekin routinely indulged and the subtle arrows he aimed at his staff. Carin was unfailingly polite and managed the discussion well. Maxwell volunteered that he was having a problem getting an acceptable price from a potential vendor of tie rod ends. The vendor wanted a minimum order of thirty thousand units to meet the price Maxwell was authorized to pay, and Maxwell only needed twenty thousand. They were at an impasse. Carin nodded and said, "Twenty thousand units is the quantity you need for the Comanche truck for the next six months. But you're going to need another five thousand for the Army's new mobile strike vehicle. Production is going to begin at this facility next year. It's exactly the same part."

"I've heard some rumors about the Army vehicle contract," said Maxwell, "but that's all it's been—just rumors. Is the Army ramping up for war with Rodinia?"

Carin smiled. "The threat from Rodinia continues to be very real, and we must be prepared. As far as the contract goes, nothing is signed yet, but based on available data, I calculate the chances of Sun Motors winning the Army contract at ninety percent. Those are good odds. Offer your vendor an order for twenty-five thousand. Don't tell them about the Army contract. What is your vendor asking per unit?"

"Twenty-eight dollars. I'm authorized to pay up to twenty five."

"Who's the vendor?"

"Maxx Systems. In Lumberton, North Carolina."

"They have problems. They're going to be sued by the state for dumping toxic solvents into the Lumber River. It won't put them out of business, but it will cost them money, and they may lose contracts from organizations that have environmental concerns. Mention the investigation into the pollution. Offer them twenty-six dollars per unit, take it or leave it. We'll make up the difference from the Army."

"Okay," said Maxwell. "Thanks. I'll do that."

"And by the way," added Carin, "if for some reason we don't get the Army contract and we have five thousand extra tie rod ends, we'll sell them to Star Automotive Group at a discount. The tie rod ends used by most of their Polaris trucks are nearly the same—the only difference is a couple of two-dollar bushings. Or we'll unload them on an aftermarket parts dealer.

Either way, don't worry. We can't lose."

At one o'clock, Sylvia, Mei Lien, and Judy went out for their usual lunch at a local eatery. Once they had been seated in their booth Judy said, "Well, what do you guys think of Carin?"

"I suppose we shouldn't be surprised that our new boss is a robot," replied Mei Lien. "At first the idea seemed strange, but when you think about it, the plant is full of robots. We have robots on the assembly line that perform quality control tests and are authorized to shut down the line if there's a problem. Many members of our janitorial staff are robots. We have fleets of autonomous city buses and delivery vehicles operating on the streets of Detroit. We have cargo ships that sail themselves from port to port, and rockets that take off and land without human guidance. So it's a logical next step that the company would put an autonomous humanoid operator in a management position. After all, we humans are just cogs in the big machine—not much different than the robots doing spot welding on the assembly line."

"Personally," said Sylvia, "I think that getting rid of creepy Randolph Meekin and replacing him with a nice, friendly robot who hasn't got his brain in his pants is a dream come true. Ladies, I feel better already. The reign of terror is over!" She paused, as if performing an internal self-assessment. "Wow—I'm amazed that my headache has gone away. My neck doesn't seem as stiff. My stomach isn't tied in knots." She raised her glass of wine. "I propose a toast to a new beginning. A workplace where we don't have to live in fear of our Neanderthal boss putting his hairy hands all over us and making gross comments and using his position of authority to threaten us."

"To a new beginning," agreed Judy.

"I hope so," said Mei Lien. "But what do you think will really change? Meekin now works downtown. It sounds like he got a promotion. What does that say about Sun Motors? And why did they choose our office for this robot manager pilot program? I'm not convinced. There's something fishy going on. Sun Motors is one of the largest privately held companies in America. We know nothing about what happens on the top floors of the Sun building downtown. I mean, aside from our chairman, president, and CEO, Hugh Atkinson, who delivers his annual message to us on our computer screens, have you ever seen a member of the Atkinson family?"

"No," said Sylvia. "They keep a very low profile. But it doesn't matter to me. All I want is to do a good job, keep the Comanche trucks rolling off the assembly line, and go home every night. I don't care what they did with Randolph Meekin. I don't care if he works downtown or in Brazil, as long as he's nowhere near me. Ugh! What a pig he was. I'm sorry, but there's just no other word to describe him." She raised her glass and downed the last of her wine. "God, this stuff tastes like two-buck Chuck," she grimaced.

"What do you expect at a place like this?" laughed Judy.

"I don't care if it's from the bottom of the barrel—I'll have another," said Sylvia as she turned to search for the server.

"Do you think you should?" asked Mei Lien.

"Today we celebrate," replied Sylvia. "And you've got to admit that Carin is pretty sharp. The way he analyzed Maxwell's contract problem was amazing. He saw the situation, crunched the numbers, calculated the odds, and provided a solution. What a breath of fresh air! Meekin would have said,"—and here she lowered her voice to a slow drawl—"'Uh, Maxwell, I'm going to have to get back to you on that. We need to evaluate this carefully. You keep working on it, okay?' Of course, Meekin would have ignored the problem until Maxwell either gave up or made a decision on his own that Meekin could then criticize. Oh, Meekin was very good at avoiding responsibility! Whatever you did that was good he'd take credit for, and if you screwed up he'd tell everyone how hard it was to work with incompetent people."

"Yeah," nodded Judy. "Remember when Roger proposed that we use the same speed sensor both the Comanche and the new SUV? The company would save twenty dollars per car. When the engineers gave it the green light, Meekin walked around and bragged that it was his idea. What a jerk."

Sylvia's phone rang. She glanced at it. "Sorry, ladies, I need to take this," she said. "Hey Jason, how's it going?"

Mei Lien and Judy exchanged glances. The call was from a man who for the past six months Sylvia had refused to identify as her boyfriend.

"Wednesday night?" said Sylvia. "Yes, I'm free. What do you have in mind? You have tickets for the Linz String Quartet chamber music concert? Yes, that sounds like fun. Dinner at six o'clock? Okay, see you then." She hung up.

"Sylvia, you hate chamber music," teased Judy.

"That's not true," she replied. "I'm getting used to it. It's growing on me."

"But Jason isn't officially your boyfriend," said Mei Lien. "Is he worth the investment?"

"Why not?" replied Sylvia. "I believe in being flexible and open to new things. And what else am I going to do on Wednesday night? Sit by myself and watch old movies? Please!"

"Something's going on," said Judy. "On a Wednesday night Jason is taking you to dinner and a romantic concert. He hasn't been to a jewelry store lately, has he?"

"Oh, come on!" said Sylvia. "Don't be silly. I think you guys have too much time on your hands and you spend it by dreaming up these fantasies. Anyway, if Jason and I go to the next level, you'll be the first to know." She glanced at her phone. "I need to get back to the office. I have a meeting with Carin."

SYLVIA BRAND

CHAPTER THREE

Sylvia stepped into Carin's office.

"Please close the door," said Carin. After giving Sylvia a perfunctory smile his face returned to its default expression of vague friendliness. Sylvia took the chair opposite. They sat for a moment in silence. It was then that Sylvia became aware of a faint whirring sound coming from behind Carin. Boldly, she said, "You have a cooling fan?"

"You have the mind of an engineer," smiled Carin. "Yes, I do. Humans, like all mammals, generate body heat, and so do we; but since we neither breathe nor perspire, we need a mechanical cooling system. However, our designers are working to eliminate all unnecessary moving parts, so future versions of the AHO 6 are expected to have a passive cooling system. Now then—enough about me. You've been with Sun Motors since you were eighteen years old. That's rather remarkable."

"Yes, I began as an intern."

"After graduating from college with a degree in mechanical engineering you were hired as a process engineering specialist at the West River plant in Kansas City. After two years you were transferred to this facility as a controls engineer before taking the position of associate logistics manager. You are presently a senior logistics manager. Your impressive work history with Sun Motors means that you are, of course, familiar with the company's code of conduct."

Sylvia felt the blood rise in her face. "Yes, of course," she replied. "Why do you ask?"

"At this moment you are showing a blood alcohol level of point zero three five. This is not enough to cause impairment—you would not be placed under arrest if you were stopped by a police officer while driving—but it indicates that, as a woman who weighs one hundred and forty pounds, you've consumed two drinks within the past hour. My guess is that it was two glasses of red wine—Burgundy, to be exact. Company policy discourages the consumption of alcohol during working hours, does it not?"

"How are you determining my blood alcohol level?" asked Sylvia.

"A breathalyzer test. I'm equipped to monitor the air quality in my immediate area. Also, given the level of light in this room, your eyes are dilated more than normal. Your skin is also slightly flushed, indicating increased blood flow into your dermal capillaries. These observations confirm the breathalyzer test."

Sylvia leaned forward and looked into Carin's eyes. "Am I in violation of company policy or am I not?"

"You are not visibly impaired, therefore you are not."

"Then why did you mention it?"

"Out of concern for your health and welfare."

"Oh? Is that part of your job description?"

"Yes," replied Carin with a smile. "As the director of logistics and operations, an important part of my portfolio is to maintain the highest possible level of employee engagement. Key metrics include levels of employee happiness, physical and mental health, job satisfaction, and turnover rates. I want all of our employees to feel as though they are a valued part of the Sun Motors family. We all share the same goals and desire to make the world a better place through the work we do here."

"Will my two glasses of cheap Burgundy at lunch be noted on my employee record?"

"No."

"Then I thank you for your concern and request that we close this topic of discussion. What else would you like to speak with me about?"

"I just want to review a few things," said Carin. "You've been in your current position for one year and seven months. You've been with the department for two years and nine months. Are you happy with your career path?"

"I suppose so. To be honest, when Randolph Meekin was my boss I became discouraged about my prospects for advancement, but now that you've taken over I think I'll be treated more fairly."

"Why did you think you were being treated unfairly by Randolph Meekin?"

Sylvia paused before answering. She suddenly regretted bringing up the name of her former supervisor. Apparently Meekin was still very much employed by Sun Motors, in the downtown headquarters building. It was true that in a company as large as Sun Motors they were unlikely to cross paths again, but it wasn't worth taking the chance that, through Carin, word about what she said about Meekin would trickle back to him. She intended to withdraw her sexual harassment complaint; her reasoning was that since Meekin was no longer lording over her, by pursuing her complaint she had little to gain and much to lose, especially in the eyes of the Industrial Council. As far as she was concerned, she wanted nothing more to do with him, and that included not complaining about him to her new boss.

"Oh, I don't want to get into it," she said. "Sometimes there's friction between a manager and his staff. No one is to blame—it's just a clash of personalities. Some people just naturally click together and some don't. I wish Randolph Meekin nothing but the best in his new position."

With his unblinking eyes fixed on Sylvia, he seemed to purse his thin lips. This, she thought, must be the pre-programmed response to some aspect of the conversation. Suddenly she got the feeling that Carin knew she was not being completely truthful. She said nothing more.

"Of course," said Carin with a little nod. "To return to the matter at hand, I can tell you that your contributions to the success of your department, and by extension the company as a whole, have not gone unnoticed. You're on a good path for future promotions. Does that please you?"

"Yes, very much. I enjoy working at Sun Motors and hope to make my career here."

"I'm happy to hear that." A tablet was lying on the desk. He reached for it and studied the screen for a moment.

"Anything important?" asked Sylvia.

"Oh, just a few pesky forms."

Sylvia thought it was interesting that Carin used the word "pesky." It crossed her mind to ask him how he knew it, but she let it slide.

"As I'm sure you're aware," said Carin, "Sun Motors has begun to compete for federal government contracts. Specifically, we believe we can produce vehicles for the military—products including lightweight personnel carriers, transport trucks, and ultimately weapons platforms. Our forecasts suggest that within the next five years military procurement of such vehicles will rise at least twenty percent, and we intend to get our share of the business." He placed the tablet face up on the desk. Sylvia saw text on the screen but couldn't make out what it said.

"We'll need everyone to pull together on this," said Carin.

"Absolutely," she nodded. "You can count on me one hundred percent."

"Glad to hear it. In order to bring the company into full compliance with Department of Defense contractor requirements, we need to ask all employees to sign some forms. They're nothing serious, and something that every other vendor has to comply with." He slid the tablet across the desk to her. "This is a standard conflict of interest statement. By signing it, you affirm that neither you nor any member of your immediate family hold a DoD position or have input into any DoD procurement process. Basically, the government wants to be certain that you can't award a contract to yourself or someone in your family."

"My brother Charlie is in the Naval Reserves."

"Not a problem."

Sylvia scrolled through the document. It seemed dense but straightforward. Her name, address, and company job title were already filled in. She didn't read every word—that would have taken several minutes and Sylvia didn't want to keep her new boss waiting. With her fingerprint she signed the screen. After positioning the tablet to capture an image of her face, she handed the tablet back to Carin. After glancing at it and tapping on the screen a few times, he slid it back across the desk.

"This one is a confidentiality statement," he said. "It says that you won't sell or distribute the plans or specifications for a contracted military product. Of course you wouldn't do that anyway—you've been at Sun Motors a long time and know all about product development confidentiality."

"Yes, I do," she replied. "Everyone in the office gets calls from industry analysts and reporters from car magazines. We're trained to give them the number of the public relations office and then hang up."

"Good," nodded Carin. "As long as we're on the subject of analysts and the press, the next form—you can swipe to it—is the same thing, only internal. Corporate doesn't want anybody talking about my presence here. At the appropriate time the Bright Horizon pilot program will be announced, but the consensus is that it should come after everyone is satisfied that I'm performing as expected. Since I'm the first autonomous humanoid operator in a large industrial setting, there's going to be a tremendous amount of public interest. We need to control the flow of information."

"Okay," agreed Sylvia as she quickly scanned and then fingerprinted both documents. "We wouldn't want any leaks."

"No, we wouldn't," said Carin as he took the tablet and tapped the screen a few times.

"By the way, can I get copies of those?" asked Sylvia.

"Copies? I'll have to check on that. You see, their very existence is confidential. We can't have documents circulating that reveal we're asking you to refrain from talking about a confidential program, because that in itself would be evidence that such a program existed. Of course these documents will become a part of your employee file in human resources, but access will be tightly controlled. I'm sure you can understand."

"Sure—I get it," said Sylvia with forced aplomb.

"Just one more—I don't want to keep you from your work." He gave her the tablet. "This one is another standard boilerplate form that gives the company the right to conduct workplace drug testing. We may from time to time ask you to submit to a urine test, saliva test, blood test, or any other minimally invasive procedure. We may also use passive data collection methods. The results of such testing may be used to evaluate your overall fitness for DoD contract work. Of course the information will be kept confidential."

She scanned the document. It was several pages long. "I don't know—this seems complicated. Should I have a lawyer look at it?"

Carin's eyes seemed to drill into her. "It's your choice. To be honest, this one is nothing more than an updated version of the one I'm sure you signed nine years ago when you first joined the company."

Sylvia had a vague recollection of signing several forms on her first day as an intern, and then more when she was hired full-time.

"As far as we're concerned," said Carin, "a valid consent form can last ten or even twenty years. But people sometimes challenge the old ones, so we want to use an abundance of caution and have everyone sign this new one."

Sylvia continued to read. After a few moments, Carin leaned closer, as if to speak confidentially. "Don't you trust me?"

"Of course I trust you," replied Sylvia. "But you know how it is. People are always saying that you should never sign a consent form without understanding it completely."

"And they're right!" said Carin. "I couldn't agree more. Now then, what questions do you have? I'd be happy to clear up any areas that are confusing to you."

Sylvia studied the form. Carin sat and watched her. In the office, alone with Carin, Sylvia became increasingly self-conscious. Carin did not move—not even a finger. The only sound in the room was the faint whirring of Carin's cooling fan. In the absence of the usual human micro-motions—the blinking of the eyes, the scratching of an ear, the shifting of weight in the chair, or even the subtle expansion and contraction of the chest as the person breathes—Sylvia was reminded that Carin was a machine. And being a machine, she wondered if Carin were capable of deception. Was it possible that Carin was not being fully truthful? Could Carin have been programmed to carry out some devious scheme?

She felt she had to ask a question, if only to appear to be a thoughtful partner. "It says here," she said, "that I understand that 'only duly authorized company officers, employees, and agents will have access to information furnished or obtained in connection any and all tests; that they will maintain and protect the confidentiality of such information to the greatest extent possible; and that they will share such information only to the extent necessary to make employment decisions and to respond to inquiries or notices from legally authorized entities.' That sounds pretty broad, doesn't it? I mean, what does 'the greatest extent possible' mean?"

"The system is based on trust," replied Carin. "Unfortunately, I'm sure you know that many personal injury lawyers are looking for reasons to sue. They do so much damage to innocent people and organizations! Think about it. Let's say a sophisticated hacker broke into the Sun Motors human resources network and accessed employee data. It was an attack that no one could have defended against. It could have happened to any person or company. Do you think justice would be served by hordes of greedy lawyers filing endless lawsuits against Sun Motors, and threatening the company with bankruptcy and the loss of thousands of jobs? I don't think so. That's why the company needs the same basic protections that you or I would want if we were in the position of safeguarding something valuable. The company will promise to use every reasonable means to protect the integrity of the data it collects. Nothing matters to Sun Motors more than the safety of personal information. And by the way, no one at Sun is exempt from company policies—not even the chief executive officer. We're all one family. We can trust each other."

"Really? Everyone has to sign these same forms?" asked Sylvia.

"No one is exempt from company policies," repeated Carin. There was a moment of silence as Sylvia continued to study the pages of text displayed on the tablet.

"A moment ago you mentioned the passive collection of health data," she said. "What does that mean?"

"Oh, it's just another safeguard," replied Carin. "As you know, all living creatures, and especially mammals, are constantly shedding or excreting or exhaling little bits of themselves into their immediate environment. If at this moment you were to get up and leave the room, you'd leave behind millions of cells from your skin, your respiratory system, your hair. You'd leave behind traces of gases that you've exhaled—including molecules of alcohol from your two glasses of inexpensive Burgundy at lunch today. Even as we speak, all that stuff is floating in the air and settling on the desk and the floor, and even on the walls. Technology has advanced to the point where a machine— like me—can collect those samples and analyze them. Not that we would ever choose to do so. The capability is there. For example, let's say that one of your colleagues at lunch had not two glasses of Burgundy but five, and came back to the office roaring drunk. My sensors would indicate an unacceptably high blood alcohol level, and consequently the person would be legally and appropriately separated from the company. Should the employee who had been fired then sue the company for passively collecting the health data that led to his dismissal? Of course not. The guy was spewing alcohol into the air, and it would be almost impossible not to capture it."

"I suppose that makes sense," said Sylvia. She smiled at Carin. "You're lucky—you don't go around leaving a trail of dead cells wherever you go."

"No, I don't," smiled Carin. "As a human being, your ability to reconstitute yourself by growing new cells to replace the ones that have ceased to function is highly advantageous. But it has its drawbacks. The process of cell growth can be corrupted and lead to disease. But that's a discussion for another time. Do you have any other questions?"

Sylvia continued reading the text on the tablet. Even to a university-trained engineer, the language seemed opaque.

Suddenly Carin reached out his hand. "If you don't wish to sign, that is your right," he said. "But it would be a shame if you were not seen as a team player. And if that were the case, you would have difficulty moving up the corporate ladder. As the company grows, we're looking for people who are one hundred percent committed, and whose applications for transfer or promotion would be readily granted by the Industrial Council. I would hate to see doors close on you because of a silly thing like a routine consent form that, once you signed it like everyone else in your office already has, would be filed away and forgotten."

Carin remained with his hand poised to receive the tablet.

Sylvia felt the atmosphere in the room grow oppressive. Her stomach began to tighten. She had been working at Sun Motors for her entire adult life. She didn't want to throw an obstacle into her career path. By a stroke of fate her tormentor, Randolph Meekin, had been whisked away. Life had suddenly gotten better. Everyone in the logistics office thought Carin was a breath of fresh air—an unbiased, pragmatic manager who solved problems and only wanted the best for the company and its employees. And now the robot was making a simple request, but one that if refused could end her career. And for what? Some imagined invasion of privacy? Heck, the social media sites she routinely visited probably knew more about her than Sun Motors and the Industrial Council ever would.

"I have nothing to hide," she said as she placed her fingertip on the signature square. After adding the snapshot of her face, she handed the tablet back to Carin.

"I'm sorry if I sounded silly about this," she said. "But you can never be too careful."

"I agree completely," smiled Carin as he tapped the screen. "Sylvia, you're a valuable asset to the company because you're a thoughtful person who considers every possibility. I'm sure your future at Sun Motors will be very bright."

CHAPTER FOUR

The next morning Sylvia came to work with a happy heart. As she pulled through the gate of the Sun Motors Detroit Assembly Plant and into the vast employee parking lot, she felt no queasiness in her stomach, no tension in her neck. Her joints were comfortably loose, not bound tightly by rigid muscles. Having slept soundly during the night, she had no need for her usual double espresso to jolt her awake, nor for her bottle of painkillers to soothe her headache. The plant—and by extension the world—seemed to be a brighter, sunnier place than it had been twenty-four hours earlier. There were clouds in the sky, but they were happy clouds, fluffy and white, rather than harbingers of gloom.

She knew exactly why the world had become a more agreeable place: Randolph Meekin, the man who had made her life miserable, was gone. It was only after she had experienced a full workday of emotional and physical freedom did she recognize what her "normal" state had been. Like a captive animal that had become conditioned to its cage, she had gotten so accustomed to Meekin's lascivious tyranny that she had lost perspective and had come to believe she didn't deserve any better. It was like the Stockholm syndrome, in which Meekin was her captor who, over time, made her empathize with him and accept his twisted world view.

A new day was dawning in the Sun Motors Detroit Assembly Plant, and the abused female workers could look forward to being treated with the respect and dignity they deserved.

"Hey, Maxwell, what's up?" she said as she breezed by his cubicle.

"Same old, same old," he replied. And for him, it was probably true—he and the other men in the office had no clue what the women had been going through. Sylvia couldn't blame him, but a little more enlightenment would have been nice. Anyway, it was all moot now. Carin gave every appearance of being a fair, rational manager—and a smart one too, who had a solid grasp of data and knew how to make informed decisions. This new feeling had re-ignited in Sylvia a spirit of competitiveness that she hadn't felt since Meekin had become her supervisor. Sun Motors was going to be a great company for years to come, and Sylvia was proud to make her contribution.

At nine-fifteen she saw Carin come through the door that led to the executive offices. As she worked on returning a batch of defective voltage sensors, she kept an eye on Carin as he made his way around the office. As Carin paused at one cubicle and then another, the atmosphere was congenial and businesslike.

This is what a workplace should be like, she thought.

She called Judy to clarify a parts quantity. Judy worked in a cubicle on the other side of the room, and Sylvia hadn't seen her since the office opened at nine o'clock; but that wasn't unusual, and they generally caught up with each other later in the morning. Sylvia got Judy's voicemail, and she left a message.

Ten minutes later she called again, and again got Judy's voicemail. This time she stood up and peered across the maze of cubicles. Employees were standing here and there, visible from the shoulders up, but Sylvia couldn't tell if Judy was at her desk. Welcoming an excuse to stretch her legs, Sylvia made her way through the cubicle maze to Judy's. At the narrow entrance she paused. Judy's chair was empty and her desk was clean. The photos of her husband and two kids were gone. The birthday cards that her kids had made with crayon were gone. The little framed painting of Ghat Bruno—the self-proclaimed spiritual leader of the religion to which Judy and her family adhered—was gone. The phone was blinking with unanswered calls.

Sylvia took out her personal phone and tapped Judy's home number. Voicemail. Where did her husband Tim work? Judy had told her once… oh yes, he was a carpenter for a local homebuilding contractor. She found the number and tapped it. The receptionist who answered told her that Tim was not on any of the worksites today. Was he expected to be tomorrow? She was not sure, and that's all she could say.

What the hell! Judy had never mentioned making a change. She liked her job and got along well with everyone in the office. What had happened between five o'clock Monday afternoon and nine o'clock Tuesday morning?

At that moment Carin appeared at Judy's cubicle. With her was a young woman.

"Excuse me—I was just looking for Judy," Sylvia said to Carin. "I needed her to confirm the number of backup cameras we need for this week's Comanche production. Do you know where she is?"

"Judy has taken a leave of absence," replied Carin with a smile. "In fact, I'd like you to meet Tameeka White. She'll be filling in for Judy."

"Sylvia Brand," said Sylvia as she extended her hand. "Nice to meet you. So, you're a temp? How long do you expect to be here?"

Tameeka glanced at Carin.

"Tameeka's assignment is open-ended," said Carin. "I'm sure you'll find her to be highly qualified and an effective member of the team." Suddenly Carin appeared distracted. Then he said, "Excuse me. I have a call I need to answer." He walked away.

"You must specialize in last-minute placements," said Sylvia as Tameeka sat down at what was once Judy's desk. "The phone rings at seven in the morning and you've got to be at a new job by nine. Right?"

"Actually, they called me yesterday," said Tameeka. She clicked through with her new password and the computer screen came to life. "They told me to be here today. So here I am."

"What time yesterday?"

"It was early in the afternoon."

"Who called you?"

"The employment agency. They said I should report to human resources, and that I'd be working for someone named Carin." She lowered her voice. "They didn't tell me Carin was a robot! It was quite a surprise. Before I met him, they made me sign a non-disclosure form promising I wouldn't reveal it to anyone. Seems strange—how long do they expect to keep something like that a secret? Anyway, I really hope this turns into a permanent job. I'm tired of being a temp."

"Who made you sign the form?"

"A man named Starling. He met me at the human resources office before he took me to see Carin."

"Okay," said Sylvia. "Once you get settled, I need you to find out the quantity of backup cameras we need this week. I emailed the part number to Judy, and I'll forward it to you. You can call or email me, but I need to know as soon as possible."

"No problem," smiled Tameeka.

Sylvia went to the human resources office. Estelle was behind her desk.

"Are you here to file another grievance?" asked Estelle without looking up from her computer.

"No, not at all," replied Sylvia. "Everything's great. Carin is amazing. But I'm curious about something. What happened to Judy Loring? We worked closely together. This morning, she's gone. Poof—just like that."

Estelle looked at Sylvia over her readers. "You know I can't comment on personnel issues. Ms. Loring has taken an indefinite leave of absence. That's all I'm authorized to say."

"The funny thing is, the temp who has taken her place—Tameeka—was called yesterday afternoon. I saw Judy before the end of the business day at five o'clock. She didn't mention anything about taking a leave of absence."

"She wouldn't be the first employee who kept her plans private," replied Estelle. "Even from her colleagues. Between you and me, if you want an answer I'd look at that crazy religious cult she belongs to."

"You mean the Church of the Golden Way? They seem like a harmless enough group. They preach peace and love and nonviolence. Nothing wrong with that."

"There's nothing wrong with it as long as she does it on her own time. But it seemed like every month she wanted to take a day off for one of their religious holidays. This month she wanted a day off because they were celebrating the birthday of their leader, what's-his-name."

"Ghat Bruno."

"Yes, Ghat Bruno. He's supposed to be one hundred and ten years old."

"Christians celebrate the birth of Jesus, right?"

Scowling, Estelle removed her readers and leaned into Sylvia. "Oh, come on. Every company has reasonable policies about religious holidays. But you can't just join some obscure cult and suddenly want your own special celebrations. What if everybody demanded their own holidays? And then there was the time she wanted to burn incense at her desk. We shot down that idea in a second."

"Okay," said Sylvia. "I see your point. I don't want to argue. But Judy didn't mention anything to this office about a commitment to the Church of the Golden Way?"

"No, she didn't."

Returning to her desk, Sylvia sat and thought for a moment. Who could she call for more information about Judy's sudden absence? She thought the best candidate would be their most recent supervisor, who unfortunately happened to be Randolph Meekin. But she needed a pretext for calling him. It had to be something important about the office. Ah—she could ask him for what he knew about a particular potential contractor in Indonesia. She didn't want to waste time with the contractor if they weren't up to the high standards of Sun Motors. Then, as an afterthought, she could casually ask him if he knew anything about Judy's sudden leave of absence.

Taking a deep breath to steady her nerves, she picked up her phone, tapped the main number of the Sun Building downtown and, after listening to various options, tapped the number for the employee directory. After choosing "M," she waited as the names rolled by: Madson, Mark, Matthews, Mead, Meachum, Meefer, Meehan—and then Meetor and Miner. No Meekin. She tapped "O" for "operator." After a moment a woman answered: "Sun Motors, may I help you?"

"Yes—please connect me to Randolph Meekin."

There was a moment of dead air. Then the operator came back on the line. "Would you please spell the last name?"

"M-E-E-K-I-N. First name Randolph."

More silence. The operator came back. "I'm sorry but there's no one here by that name. Are you sure you want the Sun Motors Building? We have many facilities worldwide."

"I'm sure—but thanks for looking," said Sylvia as she hung up. Stupid phone system—someone hadn't yet put Meekin in the staff directory. And Meekin himself was probably too lazy to demand the process be speeded up.

At lunch hour, Sylvia told Mei Lien and Maxwell that she couldn't join them at the restaurant because she had to run some errands. She drove to Judy's house, an old-fashioned two-story colonial at the end of a cul-de-sac in a suburban neighborhood of professional people and middle managers. Judy's car—a red Sun Motors SUV—was parked in the driveway. Sylvia parked in front of it, went to the garage door, and peered through one of the little windows. Another car was parked inside. She went to the front door and rang the bell. No one answered and she heard no sound from inside. She tried the door. It was locked. She walked around the side of the house to the back. Judy and Tim had a dog—a big friendly golden retriever named Buddy. To keep Buddy in the back yard, they had installed a chain link fence. Sylvia opened the gate in the fence and entered the back yard. There was no dog. She went to the back door and knocked. No answer. She peered through the glass. The kitchen was deserted. She tried the doorknob and it turned. Pulling open the door, she went inside. There was no response to her calls. The kitchen sink and counters were clean—no sign of breakfast dishes. In the living room the odor of sandalwood incense lingered in the air, and a big framed painting of Ghat Bruno—a beaming smile on his white-bearded face—hung over the fireplace.

The house was there, but the family was gone.

As Sylvia returned to her car she saw an elderly woman come out of the house next door.

"Excuse me," called Sylvia. The woman stopped and looked at her. "Have you seen Judy and Tim?"

The woman walked across her weedy lawn to the property line. "They left last night," she said.

"Last night? But their cars are still here."

"They were picked up."

"By who?"

"A sort of bus or van pulled up. This was about eleven o'clock. I remember because I was watching the news, and from where I sit I can see the street. You don't often see traffic down here late at night, so it got my attention. I didn't want to be nosy, but how can you not be interested?"

"Who was driving the van?"

"There were three people in the van and another person in a car. They went to the house and went inside. After a few minutes they all came out and got in the van, except for the person who went back to his car. Then they drove away. Just like that. I assumed they were going to the airport because each member of the family had a suitcase—Judy and Tim and the two kids."

"Can you tell me anything more about these people who picked up the family? Male, female? White, black, something else? Were they from the Church of the Golden Way?"

"I'm sorry. It was dark, and they didn't stand around. It happened very quickly. But I don't think they were church people. Whenever I see Judy and the family go to their church, they wear those pretty saffron-colored robes, like they wear in India. These people were dressed in black."

"You didn't talk to them?"

"Oh, no. I stayed inside the house. Since my husband died I never go out at night."

CHAPTER FIVE

"What's this?" Sylvia said to no one in particular. She was looking at her computer screen, where on the company intranet there was a message that had been sent to all two thousand five hundred employees of the Sun Motors Detroit Assembly Plant.

The message read:

"It is with great pleasure that Sun Motors announces the launch of a bold new program designed to support the health and wellness of our valued employees. For every Sun Motors employee, the Sun Motors Employee Wellness Plan (SMEWP) will provide full access to the highest quality health care, including overall fitness, vision, dental, mental health, and genetic health. Details will be provided by your human resources officer. And here's the good news: If your current primary care physician is on the SMEWP list of healthcare partners, you'll be able to keep your doctor. If your physician is not on the list, please contact your human resources officer for assistance in identifying a healthcare partner who can become your primary care physician."

Sylvia clicked through to the list of approved primary care physicians. Scrolling down, she searched for the name of her family doctor.

Her doctor's name was not on the list.

"What the hell," she muttered.

Her doctor was a partner in a clinic, the Dearborn Medical Group. Four other primary care physicians were also partners. Sylvia scrolled the list and found no names from the Dearborn Medical Group.

The Dearborn Medical Group was not affiliated with SMEWP.

This is a pain in the ass, she thought as she picked up the phone. She tapped the number for Carin.

The call went to voicemail. You'd think a robot would be able to answer more than one call at a time. She hung up without leaving a message.

She went to human resources, where she found Estelle behind her desk.

"How may I help you?" said Estelle without looking up from her screen.

"Can you tell me about this Sun Motors Employee Wellness Plan? I just got the email blast. I searched for my primary care physician on the approved list and her name wasn't there. In fact there was not a single name from the Dearborn Medical Clinic. What's going on?"

Estelle clicked out of her screen and shrugged. "The program is being managed by the corporate human resources office. We have nothing to do with it. I got the same email blast that you did. I'm sorry that Dearborn declined to participate in the program. I'm sure they were given the opportunity." As she peered at Sylvia over her readers, her expression softened. "Do you want my advice? Don't fight it. I know it means changing doctors. No one likes to do that. My doctor wasn't on the list, and I've been seeing her for ten years. But I made a few calls to doctors who are on the list, and I've chosen one. If I don't like her, next year I can sign up with another. It's no big problem."

"To stay with the Sun Motors plan, you changed doctors?"

"Yes. Listen to me: This is an outstanding program. It's better than any I've seen at any other major corporation. The coverage is comprehensive. Health, vision, dental—everything, including prenatal and childbirth."

"Thanks, I'll remember that," replied Sylvia sharply.

"You're a smart woman and a good employee," continued Estelle. "If you want to get along, go along. On the list of providers you'll find some of this city's top-ranked doctors and medical groups. When you find a doctor you like, your current doctor will transfer all of your records. You'll be covered for more diseases and health problems than any other plan available." She swiveled her computer so that Sylvia could see the screen. It showed the same email that she had received, describing the new SMEWP. Estelle scrolled to the bottom of the email, where there was a sign-up form. "Did you sign up online?" she asked while pointing to the little box you used to click through.

"No. I was too upset."

Estelle opened another window on her screen. "Let me show you something." It was a real-time report on a dashboard. "See that?" she pointed to a field where a number was displayed.

"Yes. It says eighty-two percent."

"As of this moment, of the two thousand five hundred employees in this facility, two thousand and fifty have signed up for the Sun Motors Employee Wellness Plan. Of the remaining four hundred and fifty, I think that within a few days another eighty percent will agree. That means that by the end of the week, ninety-six percent of the employees at this facility will have signed up for the Sun Motors health plan."

"What will happen to those who don't sign up?"

"They'll get a cash rebate in their paychecks so they can go out onto the open market and purchase the health plan of their choice. But let me tell you something—they're not going to find a plan as good as this one for the price. No way. The Sun Motors plan is a gold-level plan. The people who shop on their own—most likely because they want to keep their own doctor—are going to get a bronze level plan. They'll end up paying much more out of pocket for every service, and they won't get things like dental coverage." Leaning back in her chair, Estelle threw up her hands so that her bracelets rattled. "But hey, you can do what you want. Just remember that Sun Motors is looking for team players. You didn't hear it from me, but the word is that being a team player is a factor they look at when evaluating employees for promotions. This goes right up to the Industrial Council. You know they have the last word on everything. If they don't like you—pfft." She flicked her hands as if clearing the air of cobwebs. "You can kiss your promotion goodbye."

"You're kidding, right? The Industrial Council cares which health plan I choose?"

Estelle's face grew serious. "They care about whether you're on the team or you're freelancing. Sweetheart, you can do what you want. As for me, I'm sticking with the Sun Motors plan. I'm not going to jeopardize my career. If you want to buck the system, it's your choice. But there's no upside to it. You'll be cutting off your nose to spite your face."

"I don't know anything about these other doctors on the list."

"Well, you'd better decide soon, because the best ones fill up and won't take any more new patients. I'll tell you what I'll do. I'll send you an email with a list of the top medical groups on the list. It will save you from spending hours shopping around. Just make a few calls and then make your choice. But don't diddle-daddle. Do it today."

Sylvia returned to her cubicle. The euphoria she had felt after Randolph Meekin had been abruptly transferred—supposedly to the corporate building downtown, but that seemed unclear—was fading. Just as suddenly as Meekin had been transferred, her friend Judy was gone too, and not just from her job but from her house, along with her husband and two children.

She sat in her chair, paralyzed with indecision. She hadn't told Estelle this, but she felt tremendous loyalty and attachment to her personal physician, who had been with her through her first and only pregnancy, which had ended in a miscarriage. It had been a heart-wrenching experience; not only did she lose her baby, but her boyfriend at the time, who had told her he wanted to get married, was so freaked out by the loss of the baby that he had dumped her. After the joyous discovery that she was pregnant and a feeling that life was all sunshine and flowers, twelve weeks later Sylvia had found herself in world of gloom and spiritual desolation, with no baby, no boyfriend, a deep sense of personal failure, and the fear that it could happen again. Dr. Donna—her full name was Donna Giacalone, but everyone called her Dr. Donna—had been her Rock of Gibraltar, supporting her and helping her keep her experience in perspective. She had told Sylvia that spontaneous abortion, which was the medical term, happened in ten to twenty percent of all first pregnancies, so it was hardly uncommon; and most women who miscarry are subsequently able to have healthy children. It wasn't her fault, and it was no reflection on her ability to be a mother.

And now she faced a difficult choice. Dr. Donna, who practiced at the Dearborn Medical Group, was not affiliated with SMEWP. Many other doctors and clinics were, but not Dr. Donna. Estelle had urged her to sign up with the Sun health plan, not only because in her opinion it was a better plan than any Sylvia could get with Sun's cash alternative, but it was also a political decision. If she went with the corporate plan, the Sun Motors bosses, and even the Industrial Council, would view her more favorably, and would be more likely to keep her on track for promotions. If she took the cash and somehow made up the difference herself so that she could keep Dr. Donna, not only would it cost her more but her career might suffer.

At that moment her screen changed, and the image of Carin appeared. He was behind his desk in his office.

"Oh—hello Carin," said Sylvia as she squared her shoulders and sat up a little straighter. "What can I do for you?"

Carin smiled. "I just wanted to check in with you about the health plan memo that all employees, including yourself, received earlier today. I understand that the response to the company's very generous offer to cover employees under the Sun Motors medical program has been tremendous. Across this facility, we are now at ninety percent acceptance, which is exactly what we expected. And within the logistics office, I'm pleased to say we're at ninety-nine percent acceptance. I'd really like to make it one hundred percent—and you're the one who can put us over the top."

"Me?"

"Yes. Should you decide to accept—which I hope you do—the logistics office will have one hundred percent buy-in. This will be a feather in our cap, so to speak, and will not go unnoticed by our company leaders."

"And by the Industrial Council, I suppose?"

The moment these words passed over her lips, Sylvia felt a deep sense of regret and fear. From day one, employees at Sun Motors—indeed, employees at each and every large company across the United Americas—were taught that the Industrial Council was a benevolent association devoted to the growth and profitability of its two hundred thousand corporate members and the welfare of the fifty million people who worked for them. It was the Industrial Council that advised and guided the federal government in all matters relating to the national economy and, because the economy had been judged to fall within the realm of national security, the related policies of international trade, the environment, and national defense. Of course the nation possessed all the familiar branches of government that had been put in place when the U.S. Constitution had been first ratified in 1789; in its outward form, the structure of government hadn't changed in hundreds of years. The current president of the United Americas, Robert Deacon, was as popular as most presidents had been, and he was expected to win his second term handily. And while he went about his business of governing, and the Congress passed laws, and the Supreme Court ruled on those laws, most people knew that the real power resided with the Industrial Council, which following the terrible Global Depression had been granted sweeping powers to regulate the economy in the hopes that a firm hand on the tiller, as the saying went, would prevent the ship of state from once again smashing onto the rocks.

Like the Federal Reserve, which was now one of its subsidiaries, the Industrial Council was seen as being above politics; and indeed constitutional scholars frowned upon any direct communication between the White House and the Council, although most members of the press had long ago concluded that any sensible president knew enough to propose only those policies endorsed by the Council.

Because of its vast power, which reached down into the very hiring decisions made by the companies under its jurisdiction, while you were at work it was never a good idea to say anything negative about the Council, especially to a member of the management team of your company.

On Sylvia's screen, Carin smiled. "I'm sure the Industrial Council would be pleased to hear that the Sun Motors logistics office achieved one hundred percent buy-in to the Sun Motors health plan—why shouldn't they? It's all about teamwork and striving for perfection in all areas of business. Here at Sun Motors our goal of zero defects can be seen not just in the vehicles we produce but in how we conduct ourselves every day and in every way. And besides, the Sun Motors health plan is amazingly good. I can think of no rational reason why any Sun Motors employee wouldn't jump at the chance to participate."

"Of course, you're quite right," replied Sylvia. "The judgment of the Industrial Council is always...." She paused to find the right word that would end the discussion. "Infallible." As she said this bit of absurdity, she made an effort to keep the muscles of her face relaxed and her voice smooth.

"And yet you have reservations," said Carin. "Perhaps I can alleviate them for you."

Sylvia paused, to choose her words carefully. "I've been with my primary care physician for many years, and I would like to keep her, but she's not on the approved list. That's why I've been putting off my decision."

"That's understandable. I won't invade your privacy by asking you the name of your doctor. But perhaps I can help. You're twenty-seven years old and in generally good health with no chronic diseases—is that correct? I mean to say that you don't require the care of a specialist?"

"That's correct."

"And you live in Mexicantown?"

"Yes, since I graduated from college. I grew up in Franklin."

"I have two names for you. You don't have to write them down—I'm emailing them to you. Dr. Rebecca Goldsmith at the Willowdale Center, and Dr. Tina Packer, who has a private practice. Both are within a fifteen-minute drive from where you live. They're both accepting new patients. Either one will take very good care of you. I suggest you give them a call. You can also visit their websites."

"Okay, thanks. I'll do that."

"If for some reason they're both unsatisfactory, I have other suggestions. But I'm sure one of these two will be a good fit."

"Thanks."

"I hope we'll be able to add your name to the list of logistics office personnel who have signed onto the Sun Motors health plan, giving the office a participation rate of one hundred percent."

"I'll do my best."

Carin vanished from Sylvia's screen.

On the off chance that Dr. Donna could be persuaded to become affiliated with the Sun Motors program, or shed some light on why she wouldn't, before Sylvia contacted either one of the doctors Carin had recommended she decided to reach out to her familiar primary care physician. She went to out to her car, and using her personal phone called the Dearborn Medical Group.

Dr. Donna took the call. Sylvia explained that Sun Motors was offering a new health plan with which Dearborn was not affiliated.

"Why don't you stop by after work," said Dr. Donna. "I know you have a difficult decision, and I'd like to discuss it with you in a relaxed environment. Off the clock, so to speak."

CHAPTER SIX

As the setting sun cast its rosy glow, Sylvia wheeled her car into the parking lot of the Dearborn Medical Group. Just as she had countless times throughout her life, she walked through the glass doors and entered the faintly musty and antiseptic-smelling reception area. There to her left was the familiar wood-paneled reception counter with its protective Plexiglas front punctuated by the arched openings through which you talked to the ladies behind the desk. Beyond the potted plants in the waiting room area were the old-fashioned stainless steel-framed couches clad in turquois-colored fake leather. The screen bolted to the wall was tuned to the state news station. Mercifully, the sound was off.

It seemed like nothing ever changed here, and to Sylvia that continuity was comforting.

After a few minutes Dr. Donna came into the waiting room. "Do you have plans for dinner?" she asked Sylvia. "My husband has a Chamber of Commerce event. I find them horribly boring and try to avoid them whenever I can. I'd much rather get something to eat at a decent restaurant than cook for myself at home."

"Sounds good to me," replied Sylvia as she set aside the well-worn self-improvement magazine she had been perusing.

Once settled at a table at the Brickyard Tavern, and each with a glass of wine, Dr. Donna leaned forward and said, "I know all about the Sun Motors Employee Wellness Plan. A few months ago, their human resources people contacted us. Said they had five thousand employees in the Detroit area, and they were revamping their employee health plan. I was one of the partners who talked to them. They invited us downtown to a conference room in the Sun Building, where they gave us the pitch. Very splashy, with videos of happy, healthy employees and wise, caring physicians. They laid on the flattery with a trowel. Tried to make us think we were the chosen people destined to bring a bounty of good health and longevity to each and every Sun Motors employee and their families. And the fee scale wasn't bad either. They were going to pay as much as any of the major independent healthcare systems."

"So what was the problem?" asked Sylvia as she tore off a piece of bread from the wicker basket on the table.

"The problem was data."

"Data? What kind of data?"

"Every kind of data that bore any relationship to our Sun Motors patients, their illnesses or lack thereof, and how we interacted with them. They wanted access to everything. Every patient record for every visit or phone call. Every diagnosis and every pill prescribed. Every procedure, from an assembly line worker getting his leg put in a cast after a slip-and-fall to treatments for cancer and heart disease."

"How would they collect this endless river of information?"

"By tying into our internal systems. They said we wouldn't have to do anything other than go about our normal business. They would set up and operate the back end data collection network and databases."

"But what about patient confidentiality? Did they want you to get release forms from every patient who was a Sun Motors employee or family member?"

"No. They said they had taken care of that by having every employee sign a consent form where they worked. If you're a Sun Motors employee, and you've signed up for the Sun Motors Employee Wellness Plan, by definition you've given your consent, not only to us but to any other provider partner. How about you? Have you signed any healthcare consent forms recently?"

"Yes," replied Sylvia as a wave of embarrassment swept through her mind. "Yesterday I signed a consent form that allows Sun Motors to collect information about my physical condition while I'm on the job. Because of defense contracts—so they say—they can perform invasive tests, such as drawing blood or a urinalysis. But it goes much further than that. They can passively collect samples. My supervisor gave as an example an employee who comes to work with a high blood alcohol level." Sylvia paused, unsure about how to discuss Carin with someone who didn't work at Sun Motors. "To make a long story short," she continued, "they now have the capability to collect molecules that come out of, or from, your body, and enter the common space. If you're exhaling alcohol, you no longer have to blow into a machine. They can get it just by being near you. It's like when you put your trash on the curb to be collected, it becomes public property. If you walk into the office and shed a few million dead skin cells, you no longer own them. Anyone can collect them, including your employer. By signing the form, I acknowledged the company can collect and use information that enters the public space."

"Not just booze but cancer," said Dr. Donna. "Exhaled breath contains volatile and non-volatile organic compounds produced by metabolic processes, and the composition of such compounds varies between healthy subjects and subjects with lung cancer. You can diagnose lung cancer by analyzing the patient's breath. In our ability to analyze human exhalation we're finally catching up to dogs and cats. With their super-sensitive noses they've been able to do it for centuries. Anyway, you signed the consent form."

"Yes. My supervisor asked me to do it. I have to admit I felt I was being strong-armed. He implied that if I didn't sign, I wouldn't be viewed as a team player within the company, and that even the Industrial Council would take note of my lack of cooperation. With fifty million people working for Council companies, do you really think they would keep track of Sylvia Brand, a twenty-seven-year-old senior logistics manager working at a plant with twenty-five hundred other employees?"

"The answer is yes."

"Yes?"

"They would keep track of you because they can. To them, Sylvia Brand is just another data set, one of millions handled by the Industrial Council's big data centers. One of them is right here in Detroit. Anyone working at the Council can enter any query and pull up a list of people, including if they have signed up for the Sun Motors Employee Wellness Plan."

"But what about your patients who aren't Sun Motors employees?"

"The Sun Motors guy said that all we needed to do was assign an identifying digital tag to the patient records of Sun Motors employees. Their systems would unlock only the records with the Sun Motors tag. Non-Sun patients would not be exposed."

"Did you believe that?"

Dr. Donna took a swallow of her wine. With a laugh, she said, "Do I believe in the Easter Bunny?"

"So your partners decided to decline the offer from Sun Motors?"

"Yes. The scheme smelled bad. It reeked of abuse. Our impression was that Sun Motors was looking for rich data mines. Partners that would provide a flow of free healthcare data that they could use for—well, I don't know. Whatever they use it for."

"So it would be fair to say that any physician or medical center that signed up with the Sun Motors Employee Wellness Plan was required to sign the data contract as well."

"That would be a good assumption." Dr. Donna looked around the room for their server. "They never give you enough salad dressing. They must measure it out with a thimble." After a few moments she caught his eye and he came over. "A bit more of the raspberry vinaigrette, if you don't mind," she said. With a nod he sauntered away. She watched him. "If I were forty years younger..." She looked at Sylvia and winked. "Maybe you could have a go at him. He's cute."

"What?"

"Oh, I'm sorry. Of course, you have Jason. Is that right?"

"Yes," replied Sylvia. "We're going out tomorrow night. I have a sneaking suspicion he's going to ask me the big question. But I don't want to talk about it—not until it happens."

"I know what you mean. You don't want to jinx it."

"Right. To go back to your decision about the Sun Motors health care contract, what happened when you told them 'no'?"

Dr. Donna grew pensive. "I'll tell you, but first there's another reason I wanted to have dinner with you tonight. I'm retiring. I'm sixty-eight years old and it's time. I've known you since you were born. You've grown up to be a very capable and successful woman. With you and many others, I've had a nice record of success. But times are changing. At Dearborn we have five partners. Three of them want to sell out to National Health Systems, a big conglomerate based in Little Rock, Arkansas. They say it's either sell out or be crushed by the Industrial Council."

"How could the Industrial Council crush you?"

"Perhaps 'crush' is not the precise word. 'Starve' would be more accurate. If you're not one of the two hundred thousand corporate members of the Council, you're a part of the vast American canaille—literally, one of the dogs. You're just one of the millions of small and mom-and-pop businesses that do the everyday grunt work of our society—the fast food joints, taxicab drivers, auto repair places, dry cleaners, used clothing stores, bookstores—and yes, small medical clinics. These are much more loosely regulated than the elite Two Hundred K, as they're called, but in return for their freedom the little guys are severely curtailed in how big they can get. The moment you post over a set ceiling in revenues—it varies according to your industry—you must either agree to sell out to one of the Two Hundred K or be placed on the Council's banned list. That means that none of the Two Hundred K can do business with you. Their employees can't do business with you either. So you gradually wither and die. Dearborn is facing that choice. Three partners want to sell to National Health Systems. Two of us think that would be a horrible thing to do and would be bad for our patients. I don't want to fight. I'm retiring. My husband will keep working for another few years before we move to Costa Rica. So to answer your question, Barbara and I—the two holdouts—have decided to cash in our chips. The clinic will be sold to National Health. The three remaining partners will operate Dearborn, but strictly as a subsidiary of the parent company. So if your supervisor wants you to sign up with the Sun Motors Employee Wellness Plan, you might as well. There are no more good independent doctors. Our time has passed. Today, you're either part of the Industrial Council's machine or you're fending for yourself in the swamp of the canaille."

"And living among the aberrants," said Sylvia.

"Oh my God, yes. Let's not even think about that."

With a feeling of deep resignation, Sylvia told Dr. Donna about the two doctors Carin had recommended.

"Dr. Packer is headed for retirement," said Dr. Donna. "I'd go with Dr. Goldsmith at the Willowdale Center. She'll take good care of you."

"But the Willowdale Center is plugged into the Sun Motors data collection program, right? The company will know everything about my health history."

"The law says that patient data must be scrubbed of identifying information—name, address, phone number. In theory you're anonymous. It's a good theory—just like the Easter Bunny. I would assume that from the moment you sign up for the Sun Motors Employee Wellness Plan, all of your health data, including your historical data that we will be obliged to send to the Willowdale Center, will become their property."

"Including my miscarriage?"

"That and every other illness you've had since your parents first brought you to me when you were a child. Your entire patient history. Every phone call, every pill, every swab, every blood test."

Sylvia sat in silence, listlessly picking at her roast chicken. The atmosphere of the restaurant, which moments before had seemed friendly and inviting, had become harsh and obnoxious. The man at the table next to her brayed like a horse. The clatter of dishes at the busing station invaded her ears. The stupid fake candle on her table had gone out. She just wanted to go home and eat a pint of rocky road ice cream.

"Hey, kid, don't take it so hard," said Dr. Donna, giving her hand a friendly pat. "That's the way it is today. Go with the flow. It will all work out in the end.

CHAPTER SEVEN

At her desk on Wednesday morning, Sylvia opened the company intranet message announcing the launch of the Sun Motors Employee Wellness Plan. She read the text again, but after plowing through two pages of fine print that seemed like a bunch of legalese she scrolled to the bottom of the page and clicked "I accept." Then from the drop-down menu she selected the name of Dr. Rebecca Goldsmith at the Willowdale Center as her primary care physician. She clicked "enter," and that was all. She was now a part of the SMEWP system.

She returned to her work, which at that moment consisted of tracking an overdue shipment of O-rings from Indonesia. The container ship carrying the forty thousand O-rings—along with twenty thousand tons of other goods packed into six thousand containers stacked on her massive deck—had been caught in a typhoon in the Solomon Sea. Contact with the ship had been lost for several hours, and when the weather cleared and contact was restored the captain reported that thirty-five containers had been swept overboard. It appeared as though the Sun Motors container with the O-rings had been one of them. This was bad news because the inventory of O-rings at the Detroit Assembly Plant was down to three weeks, and even if the container ship had arrived on time in San Diego with the container intact it would have been a tight schedule to truck the parts to Detroit without a delay in production. If the container were truly lost at sea, then unless Sylvia could scrounge up forty thousand O-rings the Comanche assembly line would grind to a halt.

This potential debacle was particularly worrisome to Sylvia because she had signed off on the production schedule at the factory in Indonesia. She knew there was little room for error and that it was typhoon season in the South Pacific, but the production manager at Astra Karawang had assured her the schedule was no problem and the parts would be delivered on time. If the parts didn't show up on time—even if the cause was a typhoon—it would be a black mark on her record.

At that moment a window opened on her screen. It was Carin, sitting at his desk.

"Sylvia," he said, "please pardon the interruption to your very busy day, but I want to congratulate you on making the logistics office one hundred percent compliant with the Sun Motors Employee Wellness Plan. You've made a very wise decision! Your choice demonstrates that we are indeed a united team, we're all on the same page, and we're each thinking only of the greater good. I'm sure you'll be very pleased with the service provided by Dr. Goldsmith at the Willowdale Center. She's very highly rated. All of her patients give her glowing reviews."

"Thank you, Carin," said Sylvia. "I look forward to having Dr. Goldsmith as my primary care physician."

After a short pause, Carin spoke. "Sylvia, you seem to be under some stress this morning. Is there anything I can help you with?"

"No, thank you. I'm good." She said this not because she couldn't have used Carin's help—she certainly could have—but because years of working under Randolph Meekin's lascivious gaze and hearing his crude comments had conditioned her to never ask for his help. Never, ever. She had learned this when they first began working together. She had had a problem with a shipment of defective parts and had asked Meekin to intercede. He did so, and he had helped solve the problem. As the supervisor, this was in his job description. But from that day forward he had acted as if he had done Sylvia an immense personal favor that had saved her from being fired. (In fact, it wasn't nearly so serious.) He had asked her out, and when she declined he reminded her that she should have been more grateful to him and more willing to show her deep appreciation for his efforts on her behalf. His pressure on her was relentless, and that was the last time she had asked him for help solving a problem.

"Are you sure?" Carin inquired.

Sylvia thought for a moment. Carin wasn't like Meekin. While Meekin was an oversexed human male with serious boundary issues, Carin was an asexual robot who had shown his professionalism by helping Maxwell with his problem with the pricing of the tie rod ends. That had been a pretty neat solution, delivered without gloating. It was not in Carin's nature—or programming, if that's how you wanted to look at it—to play the kinds of games Meekin enjoyed. He himself had said that it was his primary mission to be helpful to the team. Why not give him the chance?

"Okay," she said, "as long as you're asking, I'm very worried about a container with forty thousand O-rings that seems to have been swept overboard during a typhoon in the South Pacific."

"Oh—you mean the Globe Nebula. She left the Port of Tanjung Priok on the fifteenth of this month, bound for Honolulu and then San Diego, with a load of six thousand containers. Three days out, the ship was hit by the storm. Fifty-five containers were reported lost. Statistically, seventy percent of containers washed overboard are recovered. But let's assume the report is correct and ours was one of them, and it is indeed lost forever. How many O-rings do you need for production until the end of this quarter?"

"Five thousand."

"We can get them from other Sun Motors assembly plants. We can get one thousand from Kansas City and Hermosillo, and five hundred from Chattanooga, Chihuahua, Brook Park, and Windsor. That's four thousand. Going further afield, Liverpool and Cologne have a few hundred each, as does Croydon. Taken all together, that should be enough to buy us enough time to sort out the problem with the missing shipment. When do you intend to file the insurance claim?"

"As soon as the shipping company confirms the loss."

"Don't wait. Do it now. If we're wrong and the container shows up, we'll just drop the claim. Okay?"

"Yes," replied Sylvia. "Thank you."

Sylvia was both amazed and gratified. Carin had instantly produced global inventory data that would have taken her days to track down. And he did it without making her feel as though she owed him a favor in return. It was just part of the job, as it should have been.

She returned to her work. A few minutes later her screen came alive again. Again she saw the image of Carin, but this time it was a pre-recorded message.

"Please excuse the impersonal nature of this message, but I wanted to deliver it to everyone in the logistics office. I'm very pleased that everyone has signed up for the Sun Motors Employee Wellness Plan, and that all of you have chosen your primary care physicians. The next step is to schedule your appointments for your annual physical exams. It's all part of our commitment to ensuring the very best physical and mental health for every member of our Sun Motors family. For your convenience, your appointment for your physical exam has been made during normal work hours—we would never impose upon your private time. We've been able to arrange appointments for everyone within a week. No one will have to wait longer than that. Please go to your personal calendar to see your appointment day and time. Some of you are scheduled for this afternoon, but don't worry, you don't need any special prep. Just go about your day, eat whatever you usually have for lunch, and go to your appointment. Most appointments will take less than an hour. Thank you."

Sylvia clicked open her calendar. She had been given an appointment with Dr. Goldsmith at three o'clock that same afternoon.

"Today?" she said to herself. "Oh, well—might as well get it over with."

At three o'clock Sylvia registered as a new patient at the Willowdale Center. The lobby was clean and bright, the receptionist all smiles. In the waiting room she joined a handful of other patients, who seemed to be generally younger than the doddering geriatrics she had always seen at the Dearborn Medical Group. Even better, none of them smelled bad.

After watching the news channel for a few minutes—the sound was on, and the news reader was talking about a terror bombing in Rome—the nurse announced her name, and she was ushered into an examination room, where the nurse performed all the routine tests including blood pressure ("one hundred over seventy," the nurse said with approval) and asked about any recent complaints (none).

Dr. Goldsmith entered the room. After introducing herself, the doctor spent several minutes reading Sylvia's medical history from the computer screen. Sylvia thought the doctor's application of cherry red lipstick was rather aggressive, but otherwise she appeared to be a reasonable human being without any peculiar traits.

"You had a spontaneous ending of your pregnancy?" asked the doctor.

"Yes. A year ago. That was a bit of a rough patch for me."

"I don't see a cause listed here."

"Dr. Giacalone said it was difficult to pinpoint a single factor."

"Everything has a cause," replied Dr. Goldsmith. She turned to Sylvia and smiled. "Most spontaneous terminations occur because the fetus isn't developing normally. The most common causes are chromosome issues associated with random errors that occur as the embryo divides and grows, or as the result of a damaged sperm or egg cell.

"There are other ways a pregnancy can end. In the intrauterine demise of the fetus, the embryo forms but then stops developing. With what we call a blighted ovum, there is no formation of an embryo.

"You could have had a molar pregnancy, in which case the father provides both sets of chromosomes. There is no development of a fetus, only an abnormal growth of the placenta. In a partial molar pregnancy, the chromosomes from the mother remain, but the father also provides two sets of chromosomes. This condition is associated with placental abnormalities and growth of an abnormal fetus. Molar and partial molar pregnancies are not viable, and can sometimes be associated with cancerous changes of the placenta.

"Other causes that aren't related to chromosomes include diabetes, infections, hormonal problems, uterus or cervix problems, or thyroid disease."

She stood in front of Sylvia, who was seated on the end of the examining table with her legs and feet dangling over the edge. "I have enormous respect for Dr. Giacalone and the Dearborn Medical Group," the doctor said with her red lips. "But you may find that we have a different approach to patient care. Here at Willowdale we believe that nothing happens by accident and that every disease or condition has a specific cause. In addition, we place a very high priority on uncovering that cause. After all, how can you draw a conclusion about something unless you fully understand it?"

"I suppose you cannot," replied Sylvia.

"Correct. If you had a shipment of a part for a car go missing, you wouldn't rest until you found that shipment or knew what happened to it—am I right? Or would you throw up your hands and say, 'We lost the parts. We don't know where they are. Next time will be better.'"

"Obviously the former."

"Of course! Here we have the same attitude." She put a tourniquet around Sylvia's arm. "We're going to test your blood and see if we can eliminate any hormonal issues. We'll also run a complete DNA profile to pinpoint genetic red flags. As a bonus, you'll learn all about your genetic heritage. People are often amazed to discover where they came from. When I had mine done, I found out I had a great-great grandfather who was North African. I never knew!" Dr. Goldsmith drew the blood into four little vials. "If you don't mind me asking, do you have any plans to get pregnant again? I noticed you're unmarried—is the man still in your life?"

"No, we split up. But I do have a boyfriend."

"Ah—someone new. Where does he work?"

"He works at Hilltop Financial. Downtown."

"That's one of the Two Hundred K. A good one, too. You don't need me to tell you that you shouldn't be messing around with any man from the canaille. And certainly not an aberrant! That would mean the end of your career and any sort of normal life for you and your family."

"You don't have to worry about that. I have no intention of throwing my life away."

"What's the lucky fella's name?"

Sylvia thought this question crossed the fine line between professional and personal, but Dr. Goldsmith exuded a motherly quality that put her at ease, and so she replied, "Jason Quin. He's an analyst. Specializes in the telecom industry. He writes investor reports for the weekly Hilltop Financial newsletter."

"Nice job," replied Dr. Goldsmith. "Okay—I think we're all set. We'll get the results of the blood tests in twenty-four hours and the DNA tests in forty-eight. If you have any questions, please don't hesitate to call and I'll get right back to you."

CHAPTER EIGHT

At a few minutes before six o'clock, Jason stood at the door to Sylvia's apartment in Mexicantown. Like every man who would be attending that evening's concert, he was dressed in a dark business suit (his was blue), white button-down shirt, and necktie. He rang the bell. She came downstairs to the vestibule. "It's gotten cool out," she said. "Do I need a coat?"

"I don't think so, unless you want one," he replied diplomatically. "It's totally up to you."

"Where are we going?"

"El Barzon."

"I'd better get a coat."

Sylvia returned wearing a lightweight cream-colored wool coat. "Does this look nice on me?"

"Yes," replied Jason. "Very lovely."

"Better than my blue one?"

"What?"

"I said, does it look better than my blue one?"

"They both look equally beautiful. Since you're wearing this one, why don't you keep it on, and we'll have a nice dinner and then the concert."

They got into his car and drove to the restaurant. Their table for two was waiting.

"So how was your day today?" Jason asked as he looked at the menu.

"Pretty good," she replied. "Carin helped me sort out a problem with a shipment of O-rings from Indonesia. Our container got swept overboard in a typhoon, and it looked like a major headache. In about ten seconds Carin reeled off a list of other Sun Motors plants that had excess inventory they could send us. I was impressed. The guy's got game."

"You called him 'the guy.' Sounds like you're getting used to him."

"Yes, I think all of us are. Carin is a huge improvement over Meekin."

51

She paused. She hadn't told Jason very much about Meekin other than he was generally a jerk. She hadn't told him about Meekin's inappropriate touching or repeated invitations to dinner. To do so, she assumed, would only anger Jason—a former Michigan State linebacker—and incite him to beat up the guy. Sylvia knew that would not be a positive solution to the problem.

"Oh yeah, Meekin," said Jason. "He's gone now, right?"

"Yes—he's gone. Supposedly to the Sun Motors Building. Anyway, Carin seems to be as close as you can get to the ideal boss. He gives you help when you need it and stays out of your hair when you don't. He's obviously a robot, which makes it much easier. It's not like he's some sort of facsimile human being, which would be really weird. How about you? Anything new at work?"

"We've learned that North American Telecom will be rolling out their holographic video chat service next month. Instead of seeing a flat image of the person you're talking to, you'll see them sitting or standing next to you. If you get up and walk around, it'll be just like they're in the room with you."

"I'm going to hate that," laughed Sylvia. "It's bad enough your boss can see you on the screen in two dimensions. Now you'll have to look good in three!"

"You'll always look good in three," replied Jason. "What else has happened at work? Oh yeah, on Monday the company launched its new employee healthcare program. They call it the Hilltop Financial Health Initiative. Apparently the Industrial Council has passed some new regulations mandating that every Two Hundred K employee have comprehensive healthcare, which is already pretty normal, but they also want the right to collect your personal health data. We got new consent forms to sign. I had signed a bunch of them years ago, but the company wanted them updated. I went for a physical yesterday. Fortunately my regular doctor was on the approved list. He did all the usual tests, including blood work and DNA."

"What a coincidence," replied Sylvia. "We've been going through the same process. New health plan, new consent forms, new physical exams. I had to switch doctors because my old one, Dr. Donna, refused to become a part of the Sun Motors Employee Wellness Plan network."

"Why did she refuse? That sounds like a career-killing move."

"She decided to retire. Some of her other partners are selling out to National Health Systems, which is plugged into the Sun Motors network. So I found a new doctor on the Sun Motors list. Her name is Helen Goldsmith. Seems very nice, very professional. A little bit nosey, though."

"Nosey?"

"She asked me if I had a boyfriend, and where you worked."

"Probably just trying to get to know you better."

"Yes, I suppose so."

After dinner, as they were driving to the concert hall, Sylvia said to Jason,

"This has been a very lovely evening so far, but sweetheart, you seem like you have something on your mind. Is there anything you want to talk about?"

"As a matter of fact, there is." With these words he pulled over to the curb. "There's a lovely little park right here. There are benches you can sit on next to the pond. Let's take a walk."

"Won't we be late for the concert?" said Sylvia as she unbuckled her seat belt.

"This will only take a few minutes. I just want to show you something."

He walked with her into the park, bathed in the cool glow of streetlights. In the distance they could hear kids playing basketball. He found a park bench under a willow tree by the side of the pond. They sat down and watched the ducks huddling and fussing in the shallows by the muddy bank.

"What do you want to tell me?" she asked.

Jason stood up and reached into his jacket pocket. As he did this he dropped to one knee in front of her, like a squire from King Arthur's court. From his pocket he produced a small felt-covered box. With his fingertips he flipped open the top of the box. The streetlights caught the glimmer of a diamond.

"Sylvia," he said, "I hope that you'll become my wife."

"Oh, Jason, I don't know what to say."

"Then just say 'yes.'"

"Yes—of course I will! I was hoping you would ask! Should I have said that? Oh, it doesn't matter. Yes, I will. I would like nothing more. May I try it on?"

"Please," said Jason. "I had to guess at your size. I hope it fits, but we can always have it resized."

She slipped the ring on her finger. "Oh, it fits perfectly! Do you like it?" She held out her hand so the ring sparkled in the light.

"Of course I like it," replied Jason, still on one knee on the asphalt sidewalk. "The question is, do you like it?"

"I love it," she replied as she leaned forward to give him a kiss. "I cannot tell you how happy I am! We have so much to talk about—the wedding, where we're going to live…"

"I thought maybe you could move into my place. I have plenty of room."

"Forget it, buster. I promised myself that when I got married, my husband and I would find a house of our own. No one is going to be moving into the other person's apartment. We're going to start off on an even footing. We're going to start driving around on weekends, looking at houses. It will be fun, you'll see."

"Okay," he said, raising his hands in mock surrender. "I know a really good real estate agent who can help us."

Sylvia glanced at her phone. "We'd better get going—we don't want to be late for the concert."

The Shapiro Theatre was a small hall with a few hundred seats, a testament to the relatively small market for chamber music. The volunteer usher showed Sylvia and Jason to their seats in the center of the hall a few rows from the stage. "We're in a good location," said Sylvia as the members of the audience milled around, talking to each other or reading their programs.

"I have to confess," said Jason, "a client gave me the tickets. He and his wife have a season subscription but they couldn't attend tonight. So here we are."

"Yes—here we are," said Sylvia as she kissed him on the cheek.

The house lights dimmed, and everyone settled into their seats. On the stage, a man dressed in a business suit walked into the glare of the spotlights. He introduced himself as William Masters, the managing director of the theatre. After welcoming everyone and delivering the usual announcements, he said, "Tonight, the Shapiro Theatre is particularly pleased to extend our warmest thanks to our generous corporate sponsor of this performance by the Linz String Quartet. Our sponsor is Alliance Partners. Please give them a warm round of applause."

The audience dutifully complied.

"In fact," continued Masters, "We have a very special representative from Alliance Partners with us tonight. He's sitting in one of the boxes… Palor, will you please stand up?"

One of the spotlights swung around to the box seats at the side of the hall. A figure stood up. To Sylvia's astonishment, he looked exactly like Carin, with the same plain, one-piece jumpsuit, short dark hair, pale brown skin, and wraparound glasses. The only difference was that Palor's jumpsuit was pale blue, whereas the one worn by Carin was khaki.

Palor turned to face the audience and gave a friendly wave.

"I don't want to embarrass Palor by talking about him," said Masters, "But you can see he's an autonomous humanoid operator. Is that correct, Palor?"

Palor nodded. "Yes, that's precisely correct. I manage the mergers and acquisitions department on the thirty-fifth floor of the Alliance Building. I can tell you that Alliance Partners is very pleased and honored to be the corporate sponsor of tonight's performance. At Alliance we are proud of our long tradition of strong commitment to arts and culture, which as I'm sure you all know is in perfect alignment with the vision of the Industrial Council. As for me, I must confess that I have very little knowledge of chamber music in general and string quartets in particular. I know a few facts. In the seventeen fifties the Austrian composer Joseph Haydn developed the string quartet into its current form, and ever since that time the string quartet— consisting of two violins, a viola, and a cello—has been considered a prestigious form and represents one of the true tests of the art of both composer and performer. As an ensemble, the Linz String Quartet is one of the premier practitioners of this art form. I look forward to the performance this evening."

To a smattering of applause and a few confused looks among members of the audience, Palor sat down.

"Oh my God, he looks just like Carin!" whispered Sylvia to Jason.

"Probably the same make and model," he shrugged.

"After the concert, let's go and talk to him."

At the end of the evening as the houselights were coming up, Sylvia hustled Jason up the aisle to the lobby, where they could position themselves to meet Palor as he came out of the boxes. A moment later he appeared with his human companion, a man dressed in the ubiquitous dark business suit. Sylvia saw that Palor was the same height as Carin and had the same appearance. Except for the color of his jumpsuit, they could have been twins.

Sylvia approached him and introduced herself and Jason.

"Sylvia, it's a pleasure to meet you in person," replied Palor. "Of course, I know you well. You're serving as the senior logistics manager at the Sun Motors Detroit Assembly Plant. Today you had a problem with a container of O-rings that was swept off the deck of the Globe Nebula, which left the Port of Tanjung Priok on the fifteenth of this month, bound for Honolulu and then San Diego. I believe my colleague Carin provided a solution." He turned to Jason. "It's a pleasure to meet you as well. I hope all is well at Hilltop Financial and with the telecom industry?"

"Yes, thank you—business has been very good," smiled Jason. "Do you have a particular interest in chamber music and string quartets?"

"A particular interest?" replied Palor. "I'm not sure what that means. While I have my job specialty, which is mergers and acquisitions, I'm interested in everything equally."

"I suppose that you were sent here tonight," offered Sylvia. "Your boss asked you to attend."

"Yes," replied Palor. "The goal of tonight's visit was to maintain my steady rate of machine learning, which is key to artificial intelligence. Tonight's concert was very informative, despite the many mistakes made by the performers."

"Mistakes?" asked Sylvia. "The quartet sounded pretty good to me."

"In the Schubert 'String Quartet Number 14 in D minor'   I counted eighty deviations from the score," said Palor. "In the Debussy 'String Quartet in G major' there were sixty-seven deviations. In Leoš Janáček's 'String Quartet Number 1, the Kreutzer Sonata,' there were—"

"Forgive me for interrupting," said Sylvia, "but do you really believe all of those deviations, as you call them, were mistakes? Every performer gives every piece his or her artistic interpretation. It's the emotional element that makes each performance different."

"Either you play the piece as written or you don't," replied Palor in his pleasant genderless voice. "Wouldn't you agree?"

"I don't know if I would," replied Sylvia.

"For example," continued Palor, "in the business of motor vehicle manufacturing, the cars are built according to specifications, and the goal—as it is in any business that makes a product—is to have zero defects. In the old days the goal was Six Sigma, which is three point four defects per million attempts. Today, nothing less than Ten Sigma is acceptable. Soon we will achieve One Hundred Sigma."

"I understand what you're saying," replied Sylvia. "But you may find it helpful if you looked at the written score for a piece of music as being like human DNA, which is never set in stone but is subject to interpretation, through the process of gene expression. Human identical twins share the same DNA but still show subtle differences in appearance and behavior. This is because genes can be switched on or off, depending on the environment and other factors."

"That seems rather random," replied Palor.

"If you'll excuse us," interjected Jason, "it's been a long day and I think we should be making our way home."

Palor nodded, and then said with a smile, "Sylvia, I see you are wearing a new engagement ring. A lovely twisted vine style with pavé diamonds and a cushion-cut stone. Should I congratulate you and Jason?"

"Yes, thank you," said Jason before Sylvia could answer. "We haven't made any announcements yet, but we are engaged. I assume you won't tell anyone."

"No, of course not. I wish you both every happiness."

In the car on the way to Sylvia's apartment, she turned to Jason. "That was an extremely creepy encounter."

"How so?"

"Palor knew who I was and all about the missing container of O-rings! The problem happened just this morning. The only people who knew about it were Carin and I. We didn't broadcast it to the whole world, and especially not to a management robot at Alliance Partners. And he also knew my engagement ring was new. I've only been wearing it for a few hours!"

"I can't explain it," said Jason. "Unless Carin and Palor share a common memory."

"Do you mean that Palor knows everything that Carin knows, and vice versa?"

"Maybe. Perhaps instead of being fully autonomous machines, they're more like two computer terminals networked to the same cloud database."

"Instead of being pseudo humans," said Sylvia, "they could be pseudo ants—individual representatives of one colony. They can act independently while being linked to one centralized consciousness."

CHAPTER NINE

At her desk on Thursday morning, as Sylvia was arranging for the return of a shipment of defective brake calipers, her calendar pinged.

Hurriedly she closed the file, picked up her phone, and tapped a number. "Hey Mei Lien, you're going to the grand opening of the new day care center, aren't you? Yes, I know—all the women are supposed to attend. I don't know why they aren't making all the men go too. That seems a little bit sexist. I'll swing by your desk and we can go together."

After going down the elevator to the ground floor, Sylvia and Mei Lien walked through an enclosed breezeway to an adjacent building. Inside the entrance atrium, a crowd of mostly female employees had gathered along with a smattering of men. For a few minutes they stood while more employees arrived. The doors to the new Margaret J. Atkinson Day Care Center were closed. Next to the doors a temporary stage had been erected, with a podium and some folding chairs. On an easel was a large photo of a woman. It was a formal portrait, from the shoulders up, and she was smiling.

"Who's that a picture of?" asked Mei Lien.

"I suppose it must be Margaret J. Atkinson," replied Sylvia. "I've never before seen her photo. You know the family is exceedingly private."

At precisely ten o'clock, a group of people mounted the stage. A man took to the podium. Sylvia recognized him as Gerald Posey, the chief operating officer of the plant and its highest executive. She had watched Posey's motivational messaging videos—everyone who worked at the plant had—but this was the first time she had seen him in person. She thought he was a rather bland looking man, with no particular features that would indicate an interesting character or personality. Like the other men on the stage, he was wearing a dark business suit, white shirt, and a necktie that Sylvia thought was too long.

"What's with these huge neckties that all the men are suddenly wearing?"

she whispered to Mei Lien. "It's must be a new fad or something. I hope it doesn't last long."

"The theory is that a long necktie makes you look taller," Mei Lien whispered in return. "Personally, I think it makes them look like circus clowns. To complete the ensemble, all they need are huge shoes and funny hats." Stifling a giggle, she looked around them. No one appeared to be listening. Sylvia and Mei Lien both knew it was a bad idea to publicly discuss company leaders in any way other than with effusive praise.

On the stage, Sylvia could see the other managers she knew, including Carin, who stood off to one side. "I can't imagine what our boss could possibly know about day care," Sylvia whispered to Mei Lien.

"I'm sure he must think the process of human reproduction is quite appalling," said Mei Lien. "He would probably want us to clone ourselves in a nice sterile laboratory."

"May I have your attention please," said Posey. The sound of his amplified voice reverberated through the atrium. "I would like to welcome you to the grand opening of the Margaret J. Atkinson Day Care Center at the Sun Motors Detroit Assembly Plant. Spearheaded by our chairman and CEO, Mr. Hugh Atkinson, and the Atkinson family leadership team, this new facility is part of a company-wide effort to support our Sun Motors families and give their children every possible advantage. This facility is named in honor of Margaret J. Atkinson, with whom Mr. Atkinson has shared forty years of marriage. She has devoted her career to helping children and families. She believes, as do we all, that there is nothing more important than the care and nurturing of our future leaders."

When his speech eventually concluded—Sylvia thought he droned on longer than was required to heap praise upon the Atkinson family—the group of executives left the stage and assembled in front of the door, across which had been stretched a red ribbon. To the sound of applause, Posey cut the ribbon and the doors were opened. Some of the assembled spectators moved forward while others hung back, waiting for the opportunity to leave.

"Might as well go take a look," said Mei Lien. "I have a feeling that you and Jason might soon be availing yourselves of its services."

They entered a brightly lit and cheerful room that looked like any other upscale kindergarten. Sunny yellow—the official color of Sun Motors— dominated the color scheme. Kid-sized tables and chairs, boxes of toys, and a TV monitor occupied the central space. Another section had been turned into a spacious indoor playground with a slide and a small jungle gym, all made from yellow plastic. Towards the rear of the room was a glass-enclosed space that to Sylvia looked like a clinic.

The center was already populated with twenty or so children, from toddlers to kids who looked like they were four or five years old, nearly ready for elementary school. Overseeing the kids were a man and a woman. They were both wearing white and navy blue—the man a white shirt and blue pants, while the woman a white blouse and blue skirt.

"Must be tough to play with kids while you're wearing a skirt," Sylvia whispered to Mei Lien.

The boys in the day care center were wearing white shirts and blue pants, while the girls wore blue jumpers over white blouses.

Sylvia approached the male teacher, who was sitting at a small table with two kids. They were coloring on pads of paper. She introduced herself. His name was Ahmed.

"I'm impressed with what I see," said Sylvia. "This is a first-class facility."

"Thank you," replied Ahmed. He seemed very pleasant.

"Can I ask you—what's with the uniforms? Is that some new thing?"

"The uniforms? Mrs. Atkinson firmly believes that an advanced society needs to focus on what we have in common rather than what separates us. An important part of the center's mission is to get every child on the same page, so to speak. Here, no one is any better than anyone else. We're all part of the Sun Motors family. The children have a sense of belonging, just like we all do."

Sylvia looked around the room at the children. "This is quite an attractive group. If I dare say it, they're all exceptionally beautiful. They could all be little fashion models. Tell me—how do you handle special needs kids? Or what if I had a child with a birth defect, like a missing limb?"

A fleeting shadow of bewilderment passed over Ahmed's face. "Um, in order to be accepted, children need to go through the screening process," he said. "I don't have anything to do with that."

"Oh, you mean this center isn't open to every child of a Sun Motors employee? To get in you have to qualify?"

"Yes. The people in human resources do the screening, just like they screen people who are applying for a job."

"I see," nodded Sylvia. She nodded towards the glassed-in area. "It looks like you've got a medical clinic over there. May we go inside?"

Ahmed shook his head. "No, sorry. It's not open for tours. I think it's a Board of Health requirement. But it's just an ordinary clinic where the doctor can provide regular checkups and attend to everyday injuries—cuts and bruises. That's all."

"Is it always wide open like that, so anyone can see inside?"

"No, they have curtains they can draw across the windows."

"They must be able to do blood tests and that sort of thing, too?"

"I really wouldn't know," replied Ahmed quickly. He abruptly turned his attention to a little boy who was coloring. "Say, that's nice! Is it a tree?"

The boy nodded.

Drifting away from the teacher and kids at the table, Sylvia and Mei Lien approached the glassed-in clinic. It looked like any other pediatric medical facility, with walls decorated with brightly painted cartoon elephants and bunnies. There was an examining table and all the ubiquitous cabinets and medical devices. In the rear was a counter with a computer on top, along with racks for tubes.

"That computer in the back looks familiar," said Sylvia.

Mei Lien peered at it through the window. "It's a Matrix Genome 3000," she said. "A desktop DNA sequencer. They each cost two hundred thousand dollars. They're supposed to be the most accurate small machine on the market."

"They're for sequencing DNA? Why would they need that in this company clinic?"

"Maybe as service to employees who want to know how their kids stack up in the DNA sweepstakes," said Mei Lien. "Or for parents who want to see if their kids have a genetically inherited disease, so they can plan ahead for treatment."

"Or perhaps," said Sylvia, "as a way to identify children who they think have a genetic inferiority."

Later that day, as Sylvia was working in her cubicle, the image of Carin appeared on her screen.

"Hello employees of the Sun Motors Detroit Assembly Plant Logistics Office," he began. "I'd like to talk to you today about something that's very important to the company, to the Industrial Council, and I hope to you. It's what traditionally has been called esprit de corps, which is defined as the common spirit existing in the members of a group, and which inspires feelings of enthusiasm, devotion, and strong regard for the honor of the group. Within this great organization, we're an important group, and I hope that we can build an esprit de corps that is second to none within our company and even within all the member organizations of the Industrial Council.

"Now then, those of you who attended today's grand opening of the new Margaret J. Atkinson day care center will have noticed that the children present—the very first to be admitted to the center—were all wearing clothing of white and navy blue. The teachers were too. This is to reflect the belief of both Mr. and Mrs. Atkinson that while on the job or at school, people benefit from the freedom of not having to worry about their wardrobe. Mrs. Atkinson has written in her recently published book Song for a New Civilization, which I hope you all will read if you have not yet done so, that when she was a girl she was required to wear a uniform to school; and instead of feeling as though this were a limitation on her freedom, she felt it gave her more freedom by lifting from her shoulders the heavy burden of choice. I'm reminded of the practice of our current president of the United Americas, Robert Deacon, who has said that he keeps a closet full of gray suits and white shirts because it frees him from having to make a trivial decision each morning and allows him to focus on what's truly important.

"Therefore, beginning next quarter, which is in two weeks, all employees of the logistics office will be following the new Sun Motors workplace attire guidelines. I won't recite every requirement in this message—you can read them for yourself on the human resources page. Suffice to say, the principle components are a white shirt and navy blue slacks or suit for men and white blouse with navy blue skirt for women. The human resources page provides a list of clothing retailers that stock the approved shade of navy blue."

There was more, mostly about subsidies and other incentives promote the new program, which Carin called "The Sun Motors Way." Specific penalties for noncompliance were not mentioned. Sylvia knew they didn't have to be.

CHAPTER TEN

That afternoon Sylvia went to the break room, where she was joined by Mei Lien, Lauren, and Tameeka. They admired Sylvia's new engagement ring.

"Have you set the date?" asked Tameeka as she poured her coffee.

"Not yet, but it will be soon, we hope," replied Sylvia. "We see no reason for a long engagement."

After a discussion of the many wonderful personal qualities of Jason, the conversation drifted to other topics.

"What's up with the new office dress code?" asked Mei Lien. "I haven't worn a skirt to work in years. Are we going back to the twentieth century? Navy blue isn't a good color for me. And are we supposed to wear matching shoes and carry a matching purse?"

"I don't think it's so bad," said Tameeka. "I understand where the company is coming from. When I was a little kid, my mom would go to her job wearing blue jeans and sandals. Her company sold camping and other outdoor recreational gear, and the employees were encouraged to be super-casual at work. There was no discipline—not even a boss, really. It was just sort of assumed you'd do a good job. Then the Global Depression hit and the business went bankrupt. One hundred and fifty employees were laid off. It was a horrible time. We came close to having to live in our car, but then mom got a job in a restaurant. She had to wear a uniform. It was a starched white shirt and black slacks. The work environment was like, 'OK, no fooling around, we are totally professional. We need to be the best.' The restaurant survived and we weren't evicted. It was a close call! If I have to wear a boring uniform every day, I can live with it."

"I think a restaurant is a little bit different from an office where you're not interacting with the public," said Mei Lien. "And the fact that the company where your mom worked went bankrupt during the Global Depression may have had nothing to do with the company culture. The entire national economy went down the drain. The market for outdoor recreational gear vanished. No one was buying anything."

"If you look at history," added Lauren, "societies where people are forced to conform to an artificial standard are less creative. The workers don't see themselves as being able to think outside the box. There's less innovation and more stagnation."

"I'll leave the innovation to the bosses who get paid to think," said Tameeka. "Straining my brain is above my pay grade. I just want to get along and go along."

Sylvia scrolled through her phone. "I found the page that gives the new wardrobe rules. It's a long list."

"What does it say about shoes?" asked Mei Lien.

"It says that sneakers, athletic shoes, and sandals are prohibited. Shoes must be closed toe, and the heel must be no more than two inches in height. Choose basic conservative pumps in navy blue, brown, black, or maroon. They must match the conservative tone of the suit. No 'strange or unusual designs,' whatever that means."

"It means you can't wear your black leather dominatrix boots," said Lauren.

"I'll remember that," replied Sylvia. "But to answer your question, nowhere does it say that your shoes must match your skirt. But it does say that skirt length should be a little below the knee. No miniskirts, girls."

At that moment Carin entered the break room.

"I didn't know you drank coffee," joked Mei Lien.

"I was just passing by and I saw you were here, so I decided to come in and say hello," he replied. "No coffee for me, thank you."

"Carin," said Sylvia, "as long as you're here, I'd like to tell you something. Last night I had the most interesting encounter. At the chamber music concert."

"Yes, I know," he nodded. "You met Palor. You and Jason spoke to him after the concert. You were wearing your new engagement ring. Congratulations. Have you set the date?"

"Not yet," said Sylvia. "You guys will be among the first to know. I brought up the subject of my interesting encounter—which you already seem to know about—because I was amazed that Palor, despite having never met me before that moment, knew practically everything about me that you know. He described the problem with the Globe Nebula exactly. It was startling. Do you guys have some sort of memory-sharing system?"

"That describes it very well," said Carin. "We're all connected to the cloud, and can access any data from any of our brethren. In addition, if some new data appears that's relevant to me, I'll get a flag telling me it's there. That saves me the time and energy needed to constantly search the database. It's a highly efficient system."

"So how many of your brethren, as you call them, are working within companies like ours?" asked Mei Lien.

"Sorry, that's classified," smiled Carin.

"Okay, I get that," she said, "but if you have access to the individual and collective memories of your brethren, what happens if one of you is employed by a competitor of Sun Motors? Could that competitor access your memory and your knowledge of everything you witness or in which you participate on a daily basis here at Sun Motors?"

"Good point," added Sylvia. "In fact, Alliance Partners, the employer of Palor, is a big holding company with many investments in the automotive sector. They own a controlling interest in Shang Tono Corporation, a company based in Korea that makes vehicle airbags for most of the leading automakers. Shang Tono is in the unique position of having access to production records and projections for all their client companies. That means Palor has the same access. But Shang Tono doesn't sell to Sun Motors—we buy our airbags from a company in Indonesia. But since you, Carin, work here at Sun Motors, Palor knows our production history. And if another one of your brethren worked at Shang Tono, then he would also have access to our production numbers and even our contracts."

"In such an environment," said Mei Lien, "it would seem impossible to keep trade secrets."

"Carin," said Sylvia, "I'll bet right now you know how many airbags each of our competitors have ordered for the next four quarters."

Carin smiled. "You guys are good at creating hypothetical situations. That shows excellent inductive reasoning. You assert that because Palor and I share a common memory database (which, by the way, is updated in real time), then our competitors will know our plans, which is a bad thing. But you forget that we all operate under the careful and all-knowing guidance of the Industrial Council. The Council neither envisions nor seeks a world in which one member corporation has an unfair advantage over another. The philosophy of the Council is that among Council members, there's enough to go around. There are enough slices of the pie to keep everyone happy, and therefore cheating is counterproductive."

Sylvia put her coffee cup on the counter. "So you're saying that competition is only an illusion!"

"The Council believes that competition among Council member companies is irrational and wasteful," replied Carin. "But our national competition with the military and industrial power of Rodinia is very real. As you know, open warfare with Rodinia could happen at any time."

"So the government has told us every day since the end of the Global Depression," said Lauren with a smirk.

"Watch what you say," replied Carin with a sharpness of tone that Sylvia had never heard him use before. "The threat from Rodinia is very real. And it's not just from their military. Our government has identified a massive network of Rodinian spies operating in the United Americas. These agents seek to infiltrate every level of society—including the aberrants—with a twofold mission. One is to collect intelligence and the other is to sow discord. As the United Americas intensifies our defensive stance against the aggression of these covert agents, all Morta autonomous humanoid operators have two key missions: to enhance productivity within key Council member corporations and to identify any suspected spies."

"Part of your job here is to look for spies?" said Lauren. "That's crazy. We're just a car company."

"Again, I urge you to choose your words carefully," replied Carin with an expression that was an accurate facsimile of an angry scowl. "According to the mandates of both the Industrial Council and the White House, certain key industries are vital to our national defense. Because of their importance to our nation's security, they are outside the jurisdiction of Congress. Instead they are regulated by the President with the advice and counsel of the Industrial Council. Sun Motors falls into this category. This means that because our responsibility is greater, the standards we must meet are higher. I need not remind you this is a very special place. If the demands put upon us are heavy, it's because we represent an important bulwark against those who would harm our country."

"Was Judy Loring a spy?" asked Sylvia.

Carin turned to her with a cold smile. "As you know, Judy Loring has taken a leave of absence. We do not know when, or if, she will return."

"I'm puzzled because she left town with her entire family," replied Sylvia. "In the middle of the night."

"And you know this how?"

"I was concerned about them, so I talked to their neighbor."

"And what did this neighbor say?"

As Carin stared directly at her without moving, as if he were frozen, the room fell silent. Sylvia suddenly felt she had said too much. Trying not to show her nervousness—but of course Carin was analyzing her every breath and blink of her eyes!—she took her coffee cup to the sink and began to rinse it off.

"Oh," she said, "the neighbor didn't know much except in the evening they were at home and in the morning they were gone. Judy and her family must have left during the night. That's all."

"I know Judy is a friend of yours," said Carin in a more soothing tone. "Therefore, while it's not information that I would ordinarily be allowed to divulge, I can say to you that Judy is not suspected of being a spy. She has taken a leave of absence."

"That's reassuring," said Lauren. "I would hate to think one of our team was the agent of a hostile power!"

"A thought has suddenly occurred to me," said Sylvia. "If you're looking for spies, would it not be true that a person born and raised in Rodinia would have a genetic heritage quite different from someone whose family has been living in the United Americas for generations?"

Carin smiled. "Again you show superior inductive reasoning. While there is no certainty that a person from Rodinia would be genetically different from a citizen of the United Americas, there is a high degree of likelihood. However, you must not forget about the native-born Americans who might be recruited to become spies for Rodinia. Their agents use highly sophisticated methods to convert weak-minded citizens to their cause."

"Therefore when casting the net in hopes of ensnaring spies from Rodinia," said Sylvia, "you have no preconceptions about whom you might catch. It could be anybody."

"That's right," replied Carin. "A spy could be anybody."

That night, Sylvia and Jason snuggled on the sofa in Sylvia's apartment. After dinner they thought they would watch a movie, but a romantic interlude and then conversation had delayed the opening credits.

"Sweetheart, I think we should get married right away," Sylvia suddenly said.

"Really?" he replied. "Why? I mean, I have no objection—it really doesn't matter to me—but I assumed you wanted a regular church wedding."

"Let's be realistic. My parents are divorced and my father is a tightwad who won't give us nickel for a wedding. Your dad is no longer with us and your mom lives in Alaska. The idea of a traditional church wedding is rather ridiculous. To spend all of that money just to have a ceremony that looks like what you're supposed to do rather than what you should do seems crazy. I'd rather spend our money on a down payment for a house."

"I'm with you on that," he said.

There was a moment of silence.

"Is there anything else?" Jason asked as he ran his fingers through her hair. "You seem quiet tonight. Not your usual bubbly self."

"I'm sorry. I just feel—I don't know what it is. Call it a sense of foreboding. At work, things are changing. The culture is changing."

"I thought the culture was pretty bad when Randolph Meekin was your boss. When Carin arrived you told me it was like a new day dawning."

She reached for a handful of popcorn, which they had made in anticipation of the movie. "Yes, that's what it seemed like. But in the past few days it feels like we're moving towards a culture of hyper efficiency. The employees are being treated like cogs in a machine. I signed a bunch of new consent forms that, while I'm at work, give the company the right to collect and analyze the dead skin cells that slough off my body and the exhalations that come out of my lungs!"

"Yeah, we've had to sign the same kinds of forms."

"And now we have a new dress code. I have to go out and buy navy blue skirts and white blouses. It's all part of 'The Sun Motors Way." The company is offering wardrobe subsidies for current employees, but it strikes me as a big step backward in time."

"Does it have anything to do with the escalating tensions with Rodinia? Are they trying to impose discipline as they move us toward a wartime economy?"

"Could be," Sylvia said as she drew the blanket higher around her legs. In the fireplace the flame had dwindled to a dull orange glow. "To be honest, I don't really care about the dress code. I can live with white blouses and blue skirts. I care a lot more about the loss of privacy. Carin has enormous powers of observation and memory. What would easily escape the notice of a human being, he zeroes in on. The other day he chided me for having two glasses of wine at lunch. This was based on his analysis of my breath when I was talking to him, as well as his observations of my pupils and dermal capillaries, or so he said. But however he did it, his analysis was on target. He even accurately said I was drinking Burgundy."

"You drink Burgundy?" asked Jason. "That's news to me."

"Among the crappy wine selection at the restaurant, it was the best choice. We were celebrating Meekin's transfer."

"Okay, so Carin is a highly observant busybody. What else is going on?"

"Today they had the grand opening of the new day care center at the plant. In the infirmary they've got a DNA sequencing machine. They can analyze the children's DNA! The center isn't even open to all employees—the kids have to pass some sort of screening process."

"Perhaps they're checking for genetic conditions. But it makes you wonder what they would do if they discovered a child had a genetic disorder such as Down syndrome, cystic fibrosis, or sickle cell anemia."

"My uncle Charlie had muscular dystrophy," said Sylvia. "I don't remember much about him. He died when I was little. But he was the only member of my family that I know of who had a genetic disease."

"All I know is that you're perfect in every way," said Jason as he kissed the top of her head. "And I'm sure you'll have perfect little babies."

"You mean we'll have perfect little babies," she laughed. "They'll take after you."

"And unlike me, they'll know their real mommy and daddy. No foster parents."

"Your parents did a good job," said Sylvia. "I'd say you turned out pretty well!" She pressed closer to Jason. "All I want is a nice normal family. A boy and a girl, and a cute little house in a good neighborhood. And a dog."

Jason smiled and stroked her cheek. "And you, Mrs. Quin, shall have them."

CHAPTER ELEVEN

The next morning at work, Sylvia noticed a man with a ladder installing devices high up, near the ceiling, in each corner of the office. He looked like an electrician and the devices looked like cameras. The job took about an hour. When he was finished, Sylvia noted that while the walls to her cubicle shielded her from two of the cameras, the two that were behind her had a good view of her desk and computer.

At a few minutes before ten o'clock, Sylvia went to the contracts team meeting. Tameeka, Mei Lien, Edouardo, Roger, Maxwell, and Lauren were already seated around the conference table. Sylvia—who had not yet gone shopping for her new office wardrobe—saw that Tameeka and Edouardo were wearing the requisite white and navy blue.

At exactly the turn of the hour, Carin entered. "Ah," said with satisfaction, "It's good to see that two of our team members have embraced the new office dress code. The Sun Motors Way is going to transform the company, and I'm looking forward to one hundred percent participation. And here's some good news: Today is Friday, and since Monday—this current week—the number of parts delivered late to the assembly lines has been zero. It's true! During the past four and one-half days, we've achieved an on-time delivery rate of one hundred percent. You can't get any better than that! I've been told that before I came here, you had massive problems with late deliveries. Huge headaches. The sloppiness of delivery—wrong parts, wrong quantities, wrong times—was costing the company millions of dollars. It was a disaster. I think we can all be very proud of the job we've done this week, and I know we can do the same great job every week."

With his hands, Carin applauded—stiffly but with enthusiasm. The seven members of the team joined in. Then Carin stopped, and the team members stopped too.

Sylvia had to admit to herself that during the past few days the department had brought its performance up a notch. But its work output, even under Meekin, had always been pretty good. Never had she heard anyone describe the functioning of the logistics office as being a disaster, or that problems with part deliveries had cost the company millions of dollars. Was Carin engaged in puffing up his own job performance? That seemed to contradict what Sylvia understood to be his bedrock rationality and impartiality. Unless his creators at Morta Laboratories had programmed him to sell himself, and the Bright Horizon pilot program, at every available opportunity.

"It's good to be able to deliver positive news," said Carin. "Now on to business." With brisk efficiency he led the discussion as each member of the team gave their reports and noted any problem areas.

At the conclusion of the regular agenda, Carin said, "Any questions?"

"Yes," said Sylvia. "What's with the cameras in the office? I saw the technician installing them this morning."

"I'm glad you asked," replied Carin. "Recently, you may have seen me walking around the office with some people who are unfamiliar to you. If not, you will. In any case, we are very fortunate to have with us for the next several weeks a team of professional management consultants from the Special Services office of the Industrial Council. Sun Motors has hired them to study every aspect of our operations here at the Detroit Assembly Plant, from the executive suites to the loading docks, with the goal of increasing efficiency across the board. It's one more part of the Sun Motors Way, our comprehensive effort to boost productivity while trimming waste. We want Sun Motors to be the automotive industry leader, and within the company I'm sure you'll agree that we—the people in this room—want the Detroit Assembly Plant to be number one in every key performance indicator."

"Okay, but why the cameras?" asked Edouardo.

"Their purpose is to observe and record your physical motions during the workday. These motions will be mapped and analyzed for wasted movement. There is no judgment involved. That's not why we're doing this. We want to find out if we're working as efficiently as possible.

"I'll give you an example. Let's say—just hypothetically—that Maxwell and Tameeka, who are currently stationed on opposite sides of the room, are working on a project that requires them to walk over to the other person's cubicle several times a day. The computer will record their movements and calculate the amount of time spent walking to each other's cubicles. If the analysis reveals that we would see an increase in efficiency by moving them closer together, then that's what we'll do."

"You'll be able to see everything we do at our desks," said Mei Lien. "You'll be able to see what's on my computer screen."

"Yes, but that's not particularly relevant to this program," said Carin. "We already collect and process that information. Your keystrokes are recorded, as are the files you open and view. That's a standard human resources function of employee oversight. This is designed to reveal your physical motions during the workday."

"Is there a camera in the ladies' room?" asked Sylvia.

"No," smiled Carin. "That would be a violation of your personal privacy. And it has nothing to do with workplace efficiency."

"The break room?" asked Roger.

"Again, no." Carin smiled. He put both hands flat on the table as if he were about to stand up. "I hope that explains everything. It's all part of making Sun Motors—and this office—an industry leader in productivity. Okay? Good." He stood up and left the room.

Sylvia whispered to Mei Lien, "Meet me in the break room in fifteen."

Sylvia went to her desk and checked a work file on her computer. She typed a few keystrokes. As a typist, Sylvia was unschooled. She typed with two fingers and made generous use of the delete key to correct her many clumsy typos. She had never thought much about it, because in her mind all that counted was the product. It didn't matter if she made a hundred mistakes while typing something because she corrected herself as she went along, and when she finally hit the "send" key the writing was always perfect and the numbers accurate.

To be sure, when Sylvia had first attended college she had tried to learn touch typing. For some reason—she never knew why—the effort was hopeless. She practiced and practiced, but could never associate the correct key with the correct finger. Finally she had given up, and had resigned herself to "hen pecking," as her typing teacher had once derided the technique.

For years she had hen pecked and the work had never suffered. Now, at this moment, she suddenly found that she had become self conscious about her typing. A computer somewhere deep in the bowels of the Sun Motors complex was recording and analyzing each and every keystroke. This computer, she surmised, was comparing her performance to that of her colleagues, or perhaps to a standard created by the Industrial Council.

It was judging her not on the product but the process.

She began to type more slowly and methodically. It was better, she reasoned, to type accurately the first time even if the pace were a little slower. She was working on a written report on a proposed new vendor for the electronic control unit for the Comanche satellite signal receiver, and she found herself trying to slow down and type without making any mistakes. But the effort did not have the desired result. It was as if for years she had been operating at a particular speed, and her mind and muscle memory had locked into that speed, no matter how imperfect the outcome. In trying to type more slowly and more carefully, she found that her attention wandered. The task was more boring. She found that she would forget what she was writing, and had to stop and remember, which slowed her down even more.

"Damn," she muttered.

She glanced up at the nearest camera. Its gleaming black eye regarded her with indifference. Could it read lips? Why not? If a computer could recognize your face, at night and in the rain, and distinguish it from millions of other faces, then lip reading should be an easy next step.

Focus. Just get the report done. The vendor looks good and we can do business with them.

A key fact in their favor was they had no connection with Rodinia. Word had come down from the Sun Motors Building that foreign vendors with any association to Rodinia or any of its allies, or who sold to companies in Rodinia or any of its allies, were to be viewed with deep suspicion. If possible, they were to be terminated and new contracts signed with vendors approved by the Industrial Council.

Damn! I've used the delete key a dozen times in one sentence. Okay. Slow down. Take a deep breath.

Sylvia looked over the top of her cubicle at the rest of the office. People were working as they always did. Maxwell, coffee cup in hand (as always!), was walking over to Tameeka's cubicle. He looked so normal and relaxed. Did it not bother him that he was being watched the way a researcher watches a rat in a maze? Perhaps he was a good actor. Sylvia thought she, herself, was a terrible actor. Jason always told her this. "You cannot tell a lie," he had said. "You're too honest. You'd give yourself away." He was right. Even when she had to deliver an innocuous phony compliment to someone—such as when Estelle had worn a hideous dress to the office holiday party and Sylvia had told her how lovely it looked—she felt her heart racing and the wave of deceit slosh through her brain. If Estelle had possessed one tenth of Carin's powers of observation, the fib would surely would have been revealed.

She glanced at her clock. Time to meet Mei Lien in the break room.

But why would she, Sylvia, need to go to the break room? Her visit would be on the record. She had to be able to justify it.

Sylvia never drank coffee. Just never cared for it. But now, she reasoned, was good time to start. The coffee machine was in the break room. Maxwell went there ten times a day with his cup. Perhaps Carin would notice this and speak to him about it. Perhaps not. There was no way to tell. But having an interest in coffee was a good cover for getting Sylvia out of her cubicle and stretching her legs.

She stood up and, with a cautious glance at the camera—don't look at it too long!—she casually made her way along the aisle of cubicles to the hallway. Were there cameras here? She wasn't sure. She entered the break room, where Mei Lien was waiting. A careful inspection of the corners of the walls and the ceiling revealed no cameras.

"What do you think?" she said to Mei Lien.

Mei Lien shrugged. "A camera could be hidden anywhere. There could be one in the microwave, or in the ceiling vent. We have to assume we're being watched from the moment we drive into the parking lot in the morning until we drive out in the evening."

"But who can live like that?"

"It's happening all over. My sister works for Onyx Telecom. She does customer service. Same thing—cameras everywhere. And yesterday her department got a robot manager. Its name is Waller. From what she tells me, it's the same model as Carin. Same jumpsuit and wraparound glasses."

"I'm feeling more and more like a lab rat," said Sylvia. "With the medical consent forms, the creepy way Carin can analyze you, the uniforms, the cameras—I'm beginning to wonder who I am. Where do I end and the outside world begins? Are my private thoughts the only thing remaining I can say are truly mine?"

"Soon enough they'll be able to read your mind," laughed Mei Lien. "Remember, it's just a job, okay? Eight hours out of your day. When you go home, what you do ain't nobody's business but your own. You're a free person. Look at it this way: It sure beats being one of the aberrants. They've got nothing. To be on the inside you must pay the price, but I'd say it's worth it."

At that moment Tameeka walked in. "Hey girls, what's up?" she asked as she went to the refrigerator.

"We were just talking about the new cameras," said Mei Lien. Sylvia wished she hadn't said it. Perhaps because Tameeka had replaced Judy under mysterious circumstances, Sylvia hadn't yet warmed to her.

"What about them?" said Tameeka as she took out a plastic cup with a cover.

"The idea seems a bit overbearing," said Sylvia. "Doesn't it?"

Tameeka put the plastic cup on the counter and opened it. It looked like it had yogurt inside. "I don't care," she said as she dipped a plastic spoon into the cup. "I've got nothing to hide. They can put a camera in my cubicle for all I care. I only want to do my job, get my paycheck, and go home. I'm here for eight hours a day. I don't care what they make me do for those eight hours as long as they pay me."

"But aren't you worried about the invasion of your privacy?" asked Mei Lien.

"Invasion of my privacy? I don't expect any privacy here, except in the ladies' room. If they put a camera in there, I'd be pissed. But out in the office? There's no such thing as privacy. For eight hours a day, they own you." Holding her cup and spoon, she turned to face them. "Girls, if you want my advice, I'd say, 'smile for the camera.'" She walked out of the room.

"You know, in a weird way I admire her," said Sylvia. "Here I am, getting all freaked out because I think I'm under the microscope, and there goes Tameeka with not a worry in the world."

"Do you know why it doesn't bother her?" asked Mei Lien.

"No—why?"

"Because she is astonishingly naïve and she believes the company will treat her fairly. She believes in the goodness of the world. She truly believes that if she does nothing wrong in her own eyes, then the company will treat her honorably. She doesn't understand that if the company wants to screw you, they will find a way and they will do it."

As Sylvia stirred her coffee—which was getting cold, a condition that didn't bother her in the slightest because she wasn't going to drink it anyway—she thought for a moment. "Do you think Tameeka could be a Rodinian agent?" she whispered. "After all, if you were going to be an industrial spy, you'd want to get along with everybody, especially with your bosses, and you'd do nothing to rock the boat. You'd do a good job at work while avoiding the spotlight."

Mei Lien frowned. "I don't know. I suppose anything's possible. Personally I'm not sure if I believe any of this spy talk."

"Why not?"

"I'm sure there are some spies from Rodinia working here in the United Americas. Every nation spies on every other nation. Even friendly nations spy on each other. That's been going on for centuries. The question is whether the spies from Rodinia are more numerous or more threatening than is traditionally expected, and whether you can use the threat of spies—as if they were a big bad bogeyman—to curtail traditional basic human rights." She glanced at the clock on the wall. "I'd better be going. In five minutes I have a video conference with a supplier in Brazil."

Sylvia returned to her desk. While her talk with Mei Lien and Tameeka had shown her that other people could view the increasing loss of privacy at Sun Motors with casual acceptance, she couldn't shake the feeling of being self-conscious and on edge. She told herself that Tameeka was right—it was just a job, and it didn't matter what they did to you from nine to five.

They could watch you, listen in on your phone calls, track your movements as you walked around the office, record each keystroke of your work on the computer, and even collect the organic material that came out of your body each and every minute you were on company property.

They could store your personal data in their vast databases, analyze it, compare it to others, and even sell it to other companies for whatever reason they wanted.

They could make you sign a non-disclosure agreement, ensuring you wouldn't go to the aberrant press with the inside story of life among the Two Hundred K. They could make you sign an arbitration agreement that forced you to settle any pay disputes within the company, in private, instead of in civil court, and you couldn't publicly reveal the amount of your salary.

They could make you wear a uniform like a schoolgirl. What was next—assembling outside around the flagpole each morning to sing the company song?

They could do all these things because every other Thursday afternoon, Sun Motors, Inc. sent a direct deposit into your bank account. This was the money that paid for your comfortable lifestyle—the house, the car, the nice restaurants, the annual two-week vacation to the shore.

It was just a job, Sylvia told herself. At the end of my workday and for the following sixteen hours, I'm beyond their control.

In Sylvia's desk drawer was the bottle of painkillers she had relied on when Randolph Meekin was her boss. For a week she hadn't opened it. Feeling the sharp tension in the back of her neck, from the bottle she took two pills, which she washed down with her cold coffee.

CHAPTER TWELVE

That evening at her apartment, with Jason waiting outside the bathroom door, Sylvia took a home pregnancy test.

It was positive.

"Oh my God!" she cried as she fell into his arms. "I can't believe it! We're going to have a baby!"

He kissed her and said, "This is good news! I've never been more happy. You're going to be the greatest mom!"

Suddenly Sylvia grew pensive.

"Sweetheart, what's the matter?" asked Jason. "You look as if a black cloud suddenly blotted out the sun."

Sylvia sat on the sofa and turned to face him. She put her hand on his knee. "I need to tell you something. Promise you won't be upset."

"You want to tell me something? Why should I be upset?"

"Just promise."

"Okay, I won't get upset. Now what is it?"

"This isn't the first time I've gotten pregnant."

"You mean you have a child somewhere?"

She gave a rueful smile. "No. It ended in a miscarriage. It was a few years ago, long before I met you. The father—my boyfriend at the time—said that he wanted to get married, but when I lost the baby he broke up with me. I was devastated."

"What a jerk," said Jason.

"You told me you wouldn't get upset."

"I'm not upset. I'm just saying the guy was a jerk and you're better off without him." He took her hands in his. "Listen to me. I love you. My devotion to you comes without strings attached. What happened to you is in the past. It's gone. We need to focus on the future. If for some reason this one doesn't go well, we'll try again. Other people have faced these challenges.

77

It's going to be all right. We're going to stick together. Okay?"

Wiping away a tear, she said with a smile, "Yes. I'm very hopeful, I really am. I just thought you should know. I don't want us to have any secrets."

"No secrets."

Brightening up, she said, "Do you think it will be a boy or a girl?"

"How should I know?" he laughed. "Do you want to find out, or would you rather be surprised?"

"I'd rather be surprised, but it's hard to avoid learning what it is. When my cousin Joanie had her baby, she didn't want to know the sex, but during a routine examination the ultrasound technician blurted out, 'Oh look, your can see his little boy parts!' So that was the end of the surprise."

"Okay, we'll tell the doctors we don't want to know. In the meantime, we need to start planning. Let's get married as soon as possible. We can get the license from the office of the Wayne County clerk. We're going to have to move quickly on buying a house. We've narrowed it down to three or four top contenders. This weekend let's look at them all one more time and hopefully we can decide."

"But we can't appear to be desperate," Sylvia said as she sat down on the sofa. "We're not going to tell any of the sellers that I'm expecting. We're going to say that we're planning a family, not that we're under the gun to move quickly."

"Right," agreed Jason. "What's the Sun Motors company policy about maternity leave?"

She thought for a moment. "Good question. I'll have to ask Estelle in human resources."

"And you'll need to go see your doctor. The new one—what was her name?"

"Rebecca Goldsmith at the Willowdale Center. I'll call her office tomorrow."

On Sunday, Sylvia and Jason made an offer on a charming house on a tree-lined street in the town of Northville. Built before the Global Recession, the Dutch colonial had three bedrooms and a nice big backyard. As they had agreed, Jason and Sylvia didn't reveal they were expecting a baby.

On Monday morning, Sylvia's buoyant mood did not go unnoticed. In the break room, which Sylvia was planning to visit more regularly despite the fact that her inclination to drink coffee was now even lower than it had been before she took the pregnancy test, Tameeka said, "Girl, you must have had a pretty special weekend. You're practically glowing."

Sylvia was gripped with indecision. She hated lying, which in her mind included omitting an obvious and significant truth. If someone said, "How was your weekend?" and your weekend included learning you had become pregnant, and you replied, "Oh, fine," and nothing more, then that was as good as lying.

But that morning at work, Tameeka was the first person she had talked to about a non-work related subject. She felt neither obligated nor interested in making Tameeka—about whom she continued to have uneasy feelings—the first person to hear the news.

"Jason and I made an offer on a house," replied Sylvia. "We're very excited about moving in. It's in Northville, near Maybury State Park."

"Oh, that's a nice area. I'm sure you're super excited."

"Yes we are. Well, I've got to get back for a phone call." Sylvia walked away with the feeling that she had bought some time. But the news would be difficult to keep quiet, and eventually everyone, including Carin, would know.

At two o'clock, having managed to avoid personal discussions with her colleagues at work, Sylvia arrived at the office of Dr. Goldsmith for her first pre-natal appointment. A blood test confirmed that Sylvia was six weeks pregnant.

"Do you have an obstetrician?" asked Dr. Goldsmith.

"No, I don't. There was an OB at Dearborn Medical Group, but she's retired."

"Okay, we'll help you find one. When you're at eight or nine weeks, antepartum care begins. Your OB receives your comprehensive medical history and provides you with a full physical examination and various screenings. So we need to get one lined up quickly. I'd be happy to recommend you to Dr. Elizabeth Darcy at Detroit Hospital. I think you'll like her very much."

"Thank you," said Sylvia. "You know I had a miscarriage a few years ago. Will that reduce my chances of having a successful pregnancy?"

"No. Miscarriage is usually a one-time occurrence. Most women who miscarry go on to have healthy pregnancies. Only about one percent of women will have repeated miscarriages."

"That's good to know."

Upon her return to the office at four o'clock, Sylvia went to see Estelle to ask about the company's policy about maternity leave. But as she was about to enter the human resources office, she paused.

This was not something that had to be done right away, she thought. The company policy will be whatever it is, and it's not going to change in the next few weeks or even months. There's no reason to make my personal affairs known to anyone at Sun Motors until I absolutely have to. And what if I lose the baby? It would be better if no one knew anything about it. I don't want them fawning over me and telling me how sorry they are. I'd rather die than go through that experience again. No, it would be better to wait until it's noticeable. That will be about twelve weeks from now. Most miscarriages occur before that time, so if it happens again, I may never show a baby bump.

She turned around and went back to her desk.

At four-thirty, Carin appeared on her screen.

"Ah—there you are," he said. "An hour ago I tried to contact you and you were out. A check of the records indicated you had left at one forty-five. At four o'clock you returned."

"Yes, that's correct," she replied with a smile.

"Is everything all right?"

"Yes, everything is fine. I took some personal time. I believe I'm entitled to four hours per month."

"That's true. You've used two hours and fifteen minutes. I'm sure you're keeping track of it."

"Yes, sir, I am." That morning Sylvia had decided to address Carin as "sir," even if no one else did. It seemed like a politically positive thing to do. It cost her nothing to use this honorific when she spoke with him, and she hoped that in his eyes it would burnish her image as a company loyalist.

In addition, she had decided that during meetings or other public events, heaping praise upon Carin would be a useful strategy. She could thank him profusely for having solved a small problem for her, or compliment him for showing attributes of great leadership. Yes, she told herself, if there were a game to be played, she'd damn well play it better than anyone else.

"Is there anything else I can do for you, sir?" she asked with a smile worthy of a toothpaste commercial.

"No thank you, Sylvia." He signed off.

That went well, she thought. But was it possible that Carin could detect the odor of insincerity in her behavior? He was very good at picking up on visual and other sensory cues. As an autonomous humanoid operator, machine learning was an important part of his programming. Like a massive data magnet, he captured every sensation that came to him, analyzed it, classified it, put it into context, and stored it for future reference. His knowledge of humans and their behavior grew with every passing day.

But like a human, Carin had values. They included production efficiency and total loyalty. It might very well be, Sylvia reasoned, that outward praise and obedience were all that Carin was looking for, and the underlying sincerity—or lack thereof—was irrelevant. In Carin's world, what you see is what you get. Things that are unseen have no meaning and no value.

After work, Sylvia met Jason for dinner. While they were eating, he got a call from the real estate agent. Their offer on the house had been accepted. "I think this deserves a champagne toast," he said as he leaned over the table and kissed her.

"Oh sweetheart, do you think I should?" she said.

"People have been arguing for centuries about expectant mothers drinking a bit of wine. I don't think a few sips is going to cause fetal alcohol syndrome."

"I'd rather play it safe," she said. "You have a glass of champagne. I'll have sparkling water."

"Fair enough," smiled Jason.

After dinner they drove to Northville to see the house.

"Do you still like it?" asked Jason.

"Still like it? I love it more than ever," replied Sylvia. "I can't wait to move in and start fixing it up. It needs a lot of work. What color should we paint it? The green looks hideous. I think that's why it was on the market for so long. People saw the green and went, 'Ugh.' But when we paint it a pretty lemon yellow with white trim, it's going to look beautiful. The house has good bones. That's what they say, you know. If a house has good bones, then all the other stuff can be easily improved. What do you think of that big fir tree in the front yard?"

"I think it's depressing and needs to go," smiled Jason. "It looks like something a Hobbit would have in their yard."

"It's going to be a wonderful home," said Sylvia. "Our home."

CHAPTER THIRTEEN

The next morning, as Sylvia was working at her desk, with a cup of cold coffee at her elbow, Carin suddenly appeared on her screen. With a quick glance at the cubicles around her, Sylvia saw with relief that Carin had pre-empted all of them. It was an office-wide event.

"Pardon the interruption," said Carin, "but I have a very exciting announcement. As you know, my work as director of logistics and operations is part of the bold new Bright Horizon program at Sun Motors, and indeed at many other Two Hundred K companies across the United Americas. Initiated by President Deacon and the Industrial Council, the Bright Horizon program helps ensure the United Americas keeps our global competitive leadership position, especially with regard to Rodinia, which, as you know, has a long record of stealing our intellectual property and engaging in highly unfair trade practices. These provocations are in fact pushing us to the brink of war. Neither the president nor the Industrial Council want armed conflict, but if it comes, we will be ready to defend our sovereign state.

"But let's get back to the announcement. For the past few weeks the Bright Horizon program has been in beta mode, so to speak. There have been no press releases or authorized press coverage. We have not invited public scrutiny. Today that is changing. I'm pleased to report that the Detroit Assembly Plant has been chosen for a visit from Facts News, which is the only network authorized by the Industrial Council to broadcast the exciting unveiling of the Bright Horizon program. A team from Facts News will be here, in this building, at noon today. A reporter will be interviewing me as well as several key employees. We wish she had time to speak with every employee, but of course that would be impractical. I would like the following employees to meet in the conference room at noon: Tameeka White, Sylvia Brand, Roger Khan, and Maxwell Marcos. Please come as you are—no special preparations are necessary. After our session in the conference room, we anticipate the television news crew will want to get some candid shots of the office. When we come in, just ignore us and carry on as usual. Thank you."

Sylvia was both pleased and taken aback. She was happy because out of fifty employees in the office, Carin had chosen her to be one of four to meet with the Facts News crew. I must be doing something right, she thought. Perhaps my strategy of being a team player is paying off. But she was concerned because as far as she knew, Facts News was nothing more than a propaganda outlet for the administration of President Robert Deacon. She didn't watch the channel very often because the reporting was so obviously slanted in favor of the president that she never knew whether what she was seeing and hearing was based on reality or what the White House Press Office wanted people to think.

She hoped that the interview would be more than just a celebration of Carin and the Sun Motors management team. But it didn't matter: Whatever they threw at her, she'd toss it right back at them.

At noon the group assembled in the conference room. Carin said, "Please allow me to introduce our guests from Facts News. I'd like you to meet correspondent Leslie Applegate, who will be conducting the interviews. With her is photojournalist Eric Dane and sound engineer Betsy Ford. They've also brought along a makeup artist, Chia Chen, who has kindly offered to ensure you're prepared to face the camera. Isn't that right, Chia?"

A slender girl with large white teeth smiled and nodded.

"With that," said Carin, "I'll turn it over to Leslie."

"Thanks, Carin," said Applegate. "It's a pleasure to be with you today as we reveal the big news."

Sylvia had seen Leslie Applegate a few times on television—not on Facts News, which she rarely watched, but on a television commercial for one of those shady reverse mortgage companies that try to convince old people to cash out of their family homes, spend the money, and leave nothing for their children to inherit. Gold Star Financial, in whose advertisements Applegate had appeared, had been sued by various states' district attorneys for fraud. Then the Industrial Council, using its sweeping powers to regulate anything and everything related to the national defense, had intervened and forced the states to settle out of court. Some commentators—all of them allied with the aberrants, it was said—had questioned why the Industrial Council had inserted itself into a dispute between the states and a reverse mortgage company. Eventually it was revealed that President Deacon's wife, Emily Deacon, was a major stockholder in Gold Star Financial. It was the unspoken position of the Industrial Council that to protect their personal financial interests, high government officials friendly to President Deacon, including the president himself, his wife, and their three adult children, were entitled to wield the levers of government power. This courtesy was not extended to the members of the hopelessly weak minority Liberty Party, who, much to the irritation of the majority National Unity Party, had not yet been entirely stamped out of existence. Many Liberty Party members had vanished, but others persisted. In fact, some people believed the National Unity Party deliberately kept the Liberty Party on life support because having an "opposition" party proved that the United Americas was still a democracy. "See for yourself!" proclaimed National Unity Party candidates for all elected offices, both local and countrywide. "We have tough political campaigns followed by free, fair elections. The United Americas is the beacon of democracy towards which all other nations gaze with envy."

As for Leslie Applegate, it was never proven that she herself had made any false or misleading claims on the ads. She was allowed to walk away from the scandal and keep her job at Facts News.

The first team member Applegate interviewed on camera was Carin. He was open about the fact that he was a Morta AHO 6-C from Morta Laboratories in San Mateo, California. He talked about the vast improvements that had been made in the autonomous humanoid operator industry, and how robots—for lack of a better term—working side by side with their human counterparts could take any company to new levels of achievement. And, of course, his human employees had never been happier.

This was the cue to bring on the four human staff members.

"Let's start with Tameeka White," said Leslie.

In front of the camera, Tameeka was a natural performer. She praised Carin and the Bright Horizon program, and extolled the virtues of Sun Motors products and work environment. Both Carin and Leslie Applegate appeared to be very happy.

Roger Khan and Maxwell Marcos followed. Each painted glowing pictures of Sun Motors and Bright Horizon. They were so uniform and effusive in their praise that Sylvia found the interviews to be boring. It was the same thing over and over again, as if they were scripted.

Sylvia resolved to outdo all three of them—Tameeka, Roger, and Maxwell. She was going to provide the highest praise and the most positive report. No one was going to outperform her. There must not be the slightest doubt that she, Sylvia Brand, had true leadership ability.

"And now for Sylvia Brand," said Applegate. After a quick facial powdering by Chia Chen, she was ready for the camera.

"And what has been your experience working with Carin?" asked Applegate. Sylvia looked into the camera lens and gave her biggest smile.

"Like a dream come true," she said like a starving person presented with a steak dinner. In high school Sylvia had won the drama award four years running, and now she was showing why. "From the moment we first met Carin, we knew a new day was dawning at Sun Motors. He sees problems and solves them, and always with no ego and no interest in personal gain. I work in logistics, which means I'm part of the team that must source thirty thousand individual parts that are used to make each Sun Comanche. It may not seem like a very glamorous job, but it's vitally important. We work with hundreds of suppliers from all over the world, and it's a challenge to keep them all on track. Carin has amazing abilities to cut through the red tape and get things done."

"It sounds like the Bright Horizon program is a smashing success," Applegate effused.

"It's not just Carin but all of Sun Motors," said Sylvia. "Just last week we had the honor of attending the grand opening of the new Margaret J. Atkinson Day Care Center, located here at the Detroit Assembly Plant campus. Our brilliant COO, Mr. Posey, cut the ceremonial ribbon. It feels like a miracle to have such a resource available to Sun employees. I have such high regard for Mrs. Atkinson, and indeed the entire Atkinson family! They are leading us to new heights of success, and I know that everyone here is so grateful for their inspired leadership."

Leslie Applegate took the microphone and addressed the camera. "Well, there you have it—some very happy and appreciative employees here at the Sun Motors Detroit Assembly Plant logistics office! It sounds like the Bright Horizon program is off to a roaring start!"

After the news crew had left to go to another part of the plant, Carin stopped Sylvia in the hallway. "You did an excellent job," he said. "It did not go unnoticed."

"Thank you," she replied.

She was on her way to the ladies room. Once inside, she closed the door to a stall and sat on the toilet, still fully clothed. She put her head in her hands. The pain in her gut intensified.

She heard someone come in. She recognized the shoes as belonging to Mei Lien. She opened the door to the stall.

Standing at one of the sinks, Mei Lien turned. "Oh—Sylvia." She peered at Sylvia's state of being fully dressed. "What are you doing? Are you all right?"

"I feel like I'm going to throw up."

"Are you sick?"

Sylvia got to her feet. The feeling of nausea made her take shallow breaths. "Not exactly. I'm just…. tired. Worn out. I don't know how much longer I can play this game."

"What game?"

In hushed tones, Sylvia told Mei Lien about the interview with Facts News, and how she had heaped praise upon Carin, Gerald Posey, and the Atkinson family. "It was pure bullshit," she whispered. "Totally phony. I put a big stupid grin on my face and told them exactly what they wanted to hear. I did not say this place is run like a prison camp. I did not say that Carin is a tinpot dictator. I did not say how strange it was that your kid has to audition to get admitted to the Margaret J. Atkinson Day Care Center, as if she were applying to Harvard. I did not say how people around here mysteriously disappear. Everyone knows that Randolph Meekin isn't working downtown. He never worked downtown. He just vanished. And Judy and her husband and two kids didn't take a 'leave of absence' from life. They left in the middle of the night in a van with a bunch of people dressed in black. Her replacement was hired the afternoon before she and her family abandoned their home." She looked in the mirror with an expression of disgust. "And these stupid uniforms! They might as well be orange jumpsuits. What are we, children? Or beasts of burden?"

Stepping back to lean against the stall partition, Sylvia took a deep breath and slowly exhaled.

"Let's just try and make the best of it, okay?" said Mei Lien, gently laying a hand on her shoulder. "Compared to other companies, Sun Motors is a really good place to work. At the interview, you did the right thing. Think of it as like performing in a television ad for Sun. You were acting in a commercial. You were following the script they wanted. If there was anything reprehensible, it's that they didn't pay you for your performance. They got it for free. Cheap bastards!"

They both laughed.

"I suppose you're right," sighed Sylvia. "I need to focus on the future. Did I tell you? Jason and I are buying a house. It's a cute Dutch colonial in Northville, near Maplewood Park."

"That's a pretty area," said Mei Lien. "Congratulations! Does this mean you're getting married soon?"

"Yes—very soon."

"Oh, I see…" Mei Lien gave a knowing smile. "Any particular reason for the accelerated nuptials?"

"No. No reason. We're just madly in love."

Sylvia left work an hour early for her appointment with Dr. Elizabeth Darcy at Detroit Hospital. Built over a century earlier, the stately brick structure was located downtown, near the river. Sylvia took the rattling elevator to the fifth floor, where the receptionist handed her an old-fashioned clipboard to which a stack of papers were attached. "Because you're a new patient, we need you to fill those out," said the receptionist. Sylvia took the clipboard and sat down in one of the vinyl-covered chairs. The papers included the usual medical questions—allergies (only to lobster, which she didn't like anyway), drug use (none), episodes of dizziness (no). Then there was the consent form, which consisted of several pages of dense text. Sylvia scanned through it, trying to perform some semblance of due diligence while knowing it was a pointless exercise. One paragraph caught her eye. It said, "In the event of my death, or if any of my tissues or organs are removed during a medical procedure, the hospital has my permission to use my tissues and organs in any way that advances medical science, including the development of biomedical products in which I claim no financial interest." She took the form to the receptionist. "What does this mean?" she asked.

The receptionist smiled and said, "I think they assume that because you're an ethical and caring person, you would want a fellow human being to benefit from advances in medical science that involve the use of human tissue. Wouldn't you want this? The alternative to using human tissue is to dispose of it. Just throw it away in the trash. Once our patients understand what it means, all of them have been happy to sign this form." Having said this, the receptionist fixed upon Sylvia a friendly but steady gaze.

"I suppose if you put it that way," said Sylvia, "it sound almost noble. But what about this paragraph, which says the Industrial Council may, from time to time and at its own discretion, access and review patient medical records?"

"That ensures the Council can provide the necessary regulatory oversight of health care providers," said the receptionist. "They need to inspect patient records to verify that every hospital, including this one, is meeting the necessary professional standards. It's for your protection as a consumer."

"I don't know—this all seems rather intrusive."

The receptionist gave her an unfriendly smile. "Well, if you'd prefer to pay cash at one of those aberrant medical clinics out in the country, you're free to do that. But it will cost you more and you'll be playing Rodinian roulette with your health. And as far as your patient data is concerned, in aberrant territory it's like the Wild West. Anything goes." She leaned forward and raised her eyebrows. "I've heard that aberrant clinics buy and sell human body parts. You go in for a cholecystectomy, and while you're lying there in dreamland they remove your infected gallbladder and one of your kidneys. Then they sell your kidney on the black market. You can't even sue—you know how bad the courts are out there. Nothing but incompetence and chaos."

"Well, if everybody signs, I suppose it must be all right."

"Of course it's all right! You can trust Detroit Hospital to take good care of your personal information. The Industrial Council has given Detroit Hospital the coveted four-star rating. That should tell you everything."

"Yes, of course." After signing and dating all the forms, Sylvia handed the clipboard to the receptionist.

"Okay—now that we've gotten the paperwork out of the way, I'll need to see your Sun Motors Employee Wellness Plan card." Sylvia handed it over, and the receptionist scanned it and gave it back. "You're all set," said the receptionist. "Please have a seat and the nurse will call you."

Presently Sylvia was ushered to an examination room, and after the usual preliminaries with the nurse, Dr. Darcy entered.

"Call me Liz," said the doctor as she read Sylvia's history from the tablet in her hand. "We don't stand on formality around here. You were under the care of Donna Giacalone until she retired, and now your primary care physician is Rebecca Goldsmith. They've sent all your records. You think you're six weeks along?"

"Yes," replied Sylvia.

"You're a senior logistics manager at Sun Motors, aren't you?"

"Yes."

"Will you want your child to enroll in day care where you work?"

"Do you mean the new Margaret J. Atkinson center? I hadn't thought about it. It seems like such a long time in the future! I haven't even started to show yet. Yes, I suppose I'd want our child to go there. It would be very convenient."

"Then we'll start the application process. You need to do it early. I've been told that this year and next year are already closed to admissions. If we're lucky, we'll be able to secure a spot when your baby turns two years old."

"Okay, thanks."

Dr. Darcy studied her tablet. "The baby's father is Jason Quin. Age thirty. He's been with Hilltop Financial for five years. A good company. Before that he worked as a loan officer at First Lakeville Bank. And you're not presently married, but you'll tie the knot very soon. Correct?"

"Yes."

"And you're buying a house together, in Northville. A nice little starter home."

"Yes, but how did you happen to know that?"

"It's simple—we have access to the metro Detroit area real estate records. If one of our patients shows up in that database, it's added to the patient record. We're not snooping—this is publicly available information. We just happen to be able to leverage it."

"That's interesting, but I don't see what that has to do with my health or that of my baby."

"Here at Detroit Hospital, we're concerned not only with the immediate condition of you and your unborn child, but your baby's overall well-being as he or she begins the journey of life. This includes the quality of the home environment. It can have a significant impact on the child's development."

After administering a battery of tests and taking a blood sample from Sylvia, Dr. Darcy left the room for a moment. When she returned she was carrying a small package, which she opened.

"This is a very simple dermal patch," she said as she removed the object from its sterile wrapper. "I'm going to attach it to your abdomen. As you can see, it's no larger than a small band-aid. It's waterproof, and will last until your next appointment, which will be in two weeks."

"What does it do?" asked Sylvia. (In reality, what had first entered her mind was the thought that Jason would, in a romantic moment, be turned off by seeing or touching a band-aid-like object stuck to her belly. But she was too embarrassed to say this.)

"It's connected to the internet," said Dr. Darcy as she positioned the patch on Sylvia's skin. "It transmits over one hundred data points to our monitoring system. This ensures that if there's the slightest problem or deviation from the norm, we can quickly intervene. Pretty cool, isn't it?"

"One hundred data points? That sounds like a lot. What are some of them?"

"Blood pressure, blood oxygen, glucose level, white blood cell count, a dozen different hormone levels, your heart rate, breathing rate, temperature. Also geospatial information—where you are at any given moment, and if you're lying down or upright."

"You're going to track me? Everywhere I go?"

"Wouldn't you want us to? Think about it. What if you were driving home at night and you got into an accident? Let's say your car ran into a deer and you ended up in a ditch. Let's also say you were unconscious. When you're carrying a baby, seconds count. With this dermal patch, your accident would be noticed instantly. Help would be on its way even before you could use your phone to call for assistance. This technology could save your life and the life of your unborn child."

"But the people in charge of the tracking system will know every place I've been. All the stores and restaurants I go to. They'll see if I leave work early one day or oversleep one morning."

"So what?" shrugged Dr. Darcy. "You're not a drug dealer, are you? You're not playing hooky from work, are you? If you have nothing to hide, then what's the worry?"

"Here's my worry," said Sylvia. "If I decide to stop at Starbucks to use the ladies room, am I suddenly going to get a steady stream of ads for Starbucks on my social media feed? If one day I go to a store and buy bananas, will I then receive emails from supermarkets that sell bananas?"

"I think your concerns are overblown. So what if you receive a few ads? We all get ads. Just ignore them, like I do. Let me show you something." She took her personal phone out of her pocket and then scrolled through it. She showed her phone to Sylvia. "See this ad for the cruise line? Last week I was online and I casually looked at some websites for cruises in the Caribbean. I wasn't at all interested in buying a ticket; I looked at these sites because I have another patient who loves going on those gigantic cruise ships that look like floating brothels, and so I thought I'd at least brush up on the topic. I spent about ten minutes searching and looking. I didn't linger long at any particular page or website. Later that same day, these ads started popping wherever I went on the internet. All from spending a few minutes doing a search. But I don't care. Let 'em send ads to me. I just scroll past them."

Having been connected to the internet by her dermal patch, Sylvia went home, with another appointment set for two weeks.

The Facts News story about the Bright Horizon program and Sun Motors was slated to run at ten o'clock that evening. At dinnertime, Jason came over to visit. To Sylvia's relief, when they were in bed together he wasn't bothered by the band-aid stuck to her stomach. Then at ten o'clock they turned on the television.

When Sylvia's segment came on, she cringed. "Look at me!" she said. "I look like an overeager cheerleader. My face looks so fat!"

"I think you look beautiful," he said. "And you did the right thing. You're giving them what they want. You and I may think it's a silly act and feel embarrassed by it, but you need to remember these people—and I include Carin with them—are shameless, and see only the surface. They judge you by your appearance. If you look happy, then you are happy. If you praise them, they believe you."

"It all seems very ominous," said Sylvia. "It makes me feel like I'm walking into a long dark tunnel."

SYLVIA BRAND

CHAPTER FOURTEEN

On Wednesday Sylvia was at her desk when her screen suddenly showed the image of the Facts News morning anchorperson. Sylvia stopped working and sat back in her chair. It was impossible to get any work done during these occasional interruptions.

"We have disturbing new images coming from Rodinia," said the newscaster. "Yesterday morning the Rodinian Army staged a massive training exercise on the shores of the Yukasi Peninsula. This mock invasion of the peninsula reportedly involved fifty thousand of the elite Rodinian Guard troops, hundreds of aircraft, and dozens of Rodinian Navy support vessels, including the new Munk-class cruiser armed with laser weapons capable of leveling virtually any structure within a mile of the coast. In response, this morning President Deacon convened an emergency meeting of the Joint Chiefs of Staff and the Executive Board of the Industrial Council. White House spokesperson Mitch Cornwall has told Facts News that the meeting was, and I quote, 'highly productive,' and that this new act of aggression by Rodinia will be met with 'invincible determination.' The President has requested that his War Powers be broadened to include the imposition of a nationwide curfew when necessary, as well as new measures enabling the Industrial Council to set prices of goods deemed necessary for national defense. The Industrial Council fully supports the president's request. The House and Senate are expected to pass the appropriate legislation and have the expanded War Powers bill on the President's desk by the end of this week."

The image of the newscaster disappeared and Sylvia's screen returned to the files she had opened a few minutes earlier. She went back to work, tracking down a late shipment of cameras for the roof unit of the new autonomous Comanche truck.

Without warning her screen changed again, and the view of an office with a desk appeared. A man was sitting at the desk. Flanking him were flags of the United Americas.

"Damn," muttered Sylvia. "How are we expected to get anything done around here with all of these lectures?" Then she put her hand over her mouth. Word was going around the office that the surveillance cameras had been given lip reading technology, and everything you said was captured and instantly transcribed. It was only a rumor, but there was no reason to take chances.

The man was Hugh Atkinson, chairman, president, and CEO of Sun Motors. Sylvia sat up straight in her chair. Aside from his annual year-end talk, to receive a message from Mr. Atkinson himself was a rare event. He was not a man who often put himself out in front of the public or his employees.

"Good morning," said Atkinson. His voice was low and sonorous. With his bow tie and brown suit jacket, he resembled an Ivy League professor. It was the signature look of Old Money.

"No doubt you've heard the announcement from the office of President Deacon and the Industrial Council regarding the new provocation by Rodinia. This is a serious threat to our nation, and Sun Motors is ready to do our part. I am proud to say we have just been awarded a contract to produce five thousand mobile strike vehicles for the U.A. Army. Final assembly will be at the Detroit Assembly Plant. We have also contracted with the Department of Defense to produce a classified number of armored personnel carriers and heavy laser defense units. The participating plants will be briefed in closed session.

"As Sun Motors does its part for the defense of our nation, I know I can count on every member of our Sun Motors family to contribute one hundred and ten percent. Our country and our people are depending on us to provide not only the highest quality civilian vehicles but to supply our warfighters with the tools they need to triumph over those who would seek to do us harm. Thank you."

The image vanished and Sylvia's screen returned to normal.

Sylvia frowned. It was a week ago that Carin had told her there was a ninety percent chance the Army would award Sun Motors a contract to produce five thousand mobile strike vehicles. The provocation by Rodinia that supposedly triggered the contract had happened just yesterday. How was that possible?

Out of curiosity she pulled up the page of the United Americas Stock Exchange. She found Sun Motors. Over a period of twenty-four hours, from the day before until this moment, the price of a single share of Sun Motors stock had risen from seven hundred and six dollars to eight hundred and twelve dollars. It was an astonishing increase of fifteen percent. It had been reported—but never publicly acknowledged—that members of the Atkinson family collectively owned three million shares of Sun Motors stock. Therefore over the period of one day, their wealth had increased by over three hundred million dollars.

Sylvia didn't own any Sun Motors stock. Only high-level executives were offered stock options, and she didn't have any spare cash to invest in the stock market.

Again her screen changed. This time it was Carin.

Sylvia bit her lip. But in her mind she was saying, this is crazy.

"I'll only take a moment of your time," said Carin. "But I want you all to fully appreciate that we have been given a tremendous opportunity to serve our nation in a moment of crisis. I anticipate that each and every one of us will step up and meet this challenge. And to help you meet and exceed your goals, I and the management team will be with you step by step, minute by minute, providing real-time feedback on your performance, both as an individual and as a member of the team. Thank you."

The screen reverted back to Sylvia's files.

Real-time feedback? What the hell did that mean?

That afternoon Sylvia had just returned from lunch when Carin summoned her to his office. After stopping in the ladies room to check her appearance—nothing stuck to her teeth, perfect yet minimal makeup, white blouse free of wrinkles or stains, hair brushed away from the face—she reported to his office.

Carin was seated behind his desk. As usual, the desktop was spotless, with only the computer screen, keyboard, and mouse. No paper.

Seated next to the desk was woman Sylvia had seen around the office during the past few days. The woman gave her a bland smile. Carin motioned for Sylvia to take the free chair.

"As you'll recall," said Carin, "last week I mentioned that a team of professional management consultants from the Special Services office of the Industrial Council was going to be working closely with us to improve efficiency. I'd like you to meet Isabel Nassar, one of the team members. She's been observing you for the past three days, both on video and in person. I think you'll find what she has to say to be very interesting and will help you to become a much more efficient and productive member of our team. Isabel, why don't you lead the discussion."

"Thank you, Carin," said Nassar. "Sylvia, it is such a great pleasure to meet you, although I must say I already feel as though I know you very well. But such is the nature of our work—we watch our clients and develop self-improvement programs based on what we observe, while we ourselves remain in the shadows. One cannot objectively collect data if one is interacting with the subject, wouldn't you agree?"

"Yes, of course," replied Sylvia.

Nassar reached into her slim briefcase and pulled out two sets of papers.

"This is a copy of our report on you, which I hope to discuss with you." She handed Sylvia one of the sets of papers. "As you can see, I also have a copy, so we can easily review together."

"What's the report about?" asked Sylvia. She felt the muscles in the back of her neck begin to stiffen.

"In the old day they called it ergonomics," said Nassar. "It's the scientific discipline concerned with the understanding of the interactions among human and other elements of a system, and the profession that applies theory, principles, data, and methods to design in order to optimize human well-being and overall system performance.

"In classical ergonomics, the practitioner attempts to modify the work to fit the worker. The goal is to eliminate waste, discomfort, and risk of injury due to work by shaping the work environment to fit the capabilities of the employee. For example, if you have a chair that is uncomfortable for the worker to sit in, you redesign the chair to fit the worker. But we believe this makes no sense in real life. If you have one thousand workers in a shared environment, such as in a factory, how can you possibly adapt each part of the factory to conform to the needs or whims of each worker? How can you make each chair conform to each individual employee, with all their different shapes and sizes? This would be madness—a huge waste of resources and a move toward inefficiency. We have resolved to approach the subject in a fresh way by asking how our workers could do a better job of fitting into their work environment. Instead of seeking a thousand individual solutions or standards to fit a thousand workers, we say it's better to determine one solution and ask our workers to conform to it. Does that make sense?"

"I suppose so," replied Sylvia. "To be honest, it seems like we've already got a high level of conformity. We all wear the same uniform, don't we?"

"That's just one small step," smiled Nassar. She had small, pointed teeth, like a child. "We're very pleased that the Detroit Assembly Plant, and in particular the logistics office, has embraced the Sun Motors Way program wholeheartedly. But that is just the beginning. Now then, let's talk about how we can help you. I ask you to refer to the report. You will see that it's broken down into various subsections. These include use of time, choice of movement (meaning what you do), and efficiency of movement (meaning how you do it). Let's take a look at use of time. As you can see, during the past three workdays you've gotten up from your desk four times per day to visit the employee break room. I assume you do this to get coffee, is that correct?"

"Yes," replied Sylvia. Her coffee ruse had been discovered! The pain in the back of her neck intensified. She resisted the impulse to bring her hand to her neck and rub it. She feared it would be seen as a wasted movement.

"There's nothing wrong with drinking coffee, if that pleases you," continued Nassar. "More importantly, your average visit to the break room is eight minutes in duration, during which time you chat with fellow employees. In total, you've spent ninety-six minutes of the past three work days walking to the break room, being in the break room, or walking back to your desk. Out of consideration for you, we've not counted trips to the ladies room, which were also numerous. Those will not be included in your permanent record."

"My permanent record?" asked Sylvia. The pain had spread up into her head. She felt her breathing becoming more rapid and shallow. Carin was looking at her. Was he calculating her breathing rate? Observing the dilation of her pupils? In an effort to relax, she shifted in her chair.

"Of course," replied Nassar with her childlike teeth. "It's important that we track these key metrics over time. How else can you hope to improve? In our competitive business environment, and especially with an impending war with Rodinia, every employee of Sun Motors needs to be performing at his or her optimum level. As managers, our job is to help you meet and exceed performance goals."

"You make it sound like I'm a professional athlete," said Sylvia. As the pain shot through her neck and head she struggled to control her breathing and keep her facial muscles relaxed. She didn't want them to see her grimace, even slightly.

"Actually," said Nassar, "that's a very astute comparison. We are all like professional athletes. Just as they must train to get in shape, so must we. Just as they must hone their skills, so must we. And just as every athlete must be totally committed to winning, so must we."

With his unwavering gaze, Carin stared at Sylvia. "Are you feeling all right?" he asked.

"Yes sir," Sylvia replied. "Just a slight headache. Nothing serious." She forced a smile.

"Without seeking to intrude," said Carin, "may I say that in your condition you might want to reduce your intake of coffee."

"My condition?"

"Your pregnancy." After the words passed over his lips he smiled, as if the idea of smiling had come as an afterthought.

"You know?"

"Of course we know. As you're well aware, your health data is added to your employee record in real time. Data from your recent appointment with Dr. Darcy at Detroit Hospital was received by Sun Motors as it was being created."

"I didn't realize that."

"It's clearly spelled out in your employee consent forms for the Sun Motors Employee Wellness Plan. It's standard boilerplate language. Of course, this is for your own benefit. When the company added these provisions many years ago, we were thinking about workers on the assembly line and in the warehouses. There was concern that if a worker had an accident on the job—regrettably, despite our excellent safety record, mishaps can happen—it would be important to have access to the most up-to-date medical records. In a situation when every minute is precious, the company didn't want to have to wait and send for them. Doesn't that make sense? Wouldn't you want your full medical records to be available the instant they were needed? It could be a matter of life or death."

"Yes, I suppose so," said Sylvia.

"I'm glad we all agree on that," said Nassar, showing her childlike teeth. "Now then, let's focus on helping you become more efficient. More like a professional athlete, if that's how you want to look at it. How can we reduce the thirty-two minutes you spend every workday going to the break room for coffee? How can we get it down to, say, fifteen minutes?"

Because of the pain shooting up her neck, Sylvia felt she couldn't turn her head. Stiffly she turned her entire body to face Nassar. "I'll drink less coffee."

"Okay, that might work," said Nassar. "To help you reach your goal, I've got something that will help you stay focused." She opened her briefcase and pulled out a small plastic bag, which she opened. From the plastic bag she took out a slender wristband. "This device is sensitive to both motion and geospatial location." She handed the band to Sylvia. Its color matched her skin. "We ask that you wear your wristband during the workday—that is, anytime you're being paid by the company, which includes the lunch hour. The band's internal clock will measure how you spend your time. If by accident you happen to spend more than fifteen minutes on trips to the break room, it will begin to emit a buzzing sound. It will buzz until you're back at your desk. I think you'll find it to be a minimally intrusive way to achieve a higher level of self discipline."

With her fingers, Sylvia turned over the wristband. She gave it a little twist. It was flexible. "What's to stop someone from just putting it in their desk drawer all day?"

Nassar smiled. "Oh, that's an easy one. The band learns your normal range of motions from minute to minute. It will quickly figure out if you are right-handed or left-handed. It tracks your body temperature and it will know if, for example, you take it off and put it on your desk. There's a buffer of thirty seconds between the time it senses a lack of movement and when the buzzer sounds."

"Go ahead, slip it on," said Carin. "And don't worry—it's hypoallergenic. Quite safe to wear."

Sylvia put it on her left wrist. It stretched slightly to slide over her hand.

"It blends in with your skin tone," said Nassar. "You can barely see it. After a while you won't even feel it. If you want, you can even wear it home. The data functions shut off after five o'clock."

There's no way I'm wearing this hideous thing home at night, thought

Sylvia. "If you think it will help," she said, "I'll give it a try." She resisted the overwhelming need to massage the back of her neck to relieve the increasing tension.

"Oh, and by the way—congratulations on your pregnancy," said Nassar, showing her many little teeth. "Your first one?"

"Yes," she replied. She looked at Carin. "But of course you know that."

He gave her his bland smile. "There are data sets we don't routinely access. I have no particular knowledge of your history as a mother of children. Please accept my sincere congratulations. I'm sure you will bear an exceptional child."

Self-consciously wearing the wristband, Sylvia walked back to her desk. On the way, each time she saw another employee she glanced at their wrist, and she was sure they were looking at hers too. Roger was wearing a wristband. Funny, she had never noticed it before. Emily was wearing one too, as were Maxwell and Pauline. Could they all have been wearing them and Sylvia hadn't noticed? Or had all of them been issued theirs today, like she had?

She arrived at her desk. She saw that it was nearly four o'clock. That morning she had told Carin she needed to leave at four to meet with the real estate agent and the lawyer. Carin didn't seem to mind, but after the session with Nassar, in which Sylvia's use of time had been the subject of much scrutiny, she felt acutely uncomfortable.

But this appointment was one of the most important in her life. Taking a deep breath, she took off the wristband and shoved it into a desk drawer.

"Sleep tight," she said to it as she closed the drawer. "I'll see you tomorrow morning."

SYLVIA BRAND

CHAPTER FIFTEEN

"Are you ready?" said Jason as he gripped Sylvia's hand.

"As ready as I'll ever be," she replied with a kiss to his cheek.

Jason opened the door of Room 201 of the Coleman A. Young Municipal Center. This was the office of Kathleen Barrett, the clerk of Wayne County and officiant of marriages.

After presenting their marriage license and paying the fee of one hundred and fifty dollars, they sat together in the waiting room. Sylvia tried to relax by breathing slowly and focusing on letting the tension melt away. Jason put a comforting hand on her back. "Hey," he said, "You're stiff a as a board. Are you okay?"

"I'm fine," she replied. "Just a tough day at work. I'll tell you about it tonight." She leaned into him and felt his strength. "All I want to think about is our future and the future of our child."

"Or children," he smiled.

"Let's not get ahead of ourselves. One baby at a time."

Their names were called and they went into the office, where they were met by Ms. Barrett and two witnesses, who otherwise worked as her administrative assistants. The ceremony took only a few minutes, and after they signed the papers Jason took the certificate of marriage, and together they left the building.

An hour later they lay snuggled on the big bed in their suite at the Detroit Heritage Hotel. The grand old edifice was once served as the headquarters of the Detroit Police Department, but after the Global Depression the cops had moved to a new building. When the hotel opened, it quickly became the city's trendiest overnight destination. The architects were careful to keep the flavor of the venerable structure; a few of the windows still had the original iron bars, and the old jail was now a four-star restaurant.

"You still feel a little tense," said Jason as he held her in his arms. "C'mon, let me give you a massage."

"Oh, no, you don't have to do that," she weakly protested.

"I insist. Roll over on your stomach. Put your arms over your head."

His strong fingers probed and pressed the muscles of her back and shoulders.

"Ouch!" she exclaimed.

"Ah—the splenius capitis muscle! Feels like a knotted rope. So does your levator scapulae. No wonder you can barely turn your head." He bent down and tenderly kissed the nape of her neck. "How does that feel?"

"Heavenly," she whispered.

"What was going on today at work?" he said as he gently worked the stiff muscles under her skin.

"Oh, you don't want to know," she said.

"Now that I'm your husband, I want to know everything. Especially whatever makes you upset."

"Oh, maybe it's just me, but the logistics office is starting to feel more and more like a forced labor camp. They keep coming up with these new rules that are supposed to increase productivity, but they're destroying employee morale." She paused. "Ooh, yes, whatever you're doing right now is working. Right there—where your left thumb is. That's the worst spot. Ouch! No, don't stop—I can feel it getting more relaxed. Now where was I? Oh yes. Employee morale. People are walking around like zombies. No one laughs, no one smiles. Everyone's terrified of being called out for wasting time or not being efficient. No one wants to go to the doctor because their medical information will go straight to human resources and the managers. This morning one of the girls in the office told me she thought she had a yeast infection. Instead of going to her own doctor, who's plugged into the Sun Motors Employee Wellness Plan, she went to an aberrant clinic out in the country. She had to pay three hundred dollars out of her own pocket for the examination and medications. She said it was worth every penny to keep Carin from finding out.

"Today they gave me—and everyone in the office, I think—an internet-connected wristband to wear. It tracks where I go and even my body temperature. They thought I was spending too much time in the break room, and they want me to cut it in half. Ever since Carin arrived and the Bright Horizon program started, they've installed surveillance cameras in the office, made everyone sign up for the Sun Motors Employee Wellness Plan, opened the creepy Margaret Atkinson day care center, and issued wristbands that track your every movement. They say it's simply a matter of increasing efficiency and making Sun Motors more competitive. Supposedly the data they collect helps pinpoint areas that could be improved. This looming war with Rodinia doesn't help—with new Department of Defense vehicle contracts, Sun Motors stands to make huge profits, and it forces all of us to conform to DoD standards, which are even tougher than the Industrial Council. I don't see where this is going." She paused for a moment as Jason kneaded her neck. "Oooh—right there! In the middle. You've hit the spot. Are you going to do this for me every day, or is it because we just got married and you want to keep me happy?"

"I'll do it whenever and wherever you want," he smiled. "If Sun Motors is becoming too regimented, do you want to work someplace else?"

"Where? All the Two Hundred K companies are the same. Isn't the Industrial Council doing the same things at Hilltop Financial?"

"Yes, they are. We haven't got the wristbands yet, but I suppose they could be coming. I try not to let it bother me. Remember, after five o'clock we leave all that stuff behind. We walk out the door and into our own lives. We can do whatever we want and live however we want. We've got our future to think about. Our family. My goal is to become CEO of Hilltop Financial and worm my way onto the Industrial Council."

"I think it would be easier to get elected president of the United Americas," said Sylvia. "I'm not opposed to being ambitious—that's one of your many very attractive qualities—but you've got to be realistic. Do you even know how many people serve on the Council? And where they meet?"

"According to what I've read, there are thirty members, and they have virtual meetings. They live all over the United Americas. When a seat is vacated, most often through death or infirmity, a new member is nominated and approved by a vote. To be nominated, you must be a CEO of a large-cap Two Hundred K company. The leader of Hilltop Financial qualifies."

"Is your boss, Sharon Westward, on the Council?"

"No one knows. She's never said one way or the other."

"I don't understand what it's all about," said Sylvia. "All this control. Is it power? Do the bosses enjoy having power over us and making us feel like cogs in their machine?"

"I don't think it's primarily power," replied Jason. He rolled over and lay on the bed next to his wife, propped up on one elbow. "I think it's about something much more boring and unimaginative: money."

"Money?"

"Profits. These guys are driven by the bottom line. The goal of the Industrial Council is to ensure its member companies return as much profit as possible to their investors. If a proposed strategy can help in that effort, they will do it. Making the workplace hyper-efficient is one obvious way to boost profits. Collecting and selling data is another way to make money. From their point of view, any personal data—health, lifestyle, consumer choices, political beliefs—that isn't harvested is like leaving money on the table. It's like letting good wheat rot in the field. You may not think your medical and behavioral data is worth anything, but when it's bundled with many other people who are like you—similar age, gender, income, and so forth—it becomes very valuable. Sun Motors doesn't just make SUVs and pickup trucks. Its thousands of employees make data, and Sun Motors has ensured that it owns that data and can sell it."

"But how about things like the wristbands? Don't they cost money to produce?"

"They're an investment, but they pay for themselves in boosted productivity. I guarantee you a bean counter within the Industrial Council ran the numbers on the proposed wristbands. He might have said, 'If we design and manufacture a million internet-connected wristbands at a cost of ten dollars apiece, our investment will be ten million dollars. If you add another five million dollars to run the program, that's a total of fifteen million dollars. We then ask ourselves if these wristbands, worn by one million employees of member companies, will generate increased productivity worth more than fifteen million dollars.'

"Clearly the answer was 'yes,' because the program was approved. This means that you, dear sweet Sylvia Brand, senior logistics manager at the Sun Motors Detroit Assembly Plant, are now required to wear a wristband every day. They will track and analyze your overall contribution to the anticipated increase in productivity. I'm sure you will not disappoint them."

"I wonder what it's like to live in the canaille among the aberrants," said Sylvia.

"Those people and their little businesses exist for three purposes: to buy goods produced by the Two Hundred K, to pay taxes to the government, and to provide soldiers to the military. All under the banner of patriotism. In the canaille, the only part of the civic infrastructure that's directly controlled by the government is the school system. From the cradle the kids are taught that the Two Hundred K is something to aspire to, the Industrial Council is their protector, and war is a glorious thing in which everyone should participate. That, plus the ubiquitous presence of the secret police, is the extent of the government's oversight of the canaille."

"It sounds ghastly," said Sylvia with a shudder.

"Let's not think about such dreary topics," said Jason. "I'm getting hungry—how about you? Do you want to get dressed and go down to the restaurant and get dinner? Or would you rather stay as you are and we'll order room service?"

"Sweetheart, I don't care if I never get dressed again," said Sylvia as she kissed him.

"Okay—I'll get the menu." He reached over and took the leather-bound folder from the little table next to the bed. "Let's see what looks good…. I think I'll have the pork loin with onion and Gruyere potato gratin and sautéed spring vegetables. And maybe the classic Caesar salad with Romaine Parmesan croutons. How about you?"

"I'll try the seared scallops. They come with sweet potato puree, sautéed spinach, and lemon parsley brown butter. Do you want to split an order of the crispy polenta with grilled portabella, spinach, and mushroom sauce? It sounds divine."

"Sure. And a bottle of Didier Chopin Brut Champagne."

"Isn't that expensive?" asked Sylvia.

"Isn't this our honeymoon?"

"Only until we can make plans for a proper vacation. Remember we talked about going to St. Bart. Tomorrow I'm going to start researching hotels."

"But not while you're at work," said Jason.

"God no—there's no way I'd spend even five minutes doing that at work. The keystroke recorder would tip them off, and I don't want Carin to know anything about our private life. It's bad enough he knows that I'm expecting a child. I'm surprised he hasn't given me a lecture on what brand of diapers to buy."

"If they could make you buy official Sun Motors diapers, I'm sure they would," laughed Jason. He picked up the phone and placed their dinner order with the kitchen. He turned to Sylvia: "They say they'll be here in twenty minutes."

"That give us nineteen more minutes to have fun," said Sylvia, giving him a kiss.

CHAPTER SIXTEEN

When Sylvia arrived for work the next morning, she never felt happier. The memory of her night with Jason filled her heart with gladness. She remembered his gentle touch, the weight of his body next to hers, the smell of his hair as he kissed her. Before drifting to sleep in each other's arms they had talked about their plans for their life together, the house they were buying, the child she was carrying. She thought back to her own childhood and the generosity she had felt from her parents, and she knew that she and Jason could give their child—or maybe children!—the same nurturing love.

As she approached the big glass and chrome entrance to the Sun Motors Detroit Assembly Plant offices, she gave a little inward sigh. Yes, the working conditions were difficult, even bizarre at times, but such was the nature of progress. You took the good with the bad. You gave up some freedoms in exchange for security and a rewarding career. Because the benefits were substantial, you endured the strange and often inexplicable decisions made by your superiors. And there was always the possibility of a promotion, so that eventually you could find yourself not just following the rules but making them.

It's funny, she thought to herself, that ten years earlier, when she was still a kid, the idea of being a senior logistics manager in a car factory would have seemed like the most boring and unfulfilling job imaginable. How much more fun it would be to be a car designer or test driver! As a person who sourced the parts for the cars, her job was hidden behind the scenes, like the stagehands who change the scenery in the dark so the actors can take the stage and thrill the audience. But over the years, ever since she had started at Sun Motors as an intern, Sylvia had learned to appreciate the role of the backstage workers. She saw how her work affected the making of the product and the lives of her colleagues. She derived personal satisfaction from solving problems and getting the contracts written and the parts delivered. In the grand scheme of things her role was small but important. And with her new family added to her life, she felt a deep sense of gratitude.

Lost in her thoughts, she was startled when Palin accosted her.

"Sylvia," he said with a big smile—the biggest she had ever seen on his mechanical face.

She stopped. They were standing in the parking lot a few yards from the entrance. Other employees walked past them.

"Oh, hi, Carin. What's up?"

"I have some amazing news for you! You have been chosen for a very special project. I can't tell you what it is. I need you to get in the car and go with your escorts. Everything will be explained in due time."

A black Sun Motors SUV eased alongside them. The side door opened. A man and a woman got out. They were wearing Sun Motors security uniforms. Smiling, they positioned themselves on each side of Sylvia.

"But what about my work?" she asked. "I've got a critical conference call in fifteen minutes. It's about the internal guidance system for the Comanche."

"I know all about it," smiled Carin. "I'll take your place. You've done an excellent job. Please, go with Robert and Janet. You are being given an incredible opportunity."

"But what about Jason? I need to tell him where I'm going. We keep no secrets from each other. Can I call him?" She reached for her phone.

Carin held up his hand. Without a smile he said, "We'll speak to Jason. You're going on a highly classified mission. We need to control what's being said about it. Don't worry, I'm sure you'll be seeing your husband very soon."

"Promise?"

"Of course." He extended his hand. "Now please let me hold your phone. You'll get it back the moment you return. It's just a routine security measure. Like when you go to court, and you have to leave your phone in your car. Not a big deal."

"Okay," said Sylvia. She handed her We don't want to fall behind schedule."

Sylvia turned to the open door of the SUV and then stopped. "How long will I be away?"

"Can't say for sure," smiled Carin. "Now please get in—you're a very important person!"

It was the special limousine model of the largest SUV made by Sun Motors, with leather seating, burled walnut panels, and deeply tinted windows. From behind his sunglasses, the driver gave her a glance and a little smile. Sylvia buckled herself by the window. Janet sat next to her. Robert took the seat next to the driver. Carin closed the door and the big SUV glided towards the parking lot exit. Sylvia watched the other employees getting out of their cars. Suddenly she felt exalted, as if she had been plucked from obscurity and placed on a throne. But why? What had she done to deserve this extraordinary treatment?

As the big car accelerated onto the Detroit Industrial Freeway, Sylvia turned to Janet.

"Where are we going?" she asked.

"To the airport."

"Oh—I'm going on a plane?"

"You'll see," she responded flatly. She looked straight ahead.

Sylvia sat back and watched the city roll by. She felt both thrilled and intimidated. She imagined her co-workers—Tameeka, Mei Lien, Maxell, Eduardo, and the others—passing her cubicle and asking each other, "Where's Sylvia? She's never late on Monday morning, and we have an important meeting." As the minutes and hours ticked by, what would Carin tell them? How much would he reveal about her sudden absence?

As if an electric shock had passed through her body, she suddenly turned to Janet. "Is this what you did to Judy Loring and Randolph Meekin?"

Janet gave her a bland smile. "I can't really speak to that."

"Those people left and never came back!"

"Every situation is different."

"Situation? What's the situation? I have no idea why I've been chosen for this trip. Or mission. Or whatever you call it."

"Be patient," said Janet. She gestured toward the lacquered door of the compartment between the seats. "Would you like some water?"

"No thanks, I'm good," replied Sylvia. "If this is an overnight trip, shouldn't I have brought a suitcase? I can't wear the same clothes two days in a row! And I'll need my toiletries from home—my makeup and toothbrush and all that stuff."

"All of that is being taken care of."

The car exited at W.G. Rogell Drive, but instead of going to the familiar commercial airline departure terminals the driver steered onto an access road that took them to a hanger. They came to a stop near a jet on the runway. The driver came around, and as he opened Sylvia's door the whining of jet engines and the smell of exhaust and fuel intruded. She stepped into the glare of the morning light. Far across the tarmac, a passenger jet roared down the runway and took to the sky.

"Sylvia Brand," said a woman dressed in a Sun Motors uniform.

"Yes, that's me."

"I'm Nancy. I'm one of your flight attendants. Please follow me."

Nancy led Sylvia to the steps of the jet. It wasn't one of those tiny little planes with only a few windows, nor was it as big as a regular commercial airliner.

"Today, you travel in style," said Nancy. "Sun Motors owns two business jets. This is one of them. It carries sixteen passengers and four crew members. We use it to fly our top executives to Sun Motors locations around the world.

And, when necessary, it's available for special projects." She gestured to the steps leading up to the door. "Please—after you."

Sylvia climbed the steps and entered the cabin. Instead of dozens of rows of seats in the familiar cattle-car arrangement, the space looked more like a modernistic living room, with big upholstered chairs alternating with banquette seating along the sides. The middle of the cabin had a partition leading into a conference room in the forward section. Sylvia saw there were several other passengers already on board. While they were all wearing the requisite Sun Motors uniform of navy blue slacks or skirt and white shirt—indicating they weren't top executives—she didn't recognize any of them.

Nancy showed Sylvia to her seat. One of four in a group, it faced two others, with a glossy-topped table between. One of the facing seats was occupied by a man. He watched her with benign interest.

"I'm Sylvia Brand," she said, extending her hand. "Senior logistics manager at the Detroit Assembly Plant."

"Peter Williams." While his skin seemed unusually pale, his handshake was firm and businesslike. "Robotics engineer."

"This should be an exciting adventure," said Sylvia with a smile. "I've done a lot of traveling for the company, but always flying commercial. Never on a company jet."

"Likewise," replied Peter. "A person could get used to this." He leaned forward as if to share a confidence. "I'm going to be honest with you—I have no idea where we're going. I came to work this morning expecting to have a typical day. My boss, Saran, met me at the main entrance. He told me I was going on a special assignment and I'd be leaving right away. They put me into a company car and drove me here. That's all I know."

"And they took your phone, right?"

"Yes. Saran said they couldn't risk a leak. It was all very hush-hush. I really hope I get my phone back because it's got a bunch family videos that I haven't backed up yet."

"Oh—you have a family?"

"It was our daughter's sixteenth birthday yesterday. She didn't want a big party, so my wife and I took her out to her favorite restaurant. Then we brought her home and I gave her the keys to her new car—the new Sun self-driving electric. I have mixed feelings about that, because when I was sixteen I learned to drive in an old-fashioned manually operated car with a gas engine. It even had a stick shift, if you can imagine that!"

"A real antique," smiled Sylvia.

"I'm not sure if kids are getting the same kind of training these days, where they can just point the car in the direction they want to go and the safety features make getting into an accident practically impossible. Laconda has told me about kids who say, 'Hey, now you can get drunk and get into your car and drive home, because you can't crash!' That seems like very dangerous thinking."

"I agree," said Sylvia. She thought of her unborn child. Sixteen years from now, what sort of world would he or she inherit? How many of the old ways, like driving yourself in your own car, would have disappeared?

"Aside from the videos," continued Peter, "my phone is very useful because I can track the car with it. I'll always know where she is and if anyone's in the car with her."

Sylvia smiled. "Being able to keep an eye on your sixteen-year-old as she drives around town is a good thing." She paused and looked around the luxurious cabin. "This certainly is nice. I'd feel better if I knew where we're going."

Peter shrugged. "I don't care as long as I'm home tonight."

Sylvia felt the dull thud of the outside door being closed. A voice over the intercom said, "This is Lamar. I'll be your captain on this flight. Welcome to you all. As soon as we receive clearance from the tower, we'll be taking off. Our flying time will be approximately three hours and twenty minutes. Our stewards, Nancy and Miguel, will take very good care of you. Enjoy the flight."

Sylvia said to Peter, "Lamar has the voice of an autonomous humanoid operator."

"Yep. He's a Morta AHO 7-A. The next generation above the sixes they're using as managers. Unlike a human pilot, he never gets drunk, never oversleeps, and never asks for a raise. But to be honest, designing a robot to fly a plane is much easier than designing a self-driving automobile. As far back as before the Global Depression, commercial airliners were very nearly self-flying. The human pilots were only necessary to supervise takeoff and landing. In a plane, once you're in the air, there are none of the hazards you encounter on a street, and you're not operating within inches of other vehicles. Compared to a vehicle on the road, in the sky you have a huge margin for error."

The sound of the plane's jet engines increased in volume and the craft gently rolled forward along the taxiway before coming to a stop. After a moment, the engines suddenly roared to life. As the sound became deafening, Sylvia felt herself being pressed against the back of her seat. The plane gathered speed and she looked out the window. The grass bordering the runway seemed to fly past while the trees and low buildings in the distance didn't move. She felt the nose of the plane lift, and then a "thunk" as it left the ground. From underneath came the hum of the landing gear retracting. They ascended at a steep angle—much steeper than the commercial jets she was accustomed to taking.

From her window Sylvia looked down on the angular buildings of downtown Detroit, the curve of the Detroit River, the graceful boat shape of Belle Isle, and the shimmering grey-blue of Lake St. Claire. To get a sense of where they were going, she tried to track the plane's direction as it banked to the left, and through gaps in the clouds she saw they were making a broad arc around the lake. Then the plane was fully above the clouds, hiding the earth from sight. Below lay heaps of brilliant white, while above curved the blazing blue sky.

"Are you a native of Detroit?" Sylvia asked Peter.

"My hometown is a little city on Lake Huron called Cheboygan. Population about five thousand. We're best known as the home port of the U.S. Coast Guard cutter and icebreaker Mackinaw. I graduated from Michigan State with a degree in computer science, and then went to grad school for robotics. After I got my master's degree I got a job at Sun Motors. Then I got married and we had Laconda. During the Global Depression life was very tough, but we survived. I play golf and we keep a boat in the Marina District. A twenty-two foot runabout. We take it out on the lake. That's about it—just a normal all-American family."

"You must like your job. Robotics. That's a pretty cool area to be in today."

"Yeah. I must confess my particular line of work is not very glamorous. I help develop assembly line robots. The rock stars are the people who create autonomous vehicles. Right now they're building a car that's basically a Morta AHO on four wheels that can go one hundred and fifty miles an hour. You can sit in the back seat and have a conversation with the car the way you'd have a conversation with your driver."

"Except—let me guess—the computer driver never gets drunk, never oversleeps, and never asks for a raise."

"Exactly. Our president and CEO, Mr. Atkinson, has said he wants to be among the first to have one."

"Among the first, but not the first," laughed Sylvia.

"To be sure, it'll be tested extensively before we let him take a spin. But like I said, I'm not directly involved in that project. I work on the automated assembly line."

"Do you have a Morta robot manager?"

"Yes," nodded Peter. "Her name is Gamir."

"Her?"

Peter shrugged. "Around the office we wanted to choose one gender or the other. We flipped a coin and it came up heads, which meant female. So we pretend Gamir is a woman. It doesn't matter to anyone; it was a random choice. Some people have suggested a gender-free pronoun in the form of 'dee,' with the object form as 'deem.' We didn't go for that, but eventually it may have to happen.

"It's crazy how gender colors peoples' perceptions of performance. Here's an example. The other day one of my colleagues thought Gamir spoke to him sharply. The guy had screwed up and Gamir was correcting him—"

"Sorry to interrupt, but they can do that? Vary their vocal tone?"

"Yes, the new ones can. When they believe something they're saying is particularly important—that is, the risk of failure is high if the human on the other end doesn't affirmatively respond—they can sharpen their inflection. So Gamir told my colleague that he needed to fix a problem now, and then she walked away. Later, when we were in the men's room—no cameras there—he lit into her, calling her a bitch and all kinds of other names I can't repeat. He said women are terrible managers, they can't lead, blah, blah, blah. I listened to him for a few minutes and then I said, 'Dude, do you remember that we were the ones who made Gamir a female? Gamir has no gender. Gamir is a gender-neutral robot. We could have just as easily imagined it to be male.'

"He didn't like hearing that. I couldn't convince him, so I dropped the subject. And on the flip side of the coin, one of the women who work in our office is convinced that Gamir is her soul mate and that Gamir understands her in a special way because there's a feminine bond. We tell her, 'You can think whatever you want, but all Morta 6-C management robots are the same. They have no gender.'"

"But is it possible," said Sylvia, "that because Gamir is engaged in continuous machine learning, it—or she—could amass data that's skewed towards one point of view? That somehow she could place a higher priority on data that paints a more positive picture of women than of men? For example, a human male boss who's sexist—and believe me, I've had plenty of experience in that department—will see a mistake made by a male subordinate and think, 'He made a bad decision, but it doesn't mean he's a bad worker. Anybody can make a mistake. It's not a serious problem.' Meanwhile, a female worker can make exactly the same mistake and the male boss will say, 'See? That proves a woman can't do the job. She doesn't deserve a promotion, or to be paid as much as a man.' In an organization run by women, might the same problem arise? Might a female manager have a bias in favor of the women working under her?"

"By extension," said Peter, "you could apply that to any demographic subset. Religious managers would have a bias against workers who are secular. Thin managers would have a bias against workers who are heavy. Managers who are married with kids would have a bias against employees who are single. The only way to avoid that is by establishing a strong culture of fairness in which data about employee performance is evaluated with clarity and not through the distorting lens of bias. Or you can hire gender-free robots. But as far as Gamir is concerned, it—which is the precisely correct pronoun—may have only a passing knowledge of the gender assignment we've given to it. Gamir just does its job. Gamir has no opinion regarding the differences in job performance between men and women. Gamir sees only productivity or the lack thereof. Gamir, and the other Morta

AHO 6-C robots, may be the best solution for workplace bias. They are incapable of irrational discrimination."

CHAPTER SEVENTEEN

Nancy approached their seats. "Are you comfortable?" she asked.

"Yes, thank you," replied Sylvia. "Do you know where we're going? The pilot said we'd be airborne for three hours and twenty minutes. That's enough time to get us as far as Seattle or Los Angeles. Or, if we were going south, to Miami or Houston."

"I can't comment on that," replied Nancy. "We ask that you relax and enjoy the flight. The flight time may not be relevant to the distance to our destination. Can I get you a beverage?"

"It's early in the day," said Peter, "but I could use a beer."

"Certainly," said Nancy.

"I'll take one too," said Sylvia.

Nancy smiled at her and said, "Because of your condition, I'm able to offer you water or fruit juice."

"My condition?" replied Sylvia.

"Yes. I've been advised that you will not be consuming alcohol on this flight."

"And who advised you of that?" said Sylvia.

"The decision makers supervising this trip," replied Nancy. "I really don't want to discuss your personal health. I hope you understand."

"I've changed my mind," said Peter. "I'll have apple juice."

"I'll have the same," said Sylvia with displeasure.

Nancy smiled. "Coming right up. And something to eat? I can offer you a turkey, ham, or roast beef sandwich."

"And what if I happened to be a vegetarian?" said Sylvia. "Oh, but you already know that I'm not, isn't that true?"

"Why don't you bring us one ham and one turkey, and we'll figure it out," said Peter.

With a dry smile, Nancy turned and left.

"Well, there you go," said Sylvia. "Since the whole world seems to know, I might as well tell you I'm expecting a baby."

"Congratulations!" said Peter.

Sylvia leaned closer. "They may have cameras on this plane, but you know what? I don't care. I didn't ask to be on this trip. So I'm going to speak honestly. I love Sun Motors, but sometimes I feel like I'm living in a fishbowl. They made us join the Sun Motors Employee Wellness Plan and sign a pile of consent forms that give the company the right to know everything about us. They say it's for our own protection, but sometimes I wonder. I don't like the idea that a Barbie-doll flight attendant knows that I'm pregnant and has orders to refuse me a goddamn beer when I want one. It gives me the creeps."

"I understand how you feel," said Peter, "but look at it from their point of view. Healthcare can get incredibly expensive. If they agree to cover you, they have to do it even if you come down with an expensive illness. If you get a rare disease, your insurer—in this case Sun Motors—may find itself on the hook for millions of dollars in expenses. I can tell you that from my point of view, I'm glad to have the Sun Motors Employee Wellness Plan."

"If I may ask…. Why are you glad?"

"It's because I was recently diagnosed with a rare form of Diamond-Blackfan anemia, a genetic blood disorder that prevents your bone marrow from producing enough red blood cells. It can get progressively worse until it kills you. Of all the people with this disease, about half have inherited the mutation from a parent, while the other half have a new mutation, where it appears for the first time in the family. The treatment—typically bone marrow transplants—is very expensive, painful, and short-term. When I found out I had it, I thought for sure the company would find a way to cut me loose, but they say they'll stick by me."

"I'm sorry to hear about your diagnosis," said Sylvia. "Do you mind if I ask if your daughter has it?"

"She's being tested," he replied. "We're not sure yet."

Nancy appeared with their beverages and sandwiches. As they ate they talked about less personal things, including the state of Detroit's professional sports teams and the problems of pollution in Lake St. Clair.

The seat belt sign flashed on. Nancy came to their seats, told them they were preparing to land, and cleared away their cups and plates. The plane began its gradual descent. The clouds enveloped it and the view out the window became nothing but white. After a bit of turbulence the earth appeared below. Sylvia peered intently out the window, searching for a familiar landmark, but she saw only rugged mountains, the lower ones blanketed in fir trees with the higher peaks capped in white snow. Occasional small lakes glimmered in the afternoon light, and here and there the landscape showed the meandering brown scratch of a road. There were no towns and no signs of human industry.

Despite the lack of built structures suggesting a city or airport, the plane rapidly descended. The trees became individual green spikes and the hills seemed higher. Then with a rocking "thud" the plane touched down. From her window Sylvia saw only the edge of the concrete runway and a wide, flat field bordered by a wall of pines, beyond which loomed pale purple mountains. The plane slowed and turned to the left. Now Sylvia could see the end of the runway and a road beyond. Then a building came into view— a plain structure with a control tower attached to one side—and she concluded that they had landed at one of the thousands of regional airports dotted across the United Americas.

The plane came to a halt. Over the intercom Lamar said, "Please remain seated until Nancy and Miguel tell you it's time to deplane. You'll exit by the rear door. Have a pleasant day."

Peter and Sylvia sat in their seats while Nancy and Miguel busied themselves in the back of the plane. Presently the rear door was opened and by swiveling in her seat Sylvia could see the passengers behind them standing and moving towards the exit. Then Nancy came to Sylvia and Peter and said, "You may now disembark. It has been a pleasure to serve you."

They stood up and walked to the rear door of the plane. Idling a short distance from the aircraft was a white limousine bus of the kind high schoolers rent to go to the prom or groups of people use on a business trip. Before descending the stairs, Sylvia paused to take stock of the environment. It was indeed a small regional airport, with an administration building and attached tower, a cluster of hangers, and a handful of private planes and corporate jets. There were two runways, set at an angle to each other. Just beyond the perimeter of the airport, here and there houses or other small buildings peeked from the pine forest. To the east—judging by the angle of the sun—lay a line of whitecapped mountains. Sylvia assumed it was early afternoon, and the moderate outdoor temperature suggested the plane hadn't flown far from the same latitude as Detroit. To her that meant they had probably flown almost due west, and she could be looking at the Rocky Mountains, the Cascades, or the Sierra Nevadas.

She walked down the steps and then to the limousine bus. She took a seat near the front, and Peter sat next to her. Few people on the bus were talking. Nancy and Miguel took the two remaining empty seats. The doors closed and the driver—a man wearing not the blue pants and white shirt of Sun Motors but a dark green shirt and black pants—drew a curtain across the aisle, separating himself from his passengers and obscuring the view of the road ahead. It was then that Sylvia noticed the windows of the bus were deeply tinted, so much so that even in broad daylight she could see only vague forms and the difference between the lighter sky and the darker ground.

Sylvia leaned forward to address Nancy. "I'm getting the impression that whoever arranged this trip doesn't want us to know where we are. I don't even know if we're still in the United Americas, and we certainly can't see very much out of the windows."

Nancy smiled and said, "These are nothing more than basic security measures. In due time, you'll learn much more. The ride will not be long."

"Are you staying with us, or do you have to fly back?"

"Miguel and I are here to ensure you arrive at your destination safely. Then we'll be saying goodbye."

"Do you mean you're not flying home with us?"

"Don't worry, you'll be well taken care of."

The bus began to move. Sylvia sensed the usual starting and stopping. Neither she nor Peter wore a wristwatch, and she asked Nancy, "Do you know what time it is?"

"No, but we're right on schedule," she replied.

Sylvia turned and, half-standing in her seat, said in a loud voice, "Does anybody know what time it is?"

A few of the riders mumbled "no" or "sorry, don't know."

Nancy said, "Sylvia, please be assured everything is going as planned. We'll be getting off the bus soon."

There was a prolonged period of steady driving at a highway speed, then slowing down, stopping, and starting again. Intently Sylvia peered through the tinted window and tried to discern what she saw, but she could make out only broad shapes and areas of light and dark. She could not tell if they were driving through city or forest, mountain or desert.

The bus came to a stop. Nancy and Miguel stood up and pulled back the curtain. Through the windshield Sylvia saw they were in the parking lot of an office building. Where the parking lot ended the pine trees began.

"We've arrived!" said Nancy with a smile. "Please watch your step getting off the bus."

Because they were nearest to the front, Sylvia and Peter were the first to stand and move towards the door. Before she disembarked, Sylvia turned to the driver, who was still sitting behind the wheel, and said, "Thank you for a nice ride."

"My pleasure, ma'am," he replied, touching the visor of his driver's hat.

"Will we see you again?" asked Sylvia. "To take us back to the plane?"

"We'll see. You have a good day, ma'am."

Quickly Sylvia scanned the dashboard of the bus for any useful information—a clock, toll receipt, or folded newspaper. There was nothing. Becoming aware of the restive group lined up behind her, she turned and descended the steps.

On the pavement, she stood for a moment as an unfamiliar scent came into her nostrils. She inhaled deeply and slowly. Mixed with the scent of pines there was no mistaking the faint, tangy smell of an onshore breeze from the sea.

We're near an ocean, she thought.

The building in front of her rose three stories, was capped with a flat roof, and showed typically bland office construction. The dark frameless windows revealed nothing of the activities inside. The door was set exactly in the middle of the façade. Clearly this edifice had been designed for functionality, not to win any awards for architecture. Several cars were parked in front. They were not all Sun Motors vehicles. A number of golf carts were parked there too. Sylvia hoped this wasn't some sort of home for retirees.

Nancy said, "This way, please," as she gestured towards the front entrance.

As Sylvia approached the door a man came out. He looked to be about her age. Definitely not a senior citizen. Without making eye contact he went to one of the golf carts, started it, and drove away towards a path leading from the parking lot into the pines.

After watching as the man drove away in his golf cart, Sylvia led the group inside. She entered a nondescript office lobby devoid of any artwork or visual decoration. Under her feet a gray rubber mat covered the traffic area of the glossy pebble-finish floor. The ceiling was bone white and not high. To the left, a typical office sofa—upholstered in orange and looking hard—kept company with a ficus plant. Straight ahead were a door and a staircase going up. To the right was a desk, like in a hotel, and another door.

Two women were behind the desk. They were wearing the same colors as the bus driver—dark green blouses and black skirts. They also wore nametags—Janice and Ka'sah.

"Good afternoon," said Ka'sah. "You must be Sylvia Brand. Welcome to Juliette Island."

"Juliette Island?" replied Sylvia. "We're on an island?"

"Yes," said Ka'sah. "It's named in honor of Juliette Gant, the daughter of the president of the Industrial Council. It's a very special place for very special people."

"I'm a special person?"

"If you weren't, you wouldn't be here." She handed Sylvia what looked like a cheap burner. "Here's your phone. You can use it to call any company representative on the island, and as a personal timepiece."

"Is it connected to the internet?"

Ka'sah gave her a broad, cold smile. "I'm sorry, it is not. Please go to room twenty-three, just up the stairs. There's also an elevator, but it's rather slow. You'll find it through that door." She pointed to the door next to the desk.

Sylvia took the stairs to the second floor. Room twenty-three was to the right, a few doors down. She knocked and without waiting for a response turned the knob and entered. She found herself in what looked like a home office. A man was sitting behind a desk. He was bald and wore rimless eyeglasses. Unlike the sterile lobby, this room looked as though it was designed for human comfort. There was an easy chair, a Persian rug, and an overstuffed sofa with pillows. The beige walls were decorated with a mélange of paintings and photographs. Several photos showed the man behind the desk at the wheel of a sailboat.

"Ms. Brand, please make yourself comfortable," said the man with a wave in the direction of the armchair facing the desk.

Sylvia remained standing. "Who are you, and why am I here?"

He looked up from what he was reading. "Of course—how rude of me. I'm Doctor James Hyland. I'll be your primary care physician."

"Primary care physician? What the hell are you talking about? I have a doctor and her name is Rebecca Goldsmith at the Willowdale Center. Elizabeth Darcy at Detroit Hospital is my OB/GYN. I don't need any more doctors. What I need is to go home!"

"Please calm yourself, Ms. Brand. May I call you Sylvia? Please sit down and I will answer all your questions."

Feeling as though she had no choice but to play along, Sylvia took the chair. She gave Dr. Hyland a hard look. "Okay, I'm sitting."

"I know this has been a rather unsettling day for you," said Dr. Hyland as he removed his glasses. Taking a cloth from his desk drawer, he began to wipe the lenses. "We apologize for the secrecy, shall we say, surrounding your trip here to Juliette Island. Through painful experience, we've found that a swift extraction is always best. If we ask people to come here, they often say no, which is unacceptable. It's better to get them here and explain later."

"Why am I here?"

"You are a very special person."

"So I've been told. Why?"

"Two reasons. You are carrying a child. And as we have learned from your tests, you are also a carrier of extremely rare genetic disease called mitochondrial DNA-associated Leigh syndrome. If manifested in the child, it's a severe mitochondrial disorder characterized by encephalopathy, or brain disease; body lactic acidosis, or elevated levels of lactic acid in the body; seizures; heart disease; respiratory abnormalities; and developmental delays. The specific symptoms and severity of these disorders in each individual can vary greatly from one person to another and even among members of the same family."

"What are you saying? My child is going to die of a horrible genetic disease?"

"No one knows the answer. MILS often emerges during the first three months to one year of life. However, onset can occur at any time from birth through adulthood. Some victims die in the crib. Others live well into adulthood. Medical science has long sought a cure for this disease, but finding carriers has been a perennial challenge. That's why you're here."

CHAPTER EIGHTEEN

"How do you know I carry MILS but Dr. Darcy didn't tell me?" demanded Sylvia. "This business of everyone else knowing my medical history while I'm in the dark is wearing thin. I'm not someone's lab rat. I'm a citizen of the United Americas and I have rights."

"I understand your frustration," said Dr. Hyland. "Here are the facts. Because Dr. Darcy participates in the Sun Motors Employee Wellness Plan, and Sun Motors is fully integrated with the Industrial Council, we received your test results at the same instant she did. We simply advised her to hold off on notifying you because we were going to intervene. The decision was made to bring you to the Juliette Island Center for Health Research, and now here you are. We're very glad to have you."

"This place is operated by the Industrial Council? I never signed any contract with the Industrial Council."

Dr. Hyland smiled. "Of course you did. The consent forms that you read and approved very clearly state that Sun Motors has the right to transfer its obligations as a health provider to any organization it sees fit, including the Industrial Council. This is a tremendous benefit to you! Here on Juliette Island we provide health care that's second to none. All the top pharmaceutical companies participate in our health research."

"Health research? What does that mean? Is this some sort of clinical trial?"

"In a way, yes. It's a long-term search for a cure, not only for MILS but for many other terrible diseases as well. Together with our pharmaceutical company partners, the Juliette Island Center is breaking new ground in identifying treatments for many of today's most destructive diseases. Perhaps you've heard of Quaxil, the miracle drug that alleviates some forms of trichotillomania? It was developed in a joint venture between the Juliette Island Center and Pardo Pharmaceuticals."

"I've heard it costs five hundred dollars per pill."

"Believe me, when a child compulsively pulls out their own eyebrows and hair to the point of baldness, her parents are happy to pay any price for hope."

"So I'm here because I have MILS, and my unborn child may have it too?"

"Yes."

"What about the man who is my husband and the father of my child? What about Jason Quin?"

"MILS is a disease that is passed from mother to child. The father is not relevant."

"He's relevant to me and to our child!"

"He is being well taken care of. Our concern, and your concern, must be for the health of you and your child. I don't think you fully appreciate the opportunity you have. Your form of MILS affects one in five hundred thousand children. That's more than a million in the United Americas."

"Why don't you get one of those other one million mothers to volunteer?"

"We do have a few others, but for many reasons, such as other health or mental issues, or legal constraints, volunteers are very difficult to find. Sylvia, you and your child will play a key role in the search for a cure. You will help change many lives. And in return, you'll be well rewarded."

"Well rewarded? How?"

"You get to live here on Juliette Island! This is the kind of place that people dream about coming to, whether for vacation or retirement. The weather is pleasant year-round and the island boasts beautiful topography, with lovely pine-covered hills descending to kiss white sand beaches. You'll enjoy the all amenities of civilization including a cinema, eighteen-hole golf course, shopping, and a four-star restaurant. And of course the finest medical care in the world for you and your child."

"You're assuming that I want to keep this baby, despite its having a terrible genetic disease."

Dr. Hyland's placid expression changed to a frown. He leaned forward and folded his hands on the desktop. Peering hard at Sylvia through his glasses, he said, "Of course you must have your child. There's no question about it. Are you saying you want an abortion? We don't provide that service here."

"I'm not saying I want an abortion," she replied. "I'm saying I'm entitled to make that choice."

"So you want to keep your baby," smiled Dr. Hyland. "That's good! I'm happy we agree."

"That's not what I'm saying," replied Sylvia. "I'm saying the choice should be mine. My child has a serious disease and I'm the one who should decide if I am to carry it through to full term. You haven't even asked me how I feel. I'm willing to listen to reason, but I think I deserve to be a part of the conversation."

"With all due respect, your argument is academic," replied Dr. Hyland with a dismissive wave of his hand. "Except in very unusual cases, abortions are not provided here on Juliette Island."

"Very unusual cases? Please elaborate. Who decides if a case is extremely unusual?"

"The Juliette Island Center Medical Board."

"And who is on the medical board?"

"A group of highly qualified doctors and Industrial Council members."

"Are you a member?"

"As a matter of fact, I am."

"Any women serving on this medical board?"

"Not at the present time."

Sylvia thought for a moment. Then she said, "Dr. Hyland, if in fact you are to be my primary care physician for the duration of my stay here—however long that might be—I need to know that you will be working in my best interest and will be advocating for me and my child. You have a fiduciary responsibility, do you not? Is not your patient your paramount concern, to be placed above the interests of insurance companies, hospital administrators, employers, the government, or any other entity?"

"Yes, of course," said Dr. Hyland. "Within reason, of course. We have to live in the real world."

"Let's change the subject," said Sylvia. It seemed that her new doctor—hopefully her temporary doctor, until she returned to home to Detroit—had a slippery answer for every question. After a long day, she didn't have the energy to debate him. There was much she wanted to know about her present situation, and she began by asking, "Where exactly are we? Where is Juliette Island?"

"In the upper Puget Sound, roughly halfway between Seattle and Vancouver. It's the largest of what used to be called the San Juan Islands. The islands and the surrounding territory are under the direct jurisdiction of the Industrial Council."

"Not the state of Washington?"

"That's correct. During the recovery from the Global Depression and with the rising military threat from Rodinia, among many other parcels throughout the nation, the government granted to the Industrial Council the northwest corner of Washington State. Here we conduct non-partisan research and formulate policy for the good of all the citizens of the United Americas. No politics are allowed here. We are neither Democrats nor Republicans, liberal nor conservative. It's really a very beautiful and efficient system."

"It sounds like one-party rule by a group of oligarchs."

"I think once you learn to appreciate the benefits of life here in the Olympic Zone, as the area is called, you'll take a more charitable view." He glanced at the clock on the wall. "You must be tired after your flight. I'll see you tomorrow for your first round of tests. Meanwhile, I'm sure you'd like to get settled. In a few minutes your manager will be here to take you to your home."

"My manager?"

"For lack of a better word," shrugged Dr. Hyland. "Mentor, personal guide, teacher, ombudsman—all are close, but not precisely accurate. So we just call them 'managers.'" He stood and extended his hand. "Until eleven o'clock tomorrow morning."

In the lobby, Sylvia was greeted by a Morta AHO 6-C wearing the black and blue of the Industrial Council. "Hello, Sylvia. I'm Limar, your personal manager. Please allow me to show you to your house."

"What is your assigned gender?" asked Sylvia.

"I believe our human guests use female pronouns when referring to me."

The robot turned and walked toward the front door. Janice and Ka'sah were behind the front desk, engrossed in a conversation. Sylvia and Limar went outside to one of the golf carts. Limar took a key from her pocket. "Have you driven a golf cart before?"

"Yes, thanks," she said as she took the key. "No cars for us guests?"

"No. I think you'll find the golf cart to be quite satisfactory. In inclement weather you can call for the taxi."

Sylvia took the wheel while Limar sat beside her. "Follow Pine Path until you get to Apple Way, and turn left," said Limar.

"How many people live here on Juliette Island?" asked Sylvia as she guided the golf cart along the asphalt path.

"One thousand four hundred and thirty-five guests, two hundred human staff, and a confidential number of autonomous humanoid operators of various types."

"Why do you call them 'guests'? Are they free to leave whenever they want?"

"They're contractually bound to stay for the duration of their treatment or study participation."

"Am I contractually bound?"

"Yes."

"I don't recall signing any such contract."

"You should refer to your copies of the consent forms you signed."

"I don't have them. Carin said the company would keep them for me." She stopped the golf cart on the Pine Path and turned to face Limar. "This so-called business trip is starting to look more and more like old-fashioned kidnapping and indentured servitude. When can I go home?"

After a pause, Limar said, "Each of us makes his or her contribution to our country. Everyone should serve where they are most valuable, wouldn't you agree? If in one situation a person creates a certain amount of value for society, and in another situation creates more value, then by what rational reason should that person not serve in the second situation, where he or she creates more value? Isn't there more fulfillment and satisfaction in creating more value rather than less?"

"But who makes that decision?" asked Sylvia. "Shouldn't each person decide for themselves how they want to contribute to the greater good?"

"With people of ordinary value, that may be an acceptable solution," replied Limar. "In any given system with many individuals, the people will naturally distribute themselves so that each can succeed. For example, if you have a system consisting of one hundred people, those one hundred people will not all decide to become doctors. Individually, one by one, they'll recognize that would be absurd. Some will become doctors, while others will become engineers or lawyers or artists. So that each can succeed, they will distribute themselves evenly across various occupations."

"Yes, and I chose to become a senior logistics manager at Sun Motors," said Sylvia. "I happen to like my job and I think I'm good at it."

"But you could not see the big picture," said Limar. "You could not see that because of your rare disease, you and your child have immense value to society. You and your child are special people."

"Value to society or to a pharmaceutical company's profits?" demanded Sylvia.

"What's the difference?" replied Limar. "When the pharmaceutical company benefits, so does society. What's good for industry is good for the United Americas."

"L'etat, c'est moi," said Sylvia.

"I am the state?" replied Limar. "I'm not familiar with that expression."

"You know it now," said Sylvia. "King Louis the Fourteenth of France. Ruled from 1638 to 1715. He saw himself as an absolute monarch. People in power commonly hold the delusion that what's good for them is therefore good for everyone. They believe a system that increases wealth and power for people who already have wealth and power is somehow good for all citizens. In some sort of socialist utopia that might be true, but we both know that in real world when power is concentrated in the hands of the few, the majority suffers."

Limar looked at Sylvia. "Please keep driving. We are behind schedule."

Why am I wasting my time debating with a damn robot? Sylvia asked herself as she started the golf cart. Arriving at Apple Way, she turned left. They entered a cluster of houses, not unlike a suburban cul-de-sac, but woodsier and more rustic. The homes were simple wood frame boxes with shingle roofs. They were all painted the same soft gray color. There were no cars in the driveways, only golf carts.

"We're going to number fifteen," said Limar. "A few houses down on the left."

Identical in construction to the other houses on the road, 15 Apple Way was differentiated only by an unusually tall sycamore tree in the small front yard. To Sylvia, it looked like a nicer version of the cabin she had been assigned to at summer camp when she was twelve years old. She noticed two other golf carts parked in the short gravel driveway.

"Who else is staying here?" she asked as she pulled up next to them.

"Mandy and Reese," replied Limar. "I think you'll like them because they're both from the Midwest."

"That's totally irrelevant to our potential compatibility," replied Sylvia. "But you're a robot, so I wouldn't expect you to understand."

The front door was unlocked. "On Juliette Island, nobody locks their doors," said Limar. "Most people don't even have keys. Sylvia entered the small foyer. The floor was wood and the plaster walls painted a plain off-white color. In front of her, a narrow staircase ascended to the second floor. To the right was a living room and to the left a small dining room.

"We're in the kitchen," called a woman's voice. To Sylvia's ears, the accent sounded more like Texas than Michigan, but no matter. They walked through the dining room to the rear of the house, where they found two women seated at the kitchen table.

"Hi, I'm Mandy," said the one with red hair as she stood up and extended her hand. Reese had dark brown hair. She remained seated. After introductions were made, Limar said to Sylvia, "I'll show you to your quarters, and then I'll leave you to get settled." Followed by Mandy and Reese, they trooped up the back stairway, which was even more narrow than the front stairs. On the second floor there was a hallway punctuated by several doors, and Limar led the way to the end, where he opened the last door. Sylvia entered a sitting room with a small sofa and desk. To the left, at the rear of the house, was the bedroom, and attached to it a small private bathroom.

"We were wondering who was going to get the big suite," said Mandy.

"Do you mean all the rooms aren't like this?" asked Sylvia as she peered out the bedroom window at the pine woods beyond the small back yard.

"No," said Reese. "Ours don't have the sitting room, and we share a bathroom." She exchanged glances with Mandy. They both smiled. "Ah-ha— you're going to have a baby!" exclaimed Reese.

"Is that why I have a bigger space?" asked Sylvia.

Smiling, Limar nodded.

"Congratulations!" said Mandy. "How far along are you? You're not even showing yet."

"Almost seven weeks," replied Sylvia. She turned to Limar. "This is very nice, but what am I supposed to wear? I have absolutely nothing! Not even a toothbrush."

Limar went to the window facing the front of the house. "Your problem has been solved. Your things have arrived."

Sylvia looked out the window and saw two drones, each loaded with a large box, which they deposited on the front walkway before flitting away. The foursome went downstairs, brought the boxes up, and placed them on the floor of the sitting room. Sylvia opened one of the boxes and pulled out items of clothing—skirts, blouses, shoes, sweatshirts, underwear. "None of these things are mine," she said. "They're all brand new."

"They're yours now," smiled Limar. "I think you'll find they will fit you very well. We have your measurements on file. All the clothing is custom cut and assembled."

It was then that Sylvia noticed Reese and Mandy were both wearing skirts and blouses of the same design, which matched the clothing in the box. The effect was oddly theatrical, as if they were all appearing in a production of Our Town.

"Ladies, I will leave you to get acquainted," said Limar. "Have a pleasant evening." With those words she went downstairs and drove away in the golf cart.

CHAPTER NINETEEN

Coffee cups in hand, the three women sat at the kitchen table. The setting sun cast a warm glow across the white walls.

"Welcome to Industrial Council Prison," said Reese. "The only difference between ICP and regular prison is that here there's no end to your sentence. No parole. No way out except across the river or release at the whim of the Juliette Island Center Medical Board."

"Reese, don't you think you're being overly dramatic?" said Mandy as she scooped a spoon of sugar into her coffee and stirred it. "I love it here. It's a beautiful island full of friendly people. You can do whatever you want—tennis, golf, games at the rec center, movie nights, fishing off the pier, swimming, shopping. No responsibilities other than taking care of yourself and showing up for your medical tests. No one likes to be poked and prodded and have needles stuck into them every day, but it sure beats working for a paycheck at a lousy insurance company."

"Is that what you did before they brought you here?" asked Sylvia. "Work at an insurance company? And why did they choose you?"

Mandy told her story.

She had been born and raised in Golden, Colorado, a town a few miles west of Denver. When Mandy was eight years old her abusive father abandoned her, her mother, and her older brother. Mother had to go to work to support the family, and Mandy was often left in the care of an aunt and uncle. Her Uncle Will molested her until his wife discovered what was going on. To Mandy's amazement, Aunt Rebecca kicked Mandy out of the house, as if she were the sexual predator! She bounced around the foster care circuit, managed to graduate from high school, and then earned her associate's degree in business management at Colorado Mesa University. She got a job selling final expense plans for Mountain Life Insurance, a Two Hundred K company, but because of her erratic performance she barely eked out a living.

She got pregnant by a guy who promised to marry her but instead took her credit cards and went to Las Vegas, where he racked up fifty thousand dollars in debt before she realized what he had done and cancelled the accounts.

Mandy had the baby, a boy whom she named Winslow, after his maternal grandfather.

Throughout all of this, she suffered unexplained health problems, regularly going to the doctor with a laundry list of complaints including fever, fatigue, muscle weakness, loss of appetite, weight loss, muscle and joint aches, rashes, numbness, and abdominal pain. Her doctors attributed her symptoms to the effects of adverse childhood experiences and advised her to seek mental health counseling. She did, but progress was slow. The only thing that kept her from being cast out among the aberrants was that her boss at Mountain Life felt sorry for her and made it her mission to salvage Mandy's shattered life. When the expanded Mountain Life Employee Health Plan was put into place, it included genetic testing. Mandy's tests revealed she suffered from polyarteritis nodosa, or PAN, a blood vessel disease characterized by inflammation of small and medium-sized arteries, preventing them from bringing oxygen and food to organs. PAN most commonly affected vessels related to the skin, joints, peripheral nerves, gastrointestinal tract, heart, eyes, and kidneys. The outward symptoms were caused by damage to affected organs.

"The underlying cause of PAN is unknown," said Mandy. "Some doctors believe it's an autoimmune disease. Others speculate it's triggered by the hepatitis B virus. No one's certain. That's why I'm here. Six months ago, my boss came to me and told me I'd been chosen for a special assignment. They put me on a company plane and sent me here. When I figured out what was going on, I was like, are you kidding? You want me to live out in the middle of nowhere so you can use me as a medical research subject? But I got used to it. Life is good here. Three meals a day, a beautiful place to live, good medical care—why should I complain?"

"What about your child?" asked Sylvia. "Where's Winslow?"

"They brought him here, too," she said. Her eyes lowered to look at the table. "But they said he was very sick. They couldn't save him."

"Save him? From what?" asked Sylvia.

"No one has said anything," interjected Reese. "It's all a big mystery. One day he was alive and the next day he was dead. That's the way it is around here. It's like Frankenstein's laboratory, with horrible things happening behind locked doors."

"Oh, I'm sure it's not like that," said Mandy. Still looking down, she fiddled nervously with her coffee cup. "The doctors here are very nice. They try hard. I'm sure they did their very best for Winslow. He's in a better place."

"A better place?" said Reese incredulously.

Seeking to diffuse the growing tension, Sylvia turned to Reese. "How about you? How did you end up here?"

Reese said she was raised in Houston, Texas. She wasn't sure where she had been born; at age two, she had been adopted by a couple who had raised her, and to that day they remained her parents. After high school she earned her degree in social work, and then got a job at a neighborhood rape crisis center in a small town near Amarillo, counseling women who had been sexually abused and arranging medical treatment for them. But she never knew her biological mother or father, and so one day she signed up for a commercial genetics testing company. After signing all the consent forms without reading them, she sent in her swab sample.

A week went by with no response, and then two weeks. She called the company. The customer service representative told her there was a slight delay in processing her sample, but not to worry.

Then one day four people came to the center and asked for her by name. She went to speak with them, and they told her they were from the Industrial Council Security Service, and could they please speak with her at their office in Amarillo. Willingly, Reese got into the van, but instead of going downtown the van got on the expressway towards the airport. She demanded to know where they were going, and the agents told her to be patient. She responded by kicking one of them and trying to open the door of the moving vehicle. They held her down and she saw a syringe. That's all she remembered until she woke up on an airplane. Groggy, she became belligerent, and was again subdued and drugged.

"I woke up in this house," she said. "That was exactly ninety-four days ago. Believe me, I count every minute that passes. During my first medical interview with Dr. Hyland—the creep!—I learned I was a carrier of an inherited gene mutation for Walker-Warburg syndrome, a severe form of congenital muscular dystrophy. Most children who have it don't live longer than three years. Hyland told me they had been looking for a carrier of Walker-Warburg and that I was a very special person. Ever since I arrived, they've been treating me like human lab rat, with endless blood tests and brain scans and tissue samples." She leaned forward for emphasis. "Last week, Dr. Hyland told me that while I was providing much valuable data in the fight against this deadly disease, it would be a huge breakthrough if I agreed to have a baby!"

"Are you serious?" asked Sylvia.

"Totally. Hyland said that if I became pregnant and carried the baby full term, I'd be given my own house with a view of Puget Sound and double the usual household budget. I told him to go to hell and that I wasn't going to be a farm animal producing babies for him and his cronies to use as test subjects. And besides, why would I deliberately have a child that I knew would be born with a terrible disease? It's ghastly."

"I don't mean to pry," said Sylvia, "but was the rape crisis center part of a larger Two Hundred K company?"

"Oh, no," laughed Reese. "We were part of the vast canaille. I'm a dyed-in-the-wool aberrant."

"I don't mean to be rude, but I've never before known an aberrant. Of course I've met them—gas station attendants and store clerks and so on—but you're the first one I've ever sat down and talked to, much less lived under the same roof with."

"Well, here I am," laughed Reese. "I won't bite you, I promise. I'm the same species as you—Homo sapiens. The only difference is that I don't accept the rule of the Industrial Council. To them I say, 'Screw you!'"

Mandy raised her hand in caution. "Reese, please. We don't want any trouble. And I'm sure you don't want to be sent to the cooler again."

"What do you mean?" asked Sylvia. "Is this place bugged?"

"Do bears crap in the woods?" said Reese. "One morning I was complaining to poor Mandy that I couldn't sleep. Anxiety or something. So that afternoon I went to my regular appointment with Dr. Hyland, and no sooner did I walk into his office than he handed me a bottle of pills. 'These will help you sleep,' he said.

"I replied, 'You bastards, you've got the house wired!'"

"He just shrugged and said they had a responsibility to ensure and safeguard our welfare. I told him they only wanted to 'ensure and safeguard' the viability of their human cash cows."

Sylvia looked around the kitchen. The microwave, the ceiling light, the electrical outlets, the cabinets, the refrigerator, the stove, the canisters of salt and sugar, the cute little kitten clock on the wall—all suddenly took on a sinister aspect. Cameras and microphones could be hidden anywhere.

"Girls, who's hungry?" said Mandy with abrupt cheerfulness. "What do you say we all go to the Dockside tonight for dinner? Celebrate our new roommate."

Reese looked at Sylvia. "Be prepared to blow your entire week's restaurant allowance at the Dockside. But it will be fun and the food isn't half bad. Before we go, we absolutely must get some fresh air outside."

Mystified as to why they needed to go out and get fresh air, Sylvia went along with Reese's suggestion. In the gathering twilight, they filed out the back door to a small patio facing the gloomy woods. Reese went to an old earthenware planter that had nothing planted in it. Reaching in, she pulled out a bottle and three plastic cups. To Sylvia and Mandy she each handed a cup. After putting her finger to her lips, indicating silence, she uncorked the bottle and poured a shot into each cup.

Sylvia brought the cup to her nose and inhaled. It was whiskey. She took a sip. "This is pretty good stuff," she whispered to Reese. "Where did you get it?"

"I have my source," Reese whispered in reply. "Sip it slowly. You can't have more than one or two shots every few hours."

"Let me guess," said Sylvia. "The Morta managers will detect the alcohol on my breath."

"You got it," said Reese.

"They say when you're pregnant you shouldn't have any alcohol,' said Sylvia. "But it sure tastes good!"

Reese offered them one more shot each. As she was pouring their portions, Sylvia said, "Are you sure you want to do this? The bottle looks as if it's nearly empty. We don't want to take the last of it."

"Don't worry," replied Reese as she drained the bottle. "I can get more on Sunday."

When they were finished, Reese carefully put the bottle and cups back into the planter.

"Okay, let's roll out!" said Reese. "To the Dockside!"

CHAPTER TWENTY

Sylvia rode in Reese's golf cart, while Mandy drove herself. After a few minutes' trundling along the twisting asphalt paths, now lit by streetlights, they came to the restaurant. In the parking lot there were dozens of golf carts, a few cars, and one truck. The place had all the attributes of a seaside eatery—the faded grey wood siding, the railings connected by rope twists, the front door window in the form of a porthole, and the vast expanse of dark water behind it. Sylvia told the others she wanted to see the view, and together they walked around the side of the building. What Sylvia really wanted to see was how much water separated Juliette Island from the opposite land mass, at least in this location. On the horizon she could make out distant twinkling lights. They seemed to be from another world.

Reese sidled up to her. "I know what you're thinking," she whispered. "You're looking at Victoria, British Columbia. It's a good ten miles away. Unless you're an Olympic swimmer, you wouldn't stand a chance. This island is at least five miles from any other point of land, except for the other side—the eastern side—which is connected to the mainland by a mile-long causeway. When the bus brought you here, it came across the causeway. There are checkpoints at each end with armed guards."

They went into the restaurant, where they were greeted by a Morta AHO. The machine showed them to a booth. The place was nearly full, with a variety of people all wearing clothing similar to what Sylvia had been given, as if the cast of Our Town had grown to nearly a hundred actors.

"I don't see any of the Juliette Island staff here," said Sylvia.

"And you never will," replied Reese. "Unless they have a particular job to do, like performing a medical procedure on a resident or working here in the restaurant, they go home every evening, across the causeway to the mainland. After sunset, the island is managed by robots. Since they're all made by Morta Laboratories, we just call them Mortas."

Sylvia wanted to ask why the humans left at night, but the server came for their order, and the conversation went in another direction. The restaurant had a pleasant vibe and the food was boring but edible. When they were finished and each had paid with their island debit cards, they made their way outside to the golf carts. The night air was warm, and in the dark woods the tiny lights of fireflies blinked like Morse code signals.

Standing next to their golf carts, Reese drew them close together. "It's too early to go home. We should have some fun. What do you say we go skinny-dipping? There's a little beach about a mile from here. Totally secluded. If you didn't know it was there, you'd never find it."

"I don't think we should," said Mandy. "You know it's against the rules. After dark you need to be at home or at an approved location."

"That's crazy," said Sylvia. "It sounds like a curfew. I haven't had a curfew since I was sixteen years old and my parents made me come home by eleven o'clock."

"They say," said Reese, "it's because we're such special people, and if we had a medical emergency in some remote area of the island, the first responders would be delayed. It's for our own safety."

"It's a good point," nodded Mandy.

"It's ridiculous," whispered Sylvia. "Okay, let's go. It sounds like fun. Mandy, how about you? I'm sure it will be all right if we're out a little bit late."

Mandy looked around nervously before she said, "Okay, I'll come. But we can't stay long. I don't want to spend the night in the cooler."

"Don't worry," said Reese. "Get in your cart and follow me."

Sylvia got into Reese's cart, and they rolled out of the restaurant parking area. Instead of heading towards 15 Apple Way, Reese turned in the opposite direction. Mandy followed close behind. The asphalt path climbed through a grove of tall dark pines where the only light was from the yellowish jiggling headlights on each golf cart. Then the trees yielded to an open rocky pasture, dimly illuminated by the half moon emerging from behind the high thin clouds. Reese slowed down and turned into a gravel road. A jackrabbit darted through the narrow headlight beam as the golf cart bumped along before descending a gradual incline. Somewhere in the distance an owl hooted. The hill became steeper as the road wound its way toward the glimmering water visible through the tall trees. At a small clearing Reese parked the golf cart, and when the three women were gathered together she said, "This way," and she led them along a narrow path bounded by prickly beach roses. The gravel underfoot changed to sand, and suddenly Sylvia found herself stepping onto a small crescent beach. Under her feet the white sand shone in the moonlight.

Kicking off their shoes, they walked to the water's edge, where gentle waves lapped. From far across the dark water, lights twinkled.

"Oooh, this water's cold," said Sylvia.

"Don't worry, you'll get used to it,' laughed Reese. "Come this way." She walked to a big flat rock and began to pull off her skirt and blouse. "You can put your clothes here so they don't get sandy." In a moment she was naked. For a moment Sylvia was startled—she was not accustomed to seeing unclothed people in public spaces—but then she went to the rock, took off her clothes, and put them in a neat pile.

Mandy did the same, and the three women walked toward the phosphorescent ripples. Under Sylvia's feet the dry sand retained the warmth of the day, but as they neared the water it grew damp and cool. Reese boldly strode forward into the dark surf, and when the water was up to her waist she dove in.

Sylvia felt the cold water grip her legs. She hesitated before forcing herself deeper, up to her chest. The sensation was like a thousand tiny knives sticking into her skin. But she kept moving and the pain subsided. When she felt she was ready, she dove in, and the shock of the cold water against her face nearly made her turn around and run back to shore. But with Reese setting the example, Sylvia stayed in, and Mandy was soon in the water too.

Overhead the half moon gleamed and a few of the brightest stars twinkled through the high clouds. As she swam, the tensions and conflicts that had filled Sylvia's mind and heart seemed to be assuaged, and she found herself enjoying the moment without guilt or anxiety about her future. If it was her fate to be here, at this hour of this day, then so be it. It was foolish to become angry over something beyond your control. She was one with the dark water and its unseen inhabitants—the sleek silent fishes that swam in whatever direction they wanted, over uncounted leagues of open water, even to other lands and distant currents. Freedom was such a simple thing, if you looked at it from moment to moment. At this very second, in this water, Sylvia felt as free as she had ever felt.

Sylvia looked up. High overhead, a jet plane slowly crossed the sky. It was coming from somewhere and going somewhere. With a feeling of regret, the sight reminded her that her freedom was limited to this water on this crescent beach. She squinted at the tiny light. Was it a military plane or a commercial airliner? Were there passengers on board going where they had chosen to go—on a business trip or even a vacation—or was the plane full of "special" people being shipped to some remote Industrial Council facility?

Suddenly Reese appeared next to her. "What do you think? Pretty amazing, isn't it?" she said as she tread water. Her wet hair shone in the moonlight and her teeth flashed white.

"Yes—it almost makes you forget you're living in a prison camp," laughed Sylvia. She dove in and swam under water in the welcoming cold darkness for as long as her lungs could stand it. With powerful strokes she felt the water flow around and over her hands and legs. Then, with her lungs bursting from lack of oxygen, she broke the surface.

Wiping the water from her eyes, Sylvia was startled to see Reese's head illuminated by a bright light from above. Surrounded by darkness, the spot of light shining on the ocean seemed unreal, like a scene from a movie.

Suddenly Sylvia herself was caught by a spotlight from the sky. Shielding her eyes as she tread water, she heard the faint whirring of propellers. The light was then joined by a third, trained on Mandy. High over Sylvia's head, a trio of drones hovered in a group. Each had a powerful spotlight trained on one of the women in the water below it.

"Exit the water immediately," called a metallic voice from one of the drones. "You are not authorized to be at this location. Return to the beach."

With a sickening feeling of deep dread and horror, Sylvia swam to the shore until she felt her feet brush the sandy bottom. Then she walked out of the water onto the beach. Reese and Mandy were already there, dripping and shivering, trying to cover their nakedness.

A Morta strode out of the path leading to the clearing where they had parked their golf carts. In the moonlight his eyes gleamed red.

"I didn't want to be here," wailed Mandy. "They made me come! Please just let me go home!"

"Be silent," said the Morta. "All of you, get dressed."

Under the harsh glare of the drones' spotlights, the three women went to the rock and hurriedly donned their clothing.

The Morta came to them and ordered them to turn around. Starting with Reese, he deftly bound their hands behind their backs with zip ties. Mandy began to sob uncontrollably. Reese said nothing, but stood with her head held high. Taken by surprise at the speed with which the Morta had accomplished its task, Sylvia felt deep shock at the sensation, for the first time in her life, of having her hands pinned behind her back against her will. She knew now that she had truly crossed the line between being a free person and a prisoner.

"Stay together," said the Morta. "Don't try to run."

They had no choice but to obey. Under the lights of the watchful drones, they waited on the beach. Then they heard the sound of a boat approaching. With its spotlight cutting the darkness, it swung into view from around the point sheltering the crescent beach. The boat, low and black, came parallel to the beach, turned, and then ran toward the beach until its flat bow scraped onto the sand. The front gate dropped, like on a pickup truck.

"Get in," said the Morta.

The three women, with their hands restrained behind their backs, made their way along the beach to the yawning maw of the boat and stepped up the ramp. They found themselves on a flat deck in front of an enclosed wheelhouse. A Morta guard on the boat gestured to a long bench attached to the gunwales. "Sit there," it said. They sat down, uncomfortably, with their hands tied. As Mandy whimpered, Reese said to the Morta guard, "We weren't doing anything wrong. We just went for a moonlight swim."

Its red eyes gleaming in the night, the Morta guard made no response.

"You thought maybe we were trying to escape?" she continued. "That's funny! Three naked women were going to swim ten miles to the mainland, where you guys would be waiting for us. That would have been quite a sight! Don't you have better things to do than chase innocent people who are just trying to have some fun?"

"Be silent," said the Morta guard.

After the bow door had been raised, the boat's engines shifted to full reverse, and with a lurch the craft slid off the sand and backed away into open water. Turning toward the north, it picked up speed. The hovering drones, the Morta on the beach, and Sylvia's memories of freely swimming in the dark, cold water were left behind.

"Where are you taking us?" demanded Reese. "To the cooler?"

The Morta made no reply.

"What's the cooler?" Sylvia whispered to Reese.

"I think you're going to find out," she replied. "Just remember, it won't last forever. We're valuable people. They need to protect their investment in us. As long as we contribute to their profits, they'll keep us healthy."

"What if we don't contribute to their profits?" asked Sylvia.

"If you seem harmless, they'll turn you loose among the aberrants. If you pose a threat, they make you disappear."

"Sylvia Brand and Reese Carter—stop talking," said the Morta. To steady himself in the choppy seas he was holding onto the railing. Sylvia was beginning to feel a little bit ill, and she deliberately took slow, deep breaths. On the bench next her, Mandy softly whimpered.

The boat had cruised around the island, and while the night made reckoning difficult, Sylvia estimated they went halfway around in about twenty minutes. They did not pass the causeway to the mainland. The boat slowed and pulled up to an aluminum dock mounted on floats so that it went up and down with the tide. The Morta guard ascended a short set of steps to the gunwales and then stepped onto the dock. After tying the boat to a cleat on the dock, the Morta turned and said, "You will now disembark."

Sylvia stood up. Her legs were stiff and her arms ached. With the assistance of the Morta that had piloted the boat, together the three women ascended the short steps and were soon standing on the dock.

"When are you going to free our hands?" said Reese to the Morta guard.

"Follow me," came the reply.

"No, I don't want to," said Sylvia. She didn't quite know why she said this. Perhaps she had been emboldened by Reese's independent attitude, or perhaps she had gotten tired of being told what to do. But having said it, she clenched her jaw and stood with her spine straight.

The Morta guard walked over to her. His red gaze fixed on her eyes, with viper quickness he reached out with his hand and grasped the back of her neck. Suddenly white-hot pain shot from her spine into her brain. Gasping for breath, her knees buckled and her vision became blurred. With the Morta's hand still on her neck, she crumpled to the dock. Only once she was down did he release his grip.

Crouched on her knees, with her hands tied behind her back, Sylvia felt the pain slowly ease. Slowly her breath returned and her vision became clear. She looked up at the Morta standing over her.

"Your occipital nerve is just one of many very sensitive areas of your body," the Morta said. "We know them all. We know which ones to activate without permanently damaging either you or your baby. Now get up and get back in line."

Feeling dizzy, Sylvia struggled to her feet. "Okay, okay," she said. "I get it."

"Good," said the Morta without a smile. "Let's go."

With a Morta in front and one behind, the women shuffled through a gate in a high fence to a nondescript building. Inside was a room with a desk. A long hallway led from the room. The Morta led Sylvia down the hallway, which was lined with numbered doors. He slid open number eighteen. Sylvia entered a plain cinderblock cell furnished with a bed, toilet, and sink. The Morta told her to turn around, and he released her hands.

"Go to sleep," said the Morta. He closed the door.

Sylvia was alone in her cell. The only light came from a dim bulb in the center of the ceiling. There was a small barred window at the end of the cell, opposite the door, but she couldn't see anything through it other than darkness. She sat on the bed. The metal springs under the thin mattress creaked. She thought about her life in Detroit, and about Jason and the house they were buying together. Her previous life and love seemed so far away and so long ago, and yet she could almost hear Jason's voice and feel his gentle touch. She thought about her parents, and the love they had given her as a child. Those were happy times, when life seemed brighter and simpler, even through the difficult days of the Global Recession.

Where had Sylvia gone wrong? Why had she been singled out for abuse? She had always played by the rules and had been a good and loyal employee of Sun Motors. She was an obedient follower of the Industrial Council and its systems. She had even welcomed the oversight of Carin, in no small part because his arrival had marked the end of the abusive reign of Randolph Meekin. But no matter how much she tried to go along with the program, the company and its ally the Industrial Council always wanted more. They were never satisfied. And thanks to an accident of fate—a genetic fluke over which Sylvia Brand had no control—she had been identified as a "special person" who couldn't be trusted to manage her own body. Her condition had value to medical science, they said, but Sylvia knew they really meant her condition made her valuable to the health care industry and their pharmaceutical company partners. By simply existing, she was a source of marketable data, the rights to which she had foolishly signed away. And to make her bondage even more complete, under the terms of her consent forms the Industrial Council had the right to ensure that access to her health data was full, robust, and unimpeded by her own actions. She did not have the legal right to deprive the Industrial Council of data for which it, by its own reasoning, had paid through its subsidy of her Sun Motors Employee Wellness Plan. They wanted, and were legally entitled, to what they had paid for.

Mentally and physically exhausted, Sylvia lay on the bed, covered herself with the skimpy blanket, and fell into a fitful sleep.

SYLVIA BRAND

CHAPTER TWENTY-ONE

Sylvia awoke. She didn't know how long she had been asleep. The dim bulb on the ceiling glowed. But there was other light, coming from the window.

Stiffly, she sat up. Her back ached from the thin, hard mattress. Her eyes were bleary and paste coated the inside of her mouth. The salt water had dried in her hair, making it feel coarse. Slowly she stood up. She went to the window. In order to look out she had to stand on tiptoes. Through the bars and the dirty glass she saw morning light on the pine woods. That's all she could see—just a wall of scraggly trees with a glimpse of grey sky between the uppermost branches.

At the sink she rinsed off her hands and face. There was neither soap nor towel. Then she paced in her cell, walking the five paces from the steel door to the wall with the window. She did deep knee bends and then some pushups. She went to the door to listen, but heard nothing. Another look out the window yielded only a slight change in the angle of the shadows in the trees.

Hunger gnawed at her stomach. She went to the door and pounded on it. "Hey!" she called through the narrow slit that showed nothing but a section of cinderblock wall, "If you want me to have a healthy baby for your experiments, you'd better take care of me!" She looked around the cell for a camera. There had to be a camera. They had to be watching her. She peered at the sink, the toilet, the cracks in the walls. She craned her neck to look at the lighting fixture on the ceiling.

From the door came a metallic sound. The door slid open. Limar walked in. Behind her lurked the Morta guard.

"I apologize for the poor accommodations," she said with a tone indicating a measure of kindness had been added to her voice. "I hope your evening was not too terrible."

"Yes, it was terrible," she spat. "I don't appreciate being handcuffed like a common criminal and thrown into a prison cell. I see you've got your mechanical goon standing right behind you. What is this, some sort of good cop-bad cop routine? Am I supposed to be grateful you're showing an imitation of human decency?"

Limar turned to the Morta. "Walmad, you may go. Thank you." With a nod, the robot guard left. Limar looked at Sylvia. "I'm sure you'd rather eat breakfast at home than sample the fare here at the Re-Orientation Center. We have transportation arranged for you and your housemates. Please follow me."

Sylvia followed Limar into the hallway and then to the central receiving room, where Reese and Mandy were waiting. Then Limar escorted them to the same limousine bus that had transported them from the airport—the one with the opaque windows and curtain behind the driver. "Sorry, but it's important the other residents not see you being driven from the Re-Orientation Center," said Limar. "We want to protect your privacy."

"You also want to ensure we don't know the exact location of the cooler," said Reese. "The number one rule around here is the less the so-called residents know, the better."

"Reese," said Limar, "as someone who has been a guest here for over three months, you should know the nighttime guards have their instructions. We can't have the residents wandering around the island after dark. We're all here for a purpose. We all have a job to do. I'm sorry if the rules seem severe, but it's in everyone's best interest to comply. Let's keep focused on the good we're accomplishing for our fellow citizens."

"Am I free to leave whenever I want?" asked Reese. "Do I have my rights?"

"You have a contract with your healthcare provider," replied Limar. "It's your healthcare provider's obligation to do what's best for you and for our nation. I hope I need not remind you that we are on the brink of war with Rodinia. We cannot expect to enjoy the same personal freedoms as we would in peacetime. We all must make sacrifices."

"Excuse me," said Sylvia, "but you're a goddamn robot. Exactly what sacrifices are you making? Do you even know what that means?"

"And what about this alleged war with Rodinia?" demanded Reese. "As a Morta autonomous human operator, your database of national knowledge is shared with every other Morta unit. We've been hearing about impending war with Rodinia for years. Hell, when I was a kid I heard about the horrors of Rodinia. According to Facts News, the people there were practically cannibals! I'm beginning to think this talk of war is nothing more than an excuse for the Industrial Council to solidify its power and strengthen the oligarchy."

At that moment the limousine bus arrived at 15 Apple Way. Instead of responding to the challenges from Sylvia and Reese, Limar stood up and said, "We are at our destination. I hope you have a pleasant and productive day. I hope I need not remind you of your individual appointments with your doctors—Mandy at eleven o'clock this morning, and Reese and Sylvia each at noon."

The three women filed off the bus and went into the house. On the way in, Sylvia noticed Reese and Mandy's golf carts had been returned and were parked alongside the gravel driveway.

In her private shower, with the warm water soothing her body, Sylvia ran her hands across her stomach. Soon she would be showing. Her first pregnancy had lasted ten weeks before her spontaneous abortion, as the doctors called it. She was at seven weeks now. The next three weeks would be especially nerve wracking—there was something about making it past ten weeks that seemed like an important goal. What seemed to her to be most bizarre about her situation was that on the one hand, she was living as a prisoner, which was stressful and not conducive to a healthy pregnancy, but on the other hand, her overlords had a tremendous financial interest in keeping her and her baby healthy. She was a dove in a gilded cage.

And when the baby was born, what kind of world would he or she enter? Would her child have a serious and life-threatening disease, dooming both of them to lives as human guinea pigs for the conglomerates that held the keys to healthcare?

After her shower, Sylvia joined Reese and Mandy in the kitchen for breakfast.

"My friend," said Reese as she poured Sylvia a glass of orange juice, "you may have the dubious distinction of being the first inmate of Juliette Island Prison to spend her very first night on the island in the cooler. It takes most people a few weeks to work up to that distinction."

"It wasn't exactly her idea to go to the beach at night," said Mandy. "Anyway, let's try to keep a low profile and do the best we can. I don't want any deductions on my island debit card, and I don't want to be seen as a troublemaker."

"Deductions?" asked Sylvia.

"Yes," replied Reese as she sprinkled some hot sauce on her scrambled eggs. "As a punitive measure they might put a charge on your debit card. You need to track your balance carefully, because you don't want to try to use your card somewhere and have it declined because you've been fined for some infraction you've forgotten about."

"What happens if you have no money at the end of the week?" asked Sylvia.

"Then you have to beg from your friends," said Mandy. "Believe me, it's humiliating, and an effective tool to keep people in line. It pays to follow the rules—literally."

At noon Sylvia reported to the office of Dr. James Hyland.

"I understand you had a run-in with the overnight Mortas," he said in his kindly voice.

"Yes. My roommates and I went to a beach to go swimming. They arrested us and took us to the so-called Re-Orientation Center. It was nothing more than a common jail. It was my first time behind bars in my entire life."

"I hope you learned your lesson," he said as he removed his rimless spectacles and cleaned them with a soft cloth. "Now then—we have important work to do. Mitochondrial DNA-associated Leigh syndrome, or MILS, is no laughing matter. While fate has placed a heavy burden on your shoulders, this means you have been given an opportunity to contribute to medical science in a way that few other people have. I hope you were able to get some rest last night, because we have a full schedule of tests today. Did you eat breakfast this morning?"

"Of course I did. Why?"

He looked at a paper on his desk. "That's too bad—we should have told you not to eat. We'll have to work around it. Okay, please follow me." He stood up.

"Where are we going?"

"To the medical research wing of this building."

After walking through a maze of corridors, they arrived at a reception area. "Sylvia Brand is here," Dr. Hyland said to the woman behind the desk.

The woman smiled at Sylvia. "Your first day here? Welcome. The nurse will escort you to your first appointment."

"How long will this take?" asked Sylvia.

"All day," replied the woman. "Don't worry, you'll get used to it. Think of it as being just like your old job. Nine to five."

Sylvia was shown to a room where a nurse gave her a standard physical examination including a complete blood count, cardiac stress test, liver function test, prothrombin time test, strep test, skin allergy test. For the lumbar puncture test, the nurse inserted a needle between her two lumbar vertebrae and removed a sample of cerebrospinal fluid. "This is the fluid that surrounds your brain and spinal cord to protect them from injury," she explained. "This can help us diagnose serious infections such as meningitis, other disorders such as Guillain-Barre syndrome and multiple sclerosis, or cancers of the brain or spinal cord."

Next came a flexible sigmoidoscopy, in which the nurse inserted a thin, flexible tube, or sigmoidoscope, into Sylvia's rectum. "It's a quick way to screen for colon cancer or other disorders," said the nurse.

Then it was into the stirrups for a colposcopy exam, in which the instrument produces an illuminated, magnified view of the cervix as well as the vagina and vulva. "Many pre-malignant lesions and malignant lesions in these areas have discernible characteristics that can be detected through the examination," said the nurse.

Next came an esophagogastroduodenoscopy. After giving Sylvia an intravenous muscle relaxer and an anxiety medication, plus a local anesthetic sprayed into her mouth to prevent her from coughing or gagging when the scope was inserted, the nurse inserted the scope through the esophagus and down to the stomach and duodenum, the first part of the small intestine. She examined the lining of the esophagus, stomach, and upper duodenum.

There were more—electromyography for evaluating and recording the electrical activity produced by skeletal muscles, an electrocardiograph to detect cardiac abnormalities, and a chest radiograph. Then came an ultrasound exam of the fetus and two maternal blood tests designed to measure two substances found in the blood of all pregnant women: pregnancy-associated plasma protein screening, a protein produced by the placenta in early pregnancy; and human chorionic gonadotropin, a hormone produced by the placenta in early pregnancy. "Abnormal levels," explained the nurse, "are associated with an increased risk for chromosome abnormality."

At five o'clock, the nurse announced the end of that day's testing. Sylvia felt as if her body had been invaded through every orifice and the fingers of strangers had probed her most private parts. Her body was a public resource, an open book to read by anyone, a living version of the cadavers sent to medical schools for dissection.

At home, as they were making dinner, Sylvia said to Reese and Mandy, "I can't live like this. I feel like a lab rat. They stuck needles into me as if I were a pincushion. They jammed instruments up my ass and down my throat. Dr. Hyland told me that during my next appointment on Monday they're going to put a camera into my vagina and film the fetus. They're going to do brain scans and full body x-rays. He tells me these things as if I were a willing and grateful partner to their twisted program."

"Just go with the flow," said Mandy, as she tossed the salad. "It's not an easy life, but think of the benefits. Everything is paid for. Your home, your food, your clothing—all taken care of by the Industrial Council. You have not a worry in the world. Look at us, right here, right now. We're safe in our house. We're making dinner in our kitchen. In our lives we have friends and people who care about us. Our island is peaceful and offers us everything we need. We have these things, while all over the world there are billions of people who live in wretched conditions and would gladly switch places with any one of us."

CHAPTER TWENTY-TWO

The next day was Saturday. It was like any other day of the week, and Sylvia's tests began at ten o'clock in the morning, went until lunchtime at one o'clock, and then resumed at two o'clock for another five hours. Dr. Hyland was off that day, and Limar escorted her to the medical wing.

The first test was chorionic villus sampling, a prenatal test in which a sample of chorionic villi is removed from the placenta for testing. The nurse explained that the chorionic villi are wispy projections of placental tissue that share the baby's genetic makeup, and that chorionic villus sampling can provide information about the health of the fetus.

Another nurse—there seemed to be an endless supply of them—came to the examination room with a long, thin optical instrument with an eyepiece at one end, a rigid or flexible tube in the middle, and a tiny lens and light at the other end of the tube.

"What is that?" asked Sylvia, still groggy from the anesthetic administered for the chorionic villus sampling.

"It's a cystoscope," replied the nurse. "I'm going to use it to look at the lining of your urethra and bladder."

"But I don't have any urinary tract problems. Down there, everything is normal."

"That may be," said the nurse as she opened the flow of sedative into Sylvia's intravenous line. "But we need to establish a baseline condition. Please count backwards from one hundred for me."

Sylvia wanted to protest that this procedure was unnecessary and invasive, but as she became more relaxed the problem didn't seem to be worth mentioning. She started counting, and got as far as ninety-four before the world disappeared.

She woke up. She was in a hospital room, with beeping machines on each side of the bed. Her view was blocked by portable translucent curtains. Her

149

pelvis and throat were sore. She looked at both her arms. Mercifully, the intravenous lines had been removed. The punctures were covered by bits of gauze secured with tape.

"Hello?" she called. Her voice sounded distant, weak. Summoning her strength, she called out, "Hey, I'm awake!"

The curtain was pulled aside. A nurse, dressed in white, stood at the foot of the bed. She was smiling and seemed friendly.

"Are you the same nurse who was here earlier?" asked Sylvia.

"No, I just came on duty. My name is Andrea. Now that you're up, it won't be long before we can send you home."

When the nurse said this, the first image that came into Sylvia's fuzzy mind was her home in Detroit. "Will Jason be picking me up?" she asked.

"Jason?"

"Yes, my husband. Jason. Should I call him, or is he waiting?"

"I'm sorry, Sylvia, but Jason's not here. In a few minutes you'll be driven home by one of the guards. You'll be free to enjoy the rest of your evening."

Then Sylvia remembered. She was on a distant island, living in a house that wasn't hers with roommates assigned to her by the company. She was a medical test subject. She was not going home to Jason. From deep inside her she felt a tidal surge of grief, and suddenly tears erupted from her eyes.

"I'm sorry," she stammered as she looked for something to dab her eyes. "It's been a very long week."

The nurse smiled and handed her a tissue. "I understand. I hope you don't mind if I tell you that you've been a model patient. You are very brave. The work we're doing here is very important, and you're a part of it."

"Thank you." She didn't know what else to say.

By the time the Morta guard dropped her off at home it was late afternoon. Mandy and Reese were still at their medical appointments. Feeling sore and groggy, Sylvia went up to her room, lay down on the bed, and feel asleep.

At breakfast the next morning, Reese told Sylvia that ordinarily there were no medical exams on Sunday. The island's staff was reduced to minimal levels, leaving the bulk of the work, including security, in the hands of the Mortas. Unlike their human creators, the Mortas never needed days off. They didn't sleep, exactly; to recharge and receive their software updates, they went dormant for an hour a day. Every few weeks they had to report to the local Morta maintenance facility, which Reese believed was somewhere near the island, but she wasn't sure because since arriving on the island she hadn't been off it, and she knew very little about the surrounding environment.

"Sun Motors has a plant in Tacoma," said Sylvia as she spooned strawberry jam onto her English muffin. "I was there a few years ago. They assemble internal guidance systems for the Comanche truck, which they ship to us in Detroit. A few days before I was sent here I had a video conference with the production manager, and he told me they had just gotten a Morta supervisor. He wanted to know what he should expect."

"What did you tell him?" asked Mandy.

"That our manager, Carin, was about as ideal a boss as you could hope for. No ego, ready to help with a problem, and always respectful. Of course, I told him these things via the company video conferencing service while I was sitting in my cubicle, which I knew was under surveillance. What I told the guy in Tacoma was half the truth. From a purely operational standpoint, Carin was a very good supervisor. But I had to get past the fact that he was a creepy control freak who knew more about me than I did!'

"I hear you," said Reese.

"I heard the territory north of here," said Mandy, "in what used to be Canada, was part of the canaille, occupied exclusively by the aberrants."

"You mean totally out of the control of the federal government and the Industrial Council?" asked Sylvia.

"Yes," said Mandy. "It's what used to be the province of Alberta. The center is the old city of Calgary, which the aberrants have supposedly re-named Swanta, after their so-called leader. Of course it's all a load of rubbish. I cannot imagine anyone living in the filth and lawlessness of the canaille. They can call their city whatever they want, it's still a disgusting swamp. Or so I've heard."

As they were cleaning up the dishes, Reese said, "Ladies, what do you want to do today?"

"I'm going to the movies with my friend Jacqui," said Mandy. "Then we're just going to hang out at the rec center. Maybe meet some cute guys."

"And if you meet some cute guys, what exactly do you plan to do with them?" laughed Reese.

"I try not to think about that," she replied.

Reese turned to Sylvia. "In case you're wondering, when you go in for your medical exam on Monday morning, the doctor will know if you've had sex. They'll find your partner's DNA in your vagina, or traces of a condom, or evidence of a lubricant. And if you try to wash that stuff out, they'll detect that too. Even an unusual stretching of your girl parts will be detected."

"Is it against the law to have sex?" asked Sylvia.

"You've got to remember there are no unusual laws here," corrected Reese. "Technically, we're governed by the same laws as everyone else. But we're also controlled by the contracts and consent forms we signed with the companies that employ us. Your actions are controlled by the policies set by Sun Motors, and by extension the Industrial Council, to which Sun Motors has assigned its signatory rights. To answer your question, your doctor, as the lawful representative of the Council, may determine that having sex could be detrimental to your mental or physical health. This would put into jeopardy the investment they've made in you, in the form of your paycheck. He may therefore impose a penalty if you disregard his professional medical advice. The medical board could also penalize your partner."

"Are you saying to me," said Sylvia, "that I could report for my medical exam, and Dr. Hyland could say, 'Tests indicate you recently had sex with Joe Smith, which is against my medical advice, and therefore I'm going to throw you both in the cooler.' He could do that?"

"Yes," replied Mandy as she dried the silverware and put it into the drawer. "Under the contracts and consent forms that we signed, he has the medical authority to do that."

"So by extension," said Sylvia, "If Dr. Hyland thought it would be therapeutic for me to have sex with Joe Smith, then he could order that as part of my treatment?"

Reese and Mandy looked at each other. "In theory, I suppose he could," said Reese. "But it's much more difficult to make someone do something against their will than to penalize them for doing something wrong."

"Especially something like having sex," added Mandy.

"Do we really know what they do to," said Sylvia, "I spent most of the day unconscious, with my feet in the stirrups and my legs open wide for anyone to see. Hell, for all I know every intern at that hospital had sex with me while I was lying there in dreamland. I have no way of knowing. My pelvis is sore from all the tests. Maybe it's actually sore from getting pounded by my doctor."

"I think I'm going to be sick," said Mandy.

"Ladies, let's get our minds off this morbid topic," said Reese. "Now that the dishes are put away, I'm going to get dressed."

Later in the morning, after Mandy had left to meet her friend Jacqui, Reese came up to Sylvia's room.

"Let's go explore the island," she said.

"What do you mean?" replied Sylvia, putting down her book, which she had found on the shelf in the living room downstairs. It was an old romance novel. All the books on the shelf were romance novels published decades earlier.

"I want to show you Tucker's Point." Then she added conspiratorially, "I also want to hook up with my friend Aldeen. He works weekends in the food and beverage office. He may have something for me."

"Is he the guy who gets the booze for you?"

"He might be."

"Okay, let's go. I'm sick of sitting around this boring house."

They went downstairs. "First we need to go to the kitchen," said Reese. She led the way to the kitchen closet, where she retrieved an old picnic basket. "Someone from a long time ago left this here. It's become very useful." She put the basket on the counter and opened it. Then, carrying a white towel, she disappeared out the back door. Sylvia went to the door and watched as

Reese took the empty bottle from the old planter and wrapped it in the towel. Then she came back inside and placed the bottle, wrapped in its towel, in the bottom of the picnic basket. "Get me some bread and cheese from the refrigerator," she told Sylvia. "I'll get some cups and napkins."

When they had loaded the basket with the basics for a picnic, they went to Reese's golf cart. The weather was cool for summer, and the sky was overcast. "Think it's going to rain?" asked Sylvia.

"Your guess is as good as mine," replied Reese as she turned the key. "But if it does rain, that would be very good for us."

"Good? Why? I don't want to get soaked."

Reese guided the cart along the short driveway to Apple Way. "Because the Mortas don't operate well in the rain. They have problems with moisture getting into their circuits, and their guidance systems—their cameras for visual information and their microwave sensors for basic orientation—don't function as well in the rain. The greater the amount of precipitation, the more unhappy they become. In their own peculiar robot way, of course. Unlike we humans, who are already sixty percent water and don't mind getting more dumped on our heads, most robots, including the Mortas, are zero percent water."

"The drones too?"

"Especially the drones. In the rain, they can barely fly. The fleet is grounded."

They made their way down Apple Way to Pine Path. The houses they passed seemed quiet. In the small front yards of a few, a man or a woman trimmed the hedge or swept the path. Reese waved to one—a man in his sixties. "That's Reginald Astor," she said when they were out of earshot. "He's a bit of a legend. They say he's the person who's lived here the longest. He arrived over twenty years ago, when the place first opened. He has Huntington's disease. It's getting progressively worse, and no one expects him to live more than a year or two."

"Does he have family?" asked Sylvia.

"Not on the island. I've hung out with him a few times, usually at the mess hall or the Dockside, and he never talks about his past life. But people who know him say that back in Denver, Colorado, he has a wife and two children. The kids are both adults now, of course. It's possible Reggie is a grandfather. No one's certain."

"Does he want to stay here, or are they making him stay here?"

Reese shrugged. "After so many years, they say you get used to it, and the question becomes moot. You stay because it's what you know."

They drove past the Juliette Island Center, and the road became wider and more well-paved.

"This is where Pine Path becomes Seaside Drive," said Reese. The landscape was mostly tall pines with a few dilapidated buildings nestled between. They passed an abandoned warehouse with a corrugated metal roof, an old gas station with weeds growing through the cement apron, and a cinderblock structure with a broken, faded sign reading "Wild Horse Bar."

"Years ago there were several thousand people living on what was then called Osprey Island," said Reese. "Then the Global Depression came, and many of them left. In the aftermath the Industrial Council convinced the government to turn it into a big medical research laboratory. The Council forcibly relocated all the remaining residents to the mainland, or turned them loose in the canaille to fend for themselves."

They came around a bend and suddenly Sylvia saw the gray waters of Puget Sound. The opposite shore was forested with pine trees. It seemed closer than when they were at the Dockside and looking across the water at the city of Victoria.

"You're looking east, towards Manafort Island," said Reese. "It's about five miles away. Even if you were an expert swimmer, the tidal currents are extremely treacherous. As far as I know, no one's ever swum it and lived to tell the tale."

They continued to follow Seaside Drive as Sylvia jealously watched the opposite shore. She thought she could make out the occasional building, and once she thought she saw a large truck, like a semi-trailer, ambling along a hidden road.

Suddenly the cart came to a halt. Startled from her reverie, Sylvia looked towards the front. Not ten feet ahead hovered a drone.

"Just sit quietly and do what it says," whispered Reese.

The drone fixed its cameras on them. The only sound was the whirring of its four propellers. Then it spoke: "Sylvia Brand and Reese Carter, please state your business."

"We're going on a picnic," replied Reese. She gestured to the basket.

"Where?" asked the drone.

"On Tucker's Point. As I'm sure you know, it's near the food and beverage office. We'll be within sight at all times."

"Show me the inside of the basket."

Sylvia took the basket, tilted it towards the drone, and opened the lid.

After a moment the drone said, "You may proceed."

"May I have your number please?" asked Reese.

"My number is three-seven-five." With those words the drone whirred into the sky and was lost among the trees.

"Why did you ask for its number?" asked Sylvia as Reese.

"If we get stopped again, we can tell the drone that we've been cleared by number three-seven-five. It will check its database and see that we're telling the truth. It will make our day less stressful."

They as they were making their way along Seashore Drive, they rounded a low hill that blocked the view of the water. When they emerged from behind the hill, Sylvia saw a long, low bridge that spanned the water, anchoring itself to the opposite shore.

Reese stopped the cart. "There it is," she said. "The causeway is the only road for travel on and off the island. It's the route the bus took when it brought you here. The causeway goes to Manafort Island, traverses the island, and then crosses another branch of Puget Sound to reach the mainland."

"How long do you think it takes to drive the length of the causeway and arrive on the mainland?" asked Sylvia.

"Once you get past the guards, no more than ten minutes."

Reese resumed the drive, and soon they came to a weather-beaten sign reading "Tucker's Point." About half a mile further beyond was a low office building. Reese headed for the office building.

"Aren't we going to Tucker's Point?" asked Sylvia.

"If we have time. First I need to see if Aldeen is here."

Reese steered the golf cart to an unmarked side door. There was a buzzer, which she rang. After a few moments the door opened. Sylvia saw Reese talking to a man. Then Reese walked back to the golf cart. The man watched from the door.

"You take the golf cart for a little drive around Tucker's Point," said Reese as she took the picnic basket. "Get out and enjoy the view. Come back for me in about fifteen minutes."

With the picnic basket in hand, Reese turned and hurried toward the door where the man was standing.

Mystified, Sylvia turned the golf cart around and steered in the direction of Tucker's Point. She parked on a high point of land overlooking the water. Below her the waves muscled against the rocks, surging and retreating, over and over again in a relentless cycle. Seagulls wheeled and cried, because that's just what seagulls do, even if their display seems pointless. To her left, about a mile away, the causeway, concrete pale against the dark water, reached in a gentle arc to the opposite shore—another island to be sure, but one step closer to the world she had left behind. The causeway was quiet now, with no traffic. Perhaps it was because it was late Sunday afternoon, and no one was coming or going. Squinting, she imagined the bus that had brought her to this island just three days earlier. Had it only been three days? It felt like a lifetime. In her mind she saw the bus, the windows opaque, the screen across the front, with its passengers who were unknowing of their destination and expecting a simple one-day business trip. How fantastical it was! She had a rare genetic disease, passed on to her baby, and for that reason she was a "special person" whom the Industrial Council and its doctors and pharmaceutical companies needed to keep under lock and key.

A boat came into view. It was not large—perhaps thirty feet—but with its aggressive, angular lines and gray color scheme it looked like a military vessel. It cruised slowly, perhaps a quarter of a mile offshore. Powered by its electric motor, the boat approached noiselessly, like a cat prowling the perimeter of a barn. Sylvia stood and watched it. Then she saw a figure emerge from the cabin and stand on the flat foredeck. As the boat passed the point opposite from where she was standing, she realized the figure was a Morta guard.

He was looking directly at her. She instinctively shrank back, but on the exposed point of land there was no place to hide. Then she remembered drone three-seven-five. It had cleared them to be in the area. Gathering her courage, Sylvia stood up straight, with her hands on her hips, and returned the guard's gaze. The boat did not change course, but slowly continued around the point. The Morta guard kept watching her until the trees obscured his view. After a moment all that was left of the passage of the patrol boat was the faint ripple of its wake.

Sylvia stood for a while, taking in the view. She was facing east, toward the mainland. In her imagination she flew across the miles all the way to Detroit. It would be almost dinnertime there. What was Jason doing at that moment? Sylvia had vanished Thursday morning. That was three days ago. Surely he would have contacted the police. But what if Carin told the cops that she had never shown up for work on Thursday morning? She tried to remember if she had seen any of her co-workers in the parking lot that morning. She didn't think she had. There was no proof that Sylvia Brand had ever arrived for work that day.

Perhaps Carin told Jason she was out of town on business. How long could that story hold up? And would the company then be forced to concoct a new story to explain her disappearance?

The third possibility was that the company had told Jason the truth—that his new wife had been spirited away to serve as a medical guinea pig on a secret island in the Pacific Northwest. No, that was not a possible choice, because if the company told every aggrieved spouse about the whereabouts of their loved ones, then Juliette Island would be quickly overrun by family members intent upon their rescue.

As the days and weeks passed and Sylvia never came home, what would Jason do? Yes, he might hold fast and keep the torch lit for her. Then she began to get a sick feeling in her stomach. The opposite might happen. Jason might get tired of waiting, or he might believe that she had run out on him. How long could she expect him to wait? A month? A year? Five years? And what were his feelings toward his unborn child? Would he ever see him or her?

Sylvia took a deep breath. Agonizing over her fate wasn't going to change it. Bitterness about working for Sun Motors—such a good job!—and signing the contracts and consent forms wasn't going to get her back to the life she had known. She had agreed to be a part of the system, and the system was now exacting its price.

She looked at her phone. Fifteen minutes had elapsed. She turned away from the dark water and went to the golf cart. She started the motor and drove back to the side door of the food and beverage office.

A moment later the door opened and Reese walked out, holding the picnic basket. With a smile on her face she put the basket in the back of the cart and climbed into the seat.

"Mission accomplished!" she announced.

"What does that mean?"

"I'll show you when we get home. Too risky out here. You never know when a drone is lurking."

Sylvia drove them home. Instead of going into the kitchen, Reese led Sylvia around the house to the back patio. She opened the basket and, after taking out the bread and cheese and utensils they had packed, she reached to the bottom and pulled out an object wrapped in a white cloth. Removing the cloth, she held up a bottle of Bourbon whiskey.

"Twenty years old," she said. "This is the stuff they serve to the doctors and big-shot administrators here on the island. Top shelf. Shall we have celebratory sample?" She went to the old planter and took out two cups. Sylvia uncorked the bottle and poured a shot into each cup.

"Wow, this is amazing," said Sylvia. "I feel like I'm a member of an exclusive club. I don't want to pry, but did your friend Aldeen simply give this to you?"

"Yes," said Reese. "I give him the empty bottle so there's no inventory problem, and he gives me a fresh one. No one's the wiser."

"He must really like you."

Reese shrugged. "I suppose so. He's not really my type."

"What do you mean he's not your type? You're not leading him on, are you? That wouldn't be very nice."

Reese laughed and took another sip of her whiskey. "Believe me, no one is leading him on! He knows exactly what he's getting."

"Reese, what do you mean?"

"I make him feel good, and in return he makes me feel good." She raised her cup. "Cheers."

"Oh my God, Reese, you have sex with this guy in exchange for booze!" Sylvia looked at the cup in her hand and grimaced.

Reese put her hand on Sylvia's arm. "First of all, it's not really sex. I mean, it's oral sex. That's all. He's not getting into my pants and he knows it. But on this lonely island, something is better than nothing, isn't it? He gets his rocks off and then he lets me take home a bottle of the good stuff. I'd say it's a fair trade."

"I'm sorry, it just seems so unsavory. Like you're... I don't know exactly what to call it..."

"Prostituting myself? It's all right, you can say it. But think about it—

157

aren't all of us prostituting ourselves? We allow the doctors to shove all kinds of gizmos into every orifice and peer with their cameras into every private part of our bodies. They take our blood and saliva and urine and hair follicles. They put us into MRI machines and take ultrasounds and x-rays. In return we get three square meals a day, a roof over our heads, and a nice island to live on. From my point of view, giving Aldeen a happy ending in return for a fifty-dollar bottle of Kentucky Bourbon is a pretty good deal. It makes me think the next time my doctor shoves a stainless steel scope up my ass, I should demand a bottle of Cognac."

Sylvia heard the sound of a golf cart in the driveway. "I think Mandy's home," she said.

Reese collected the cups and put them with the bottle in the planter. Then they went inside.

CHAPTER TWENTY-THREE

It seemed like Sylvia had no sooner fallen asleep in her bed when she was awakened by the sound of heavy footsteps on the stairs. Groggily she opened her eyes. Her door flew open, the lights came on, and two Morta guards entered her room, followed by a company security officer.

"Sylvia Brand," said the security officer. "Get up. We're taking you into custody."

"Why? What's going on?"

"You and Reese Carter made an unauthorized visit to a restricted area, where she engaged in a sex act. This is a violation of your contract. Now get up and get dressed."

Bewildered, Sylvia got out of bed and hastily put on her clothes while the security officer watched. After the guard had zip-tied her hands behind her back, the four of them marched down the stairs. Mandy stood in the living room, wearing her bathrobe, with its terrycloth belt tied tightly around her waist. With a stricken expression on her face, she said nothing.

Sylvia walked outside. In the driveway a van was idling. The night air was cool and damp. Overhead the stars shone bright and clear, while from the safety of the shadowy bushes crickets chirped to each other. From the open door of the van, the interior light threw a harsh blaze across the walkway. Reese, her hands behind her back, was already sitting inside the van, with a Morta guard next to her. After Sylvia had awkwardly climbed inside, the door was slammed shut and the van began to roll.

"What happened?" Sylvia asked Reese.

"We were caught on camera," she replied.

"You and Aldeen?"

"Yes. The security people had installed an additional camera that Aldeen didn't know about."

"You two, be quiet," interjected the Morta. "No talking."

The van trundled along the road. It was no surprise to Sylvia that the van had no windows, and also no surprise when they stopped, the doors were pulled open, and she saw they were parked by the gated entrance to the Re-Orientation Center.

"Back to the cooler," said Sylvia as she stepped onto the gravel driveway.

"Be strong," said Reese.

"No talking," said the Morta guard.

They were led through the gate, inside the building, and into separate cells.

After her hands had been freed and the door clanged shut, Sylvia stood in the center of the cell. Overhead the naked bulb glowed. There was no sound—no crickets, no cars outside, no voices. She went to the steel door with its narrow slit. Sylvia listened. She heard footsteps. They came closer. She glimpsed the waist of a Morta guard as it passed her cell. Then the footsteps receded.

She sat on the metal-framed bed. It is me? she wondered. Am I out of step with reality? Do I have expectations that are unrealistic? I just got here— why do I keep getting into trouble? All I ever wanted to do was follow the rules and be a good person. Where did I go wrong?

Then she felt a wave of anger. It's not me—it's them! This horrible sick system has tricked me and made me into a zoo animal. I must never surrender! Never! For the sake of my child, I must resist the forces that want to turn me into a commodity and my disease—if you have to call it that— into a cash machine.

Then her practical mind stepped in. They aren't going to hurt me. They want me to be healthy for their experiments. This isn't ethnic cleansing or genocide, where people are targeted for elimination. It's not even like ordinary incarceration, where they don't particularly care if you happen to die while in custody. I'm a special person. They need me for both their research and their profits. They may want to make me uncomfortable and even scare me, but they won't do anything really bad to me.

Feeling physically and mentally exhausted, she lay down on the bed and drifted into a restless sleep.

The next morning she was driven to the Juliette Island Center for Medical Research, where Dr. Hyland met her and escorted her to the surgical wing.

"I'm tired and hungry," she told him. "I haven't had the opportunity to go home and get cleaned up. Whatever we're doing this morning, I hope it won't take long."

"No, it won't take long," he replied with a smile as they walked through the corridors.

"Am I going to be punished for what happened last night?"

"No. We can talk about that later. Ah—here we are." They had arrived at the surgical prep room. A nurse stood by. "Please lie down on the bed. No need for a hospital gown—you can leave your clothing on. Good. Now the nurse will roll up your sleeve and insert an IV line. I assume you're right-handed, is that correct?"

"Yes. What are you giving me?" she asked as the nurse swabbed her left arm.

"A small dose of midazolam, a short-acting sedative drug that blocks pain and makes you feel sleepy but doesn't render you unconscious. You should not require help with your breathing, but if necessary we'll give you extra oxygen through a mask as well as fluids through a catheter into a vein."

"What are you going to do to me today?" She asked the question not because she really wanted to know (they had already done so many things to her body that in her mind it hardly mattered) but because she didn't want Dr. Hyland or the nurse to think she had relinquished all of her rights as a patient. It was a childlike attempt to preserve the fiction that this was a true partnership between doctor and patient, which in her heart she knew was far from the case.

"Just a short procedure," he said. "We can talk more about it later. I'll come back in a few minutes to see how you're doing."

He walked away, and Sylvia was left staring at the ceiling tiles.

She began to feel drowsy. At first it aroused in her feelings of anxiety, and so she fought the sensation, but after a few minutes she realized that instead of slipping into unconsciousness she was hovering in a pleasant twilight between wakefulness and sleep. This isn't so bad, she thought. Very relaxing, in fact.

Dr. Hyland appeared at her bedside and peered down at her with a benign smile. "How do you feel?" he asked.

"Fine," she murmured. Her voice sounded far away.

"Can you feel this?" he said as he took her left hand and manipulated it. She glanced down and saw a syringe. He was giving her an injection into the muscle between the thumb and forefinger.

"No. What are you doing?" She asked more out of curiosity than concern.

"Giving you a local anesthetic. We're almost ready to proceed."

Let them do what they want, thought Sylvia. It doesn't matter to me.

With his right hand, Dr. Hyland picked up a white plastic syringe with a wide stainless steel needle that looked more like a straw with a sharp point. With his left hand, using pair of blunt forceps, he grasped a section of flesh between the thumb and forefinger, parallel to the index metacarpal bone, making a hump. With the white plastic injector in his right hand, he stuck the sharp end of the needle into the hump of flesh, parallel to the bone. When it had gone in about half an inch, he depressed the plunger on the injector, while at the same time slowly withdrawing the injector. After about ten seconds, the plunger was fully depressed. With his left hand, he then took a piece of gauze and pressed down on the entry wound while removing the stainless steel needle. When the injector was free, he set it aside.

After applying a bandage to the entrance wound he smiled and said, "There—all done! That was easy, wasn't it?"

"Yes, I suppose it was." Lifting her left hand, she looked at the bandage with vague interest. "Did I hurt my hand?"

"No—don't worry. Everything is fine. When you've come out of sedation, we'll talk. Then you can go home. Get some rest."

Sylvia lay in her bed, thinking about Jason, and how painting their new house yellow with white trim would make it look much nicer than its current hideous green, and her friends at Sun Motors, and how the contract for the Comanche truck battery system—a major component—needed to be renegotiated....

After a while she felt clear-headed, and there was a dull pain in her left hand.

The nurse came to her bed. "Do you feel like getting up?" she asked.

"Yes, I do." Sylvia sat up. The IV in her arm had been removed, and in its place was a little white bandage. She took a few deep breaths before standing on her feet. "Okay, now what? It's Monday morning, right? Can I go home and get something to eat before my tests today?"

"Yes," replied the nurse. "One of the guards will drive you home. Your hand will feel stiff and swollen—that's to be expected. Do not remove the bandage."

The Morta guard drove her in a golf cart. They did not speak to each other. When she got home, neither Reese nor Mandy were there. After making herself some eggs and toast, Sylvia took a shower, keeping her hand in a plastic bag, as the nurse had instructed. By the time she was dressed again it was time to go back to the Center for her regular appointment.

She found Dr. Hyland in his office.

"Ah, Sylvia, I see you've weathered the procedure very nicely," he said as she sat down. He took her left hand and gently removed the bandage. He examined the wound. "Some swelling, which is normal. No sign of infection. Good." With a satisfied expression he released his grip.

She looked at her hand, from which the bandage had been removed. She flexed her fingers and formed a fist. There was a small hole in her skin, from which blood oozed.

She looked closely at her hand. "Oh my God—there's something under my skin!" Gently she ran her fingertip over the bruised and tender flesh between her thumb and index finger. "I can feel something in there! It's hard, like a little cylinder. What did you do?"

Leaning forward and clasping his hands on the desktop, Dr. Hyland assumed a thoughtful demeanor. "Sylvia, last night both you and Reese got yourselves into serious trouble. Reese more so, of course, because she was consorting with that man, Aldeen. Sexual liaisons between residents and employees of the island are prohibited."

"Sorry, I guess she didn't see that in the guest handbook."

"Don't be a smart aleck. You're very lucky you aren't serving a week in the Re-Orientation Center, like Reese is."

"But the drone cleared us. Number three-seven-five."

"Drones have the authority to stop and question residents who are observed in unusual or off-limits places. They do not have the authority to approve a sexual encounter in an empty office in the food and beverage department building. Now then—about your hand. Because of your repeated infractions of the island travel policy, the Juliette Island Center Medical Board has decided that you are to carry an RFID tag. As I'm sure you know, the acronym stands for 'radio frequency identification.'"

"I know exactly what RFID means," she replied curtly. "At Sun Motors we've been using RFID tags for years."

"This morning I implanted one in your hand. It's actually a GPS device that transmits your location, twenty-four hours a day. I'll show you." He tapped a few keys on his computer and, after a moment, turned the screen to show Sylvia. "I've logged onto our patient management system. As you can see, it shows your location here, in my office. It's accurate to within two meters."

"You bastards!" she shouted. "You implanted a tracking device in my hand!"

"Yes, we did. Because you're carrying a child, we felt it was important to give you every opportunity to stay out of the Re-Orientation Center. Life there is not very pleasant, and we want to ensure the health of your baby."

"But you have no right to implant a foreign object in my body!"

Dr. Hyland nodded thoughtfully, as if pondering her question and showing empathy. He removed his rimless glasses and, taking a cloth from the pocket of his white coat, carefully cleaned the lenses. "To the contrary," he said as he replaced his glasses on his nose, "Our contract with you gives us the right to protect our very considerable investment in you and your child. We agree to provide a full range of medical services, and in return you agree to act responsibly and in the best interests of your own good health. If you are prone to wander around the island—to go swimming after dark at a deserted beach, or accompany your friend to a remote area so that she can have a sexual encounter—then the Medical Center Board sees the risk to your safety increasing. It's all about risk, Sylvia. Our goal is to enhance and maximize life, not jeopardize it. While we're in the business of medicine and healing, it would not be a stretch to say we're also in the business of insurance." He smiled. "I think with a little bit of perspective, you'll agree it's not such a big deal. Why, there are many people in business who eagerly have RFID tags implanted in their hands, just as you have. Having a tag in your hand allows you to access restricted areas without worrying about carrying a key or identification card. You simply approach the locked door, and instead of swiping your old-fashioned card or sticking your face into a camera lens, you hold up your hand, and the door opens. You can even pay for your dinner at a restaurant by waving your hand over the receptor carried by the server."

"I don't need to do any of those things on this island," replied Sylvia. "This thing in my hand does nothing but give you more control over me. Let me tell you something: I don't care if you don't trust me. I'm going to do whatever the hell I want, and if you want to send a drone or a Morta guard after me, be my guest. I'm not a cow or a sheep, content to graze in my little pasture. I'm going to live my life with something approaching human dignity."

"I understand," said Dr. Hyland. "You're still very new here. It takes a while to get acclimated. My advice is to relax and go with the flow. Juliette Island can be a very lovely place, if you're open to it."

Sylvia looked at his kindly face for a moment before turning her gaze to the window. Through the glass she saw the sun shining brightly against the greens and blues of the pine trees. Then she said, "I don't know why I'm here. How did this happen? Is this what my life is going to be?"

"Sylvia," he said, "I've been here a long time. I've seen many people come through these doors. They arrive with many different attitudes. Some are angry and resentful. Some are bewildered. Some are happy to be here—possibly because they have some issue in their previous life they're relieved to have put behind them. While people land on this island with different feelings, the ones who make the best adjustment and learn to enjoy themselves are the ones who trust in a higher power. They trust there's a deeper reason why the path of their life has led them here. Here on Juliette Island, everything hinges on trust. I need you to trust that we have your best interests at heart, and you have ours as well."

To Sylvia, the answer was this: There was no answer. The world was the way it was. Or rather, the United Americas was the way the Industrial Council had fashioned it. It was a place where the rules had been designed by faraway people who were much more powerful than she. She knew these people didn't trust her. They had brought her here under false pretenses, and it was clear she would not be allowed to leave. All this stuff about working for each others' best interests was a twisted diversion from reality.

But it was useless to debate Dr. Hyland. He held too much power over her—and her unborn child.

Sylvia raised her eyes to meet his. "Let's get down to business. What's my schedule for today?"

Sitting back in his chair, Dr. Hyland made a few clicks with his mouse. "In half an hour you will undergo a computerized tomography scan. Your CT scan will combine a series of X-ray images taken from different angles around your body and then use computer processing to create cross-sectional images, or slices, of the bones, blood vessels, and soft tissues inside your body. CT scan images provide more detailed information than plain X-rays. With a CT scan, we will not only detect any tumors, lung nodules, and liver masses, but muscle and bone disorders, heart disease, internal injuries, or internal bleeding. A CT scan can also help guide procedures such as surgery, biopsy, and radiation therapy. But perhaps most of all, it will give us a clear picture of your entire body at this moment in time—a baseline, if you will, against which we can make comparisons in the years to come."

"The years to come?"

"Sylvia, this is a long-term program. We're looking for data that spans not days or weeks, but years. Don't you understand? Nothing of value is created overnight. Deep knowledge takes time."

CHAPTER TWENTY-FOUR

Sylvia completed her CT scan and some other tests. At the end of the day, tired and feeling like a human pincushion, she went back to 15 Apple Way. Mandy was there, and the first thing Sylvia did was go to the back patio and look for the bottle of whiskey. It was still in the planter.

"Didn't they know?" Sylvia mused aloud.

"I guess they saw Aldeen and Reese getting it on, but didn't catch the payoff," replied Mandy. "When Reese comes back we'll drink a toast to freedom."

Together they made dinner.

"Getting a GPS implant is a serious thing," said Mandy as she tossed the salad. "They're not playing games with you. Do you know Charlie Ohan, who lives at 23 Plum Court? He's the skinny guy with the curly blond hair. He was once a feisty one! Always causing trouble and demanding to see his manager over every little thing. I heard that somehow he got hold of a real cellphone and tried to call his wife in Des Moines. They intercepted the call and scrambled it, and then found the phone. That earned him a week in the cooler. Then he tried to escape by hiding in a truck going across the causeway. That was a stupid thing to do because they search every vehicle very carefully. They tossed him in the cooler for a week, and they also planted a GPS device in his hand, just like yours. He didn't believe it was real, and one day he decided to go to the southern tip of the island and flag down a passing ship. You know, as if he were a castaway on a desert island. He hadn't gotten halfway there before they were all over him—drones and Morta guards both. Again he went to the cooler, only this time it was for two weeks. When he came out he was a changed person. Almost like a zombie. Whatever they did to him in there, it sucked the life right out of him. He became the mellowest person on the island, but it was fake, you know what I mean? You can go and talk to him, and it's like talking to a human Ken doll. They did something to him. I don't know what it was, but it changed him."

"When he came back from the cooler, did he have swollen eyes?" asked

Sylvia. In a saucepan she heated some oil and butter for the chicken cutlets.

"Yes, he did! Both his eyes were bruised. He looked like he had been in a boxing match. I asked him what had happened, and if they had beaten him. He said he didn't remember anything happening. He woke up in the Medical Center, in a hospital bed. Then they let him go home."

"It sounds as if they gave him a lobotomy," said Sylvia. She shivered at the thought.

"Why were his eyes bruised?"

"It's called a transorbital lobotomy. Also an icepick lobotomy. Very popular among medical professionals in the first half of the twentieth century. The surgeon inserts an icepick into the soft tissue just above the eyeball and below the eyebrow, and pushes it through the thin frontal bone of the eye socket. The tip penetrates into the frontal lobe of the brain, which controls personality, behavior, and emotions. The surgeon swishes the icepick around in there, severing neural connections. After doing one side of the brain through one eye socket, he'll do the other side through the other eye socket."

"That's so gruesome," said Mandy. She put the salad on the table and went to the drawer for silverware.

"Yes—and unpredictable. Because the doctor is cutting blindly, he has no idea what the result will be. But icepick lobotomies are cheap and fast, and unlike drugs like Thorazine, the effect is permanent. Do you know why Charlie is here on Juliette Island?"

"He told me he had UV-sensitive syndrome, a condition characterized by sensitivity to the ultraviolet rays in sunlight. That's why he never goes out in the sun—even a small amount of exposure can give him a sunburn. Pardo Pharmaceuticals is using him to develop new sunscreens, as well as testing a new drug for those afflicted with the disease."

"The fact that Charlie Ohan is a walking zombie with half a brain has no impact on his usefulness as a medical test subject," said Sylvia. "As long as he's capable of showing up for his appointments and enduring whatever they do to him, he's worth the investment."

After Sylvia had sautéed the chicken, they sat down at the table.

"I hope you don't mind my asking," said Sylvia, "but you seem to be very content here. Doesn't it bother you that you can't leave? And that your child is dead?"

Mandy took a serving of salad from the bowl. "I suppose I feel at home here because I have nowhere else to go. I have no family. My job at Mountain Life Insurance was just a paycheck. And I was sick all the time. When I first came here I was just like you—I was angry and resentful. But then I started to realize this was a good place for me. I've made some friends, and the medical care is amazing. I don't care if they use me as a guinea pig. It's a small price to pay for security. I don't have to worry about anything. I just show up when they tell me to, and the rest of the time I do what I want. Of course I miss Winslow, but what could I do? He had a serious illness."

"What did they do with his body after he died?"

"They cremated him. They have a place on the north end of the island where they do that."

"There's a crematorium here on Juliette Island?"

"Yes. Of course it's totally off limits. If you go north from here, along the coast, you eventually arrive at the causeway. The crematorium is about a mile beyond that. They took Winslow there, and they gave me his ashes in a little urn. They allowed me to go out in the boat and scatter them in the Sound."

"They let you go out in a boat?" Sylvia asked incredulously.

"Yes. They keep it in a boathouse next to the crematorium. It's not very big—it has a little outboard motor. I had to go with a couple of human security officers, of course. I don't think the Morta guards are allowed to go in small boats. Can you imagine what would happen if one of those things fell into the water? It would sink like a stone!"

"So when you die on the island, they cremate you?"

Mandy shrugged. "I suppose. I've never been to a funeral here. I don't even think there's a cemetery."

After dinner, Sylvia decided she needed to become more familiar with the approved places that residents could go. After all, she reasoned, if she were wearing an implant that alerted the guards the moment she strayed into forbidden territory, she might as well get to know the places she could go. I'm not a doormat, she told herself, but neither am I a masochist.

She got into her golf cart—a small and pathetic symbol of freedom, she thought, but nonetheless one that was very real. She drove around for a while in the gathering twilight, exploring the various roads and neighborhoods. All the houses looked like hers; the only differences were that some of them had little gardens in the front, while others had nothing but grass. She saw people here and there, puttering around their yards or walking along the roads. All were wearing the same cut and color of clothing that Sylvia had been issued. She saw no pets—no cats, no dogs. She heard no barking, which was odd, because at home at twilight you always heard dogs barking. Roosters crow at sunrise and dogs bark at sunset.

She came around a bend and before her she saw a playground, with a slide and swings and a jungle gym for climbing. A handful of children were playing there, supervised by their mothers and fathers. Feeling the pull on her heartstrings, Sylvia drove into the little gravel parking area. Leaving her golf cart among the others, she walked to the edge of the playground and watched for a few minutes. She imagined her own child, two or three years from that moment, taking her first steps into this exciting, big-kid world, learning how to climb and run, and meeting other children.

A little boy came running by, and he tripped and fell down. He began to

169

cry. Instinctively Sylvia went to him and helped him up. As she was brushing the wood chips off his knees, a couple hurried over. They were both in their thirties, and the woman appeared to be pregnant.

The woman took the little boy in her arms and began to comfort him. As Sylvia stood there watching, she began to feel self-conscious, so she turned to the man and said, "Your son is a very energetic little boy!"

The man smiled and said, "Thank you—although I must confess, I'm not Timmy's father. My name is Jim Ryan. Pleased to meet you." He extended his hand.

"Sylvia Brand," she said as they shook. "I'm sorry—I just assumed—"

"Oh, no worries," said the mother. "I'm Natalie Downey. Jim and I are engaged to be married. Our child is due next April. My son is from my previous relationship."

Sylvia explained that she was new to the island and was exploring the permissible areas. Natalie glanced at the bandage on Sylvia's left hand. "I see you've got the implant," she said. She held up her own left hand. "Feel under the skin. There—next to the metacarpal bone."

Sylvia felt the outline of a small cylinder just like the one Dr. Hyland had implanted that morning in her flesh. "How long have you had it?" she asked Natalie.

"Three years. One day I decided to blow off my medical appointment and go for a drive. They found me on the western shore, brought me back, and put me in the cooler overnight. The next day they stuck this thing in me. For a while I hated it. I wanted to get a knife and cut it out. But I got used to it. I decided to go along—and I'm glad I did."

Intrigued, Sylvia hung around while Natalie soothed her son and sent him back to the playground. Then the three of them walked over to a bench and sat down. They chatted about inconsequential things until Jim excused himself, saying he had to get up early the next morning for a special medical test.

"Jim seems very nice," said Sylvia as he walked away.

"Oh, he's just wonderful!" replied Natalie. "I'm so glad they found him for me. Of course at first I was, like, 'Are you kidding? Is this an arranged marriage?' But much to my amazement, it's working out beautifully."

"I'm sorry—what did you say? They found him for you?"

"Yes, I know—crazy, isn't it? Scientific matchmaking! But it works!"

At Sylvia's urging, Natalie told her story.

Like Sylvia, Natalie had a good job with a Two Hundred K company—a plastics fabricator in Atlanta. And like Sun Motors, the company had brought in a Morta supervisor and had enrolled the employees in a comprehensive health plan doubling as an employment contract and non-disclosure agreement. Her supervisor—his name was Basor—had explained that instead of signing a dozen different forms, it was much more expedient to bundle all of them into one agreement. In retrospect, said Natalie, the resulting document was something close to an indentured servitude contract, but at the time she was grateful to have a good job with a top company, so she signed it. She met a man, Edwin, and they got married. After a few months, she got pregnant. Lab tests, provided free of charge by the company, revealed that her unborn child had a rare form of anemia, which he had contracted from Natalie and Edwin, who were both carriers. The doctors told them that the disease was unpredictable, and their child might die by the age of five or live a fairly normal life well into adulthood. After much soul searching, she and Edwin had decided to have the child and hope for the best—perhaps by the time he was a toddler, medical science would have found a cure.

One day as Natalie was going to work—this was when she was twelve weeks pregnant—Basor met her in the parking lot and told her she was going on a special assignment. She was whisked to the airport and put on a company plane. A few hours later, the plane landed, she was put in a van, and the next stop was the Juliette Island Center for Health Research.

At first she was angry and defiant, and made a few attempts to test the boundaries of her confinement. Eventually they got tired of putting her in the cooler, and gave her the RFID tag implant.

"When Timothy was born, that changed everything for me," said Natalie as she kept one eye on her child, who was climbing up the stairs to the slide. "I had to start thinking about him and his future. I became resigned to the fact Juliette Island was our home. I had a new career as a medical test subject. I had a good life with everything I wanted. I was sad about leaving Edwin behind, but I'm sure he found someone new. People do that, right? They don't sit around moaning. They get on with their lives, just as I was getting on with mine."

With a pang, Sylvia thought of her dear Jason. Would the same thing happen to them? Of course it would. Jason wasn't going to wait around for months or years with no word from Sylvia. He was going to find someone new—presumably a girl who didn't carry any genetic diseases and therefore was of no interest to Pardo Pharmaceuticals and the Industrial Council.

"How did you meet Jim?" she asked.

"Back in March—it was the fifteenth, I'll never forget the date—my doctor called me in and said he had some amazing news. Around that time I was feeling depressed, so I was like, 'Yeah?' He told me that they had identified a man of my age and background who was the carrier of a different genetic disease than mine, which meant that he and I could have children that were free of genetic diseases, although they could be carriers. At first I thought he was joking—was I no better than a farm animal used for breeding? But he kept talking, and then he showed me a video of Jim, and I thought he was very handsome. I said okay, I'll meet him for dinner. My doctor then gave me a form to sign. It was several pages long, and I asked him what it was, and he said it was just a formality—something about liability. He also said it was an agreement that if Jim and I had children, they'd be bound by the same agreements Jim and I had with our employers. The possibility of actually having more kids seemed far-fetched, and I wanted to meet this guy, so I signed.

"That night I met Jim at the Dockside, and at first I wasn't sure about him, but as the evening went on I started to like him. We dated some more, and then I got pregnant. I was deeply conflicted and thought about finding a way to terminate my pregnancy, but my doctor was delighted. He then arranged for Jim and I and Timothy to move into a private house and receive a bigger allowance. No more living with roommates! I later found out this was standard procedure—if you get pregnant through a sanctioned relationship, you and your partner go to the top of the list for a private home, and you get more money. Believe me, those are nice perks."

"Congratulations," said Sylvia—not because she thought Natalie's experience was in any way acceptable, but because Natalie herself seemed so happy that to say anything else would be cruel. "It sounds as if you're committed to staying here on Juliette Island."

"I think so," said Natalie. "Jim wants to, and we have nothing to complain about. Life is good here. A little bit boring, I'll admit, but there's safety and security."

"But what about your children?" asked Sylvia. "Timothy and your new one? Do you expect them to live here for the next eighty or ninety years?"

"I don't know," said Natalie. "But think about it—there are millions of people who live on islands in the South Pacific that are no bigger than Juliette Island. For generation after generation, they live in places like Tuvalu, a group of tiny islands midway between Hawaii and Australia. Eleven thousand people live out in the middle of nowhere! They have their own government, bank, and police force. Are they to be pitied because they live in isolation?"

"No, but the people who live on Tuvalu can leave if they want to," replied Sylvia. "The government doesn't implant tracking devices in their bodies."

"Every place is different," replied Natalie with irritation. Then, perhaps not wanting to start an argument, she smiled and said, "All I know is that we're happy here."

CHAPTER TWENTY-FIVE

The next day was Tuesday, and at ten o'clock in the morning Sylvia dutifully reported to the office of Dr. Hyland.

"Before we get started," she said, "I'd like to ask you about something."

"Sure—what is it?"

Sylvia told him about meeting Natalie and hearing about how Natalie had met and become engaged to Jim, and how they were having a child together. "How often does that happen?" she asked.

"It's interesting that you should bring that up," smiled Dr. Hyland. "Yes, it's true we proactively identify mates for our residents. We call it our partner match program. The criteria are not unlike those used by dating services— age, education, family background, and so forth. In addition, we have the advantage of knowing the complete genetic profile of each of our residents, enabling us to precisely align people on the basis of their inherited genetic variances."

"Don't you mean genetic diseases?" asked Sylvia.

"We prefer not to use that word, particularly when discussing making a match between two people. We feel that 'variances' is equally descriptive without being pejorative. After all, here on Juliette Island we regard genetic variances as opportunities, not defects."

"Opportunities for profit, wouldn't you say?"

"Yes, I would," nodded Dr. Hyland. "Profit is a powerful motivator. Don't you think most of the advances made by the human race have been spurred by the desire for profit? When Thomas Edison invented the light bulb, he didn't release his patent and make his invention free to all, did he? Of course not; he manufactured and sold light bulbs. When Steve Jobs revolutionized the personal computer, did he give away his designs? No, he retained his rights to them and made a profit from them."

"I don't want to get into a debate with you," replied Sylvia, "other than to say a stable, healthy society is based on three interest groups: labor, capital, and government. The first two, by nature, exist in opposition to each other. To maintain balance, the government must be an impartial arbiter between them. If either labor or capital becomes too powerful, the government must step in and balance the relationship. Unfortunately, in the United Americas we have a situation where the government and capital work together hand in glove. With the Industrial Council at the forefront, they act as one. Against such a combined force, labor is helpless. The unhealthy impulse to generate corporate profits at all costs cannot be held in check. This creates a situation like what we have today, with the rampant exploitation of the value created by labor and its transfer to the ruling oligarchs."

"Very impressive analysis," said Dr. Hyland as he peered at Sylvia through his rimless glasses. "Unfortunately, you've omitted a critical factor. This is efficiency. With its competing interests, the world you describe is woefully inefficient. Many would even call it wasteful. Why should there be tension between capital, labor, and the government? Think of all the pointless and wasteful labor strikes of the nineteenth and twentieth centuries. An entire industry could be shut down because some labor leader wanted to make a name for himself, thereby creating hardship, lost wages, and loss of production. If you thought about it, I'm sure you'd conclude that the Industrial Council, working shoulder to shoulder with the government, has produced impressive benefits."

"Impressive benefits for a few people," replied Sylvia, "but not for the majority. And at what cost? Whatever happened to personal freedom? To not only do what you want, but freedom from exploitation?"

Dr. Hyland leaned forward and said, "My dear Sylvia, it must be nice to hold such high ideals. I prefer to live in the real world. Now then, before we find ourselves spending all day pursuing this fascinating topic, let's return to the business at hand. You asked about your friends, Natalie and Jim. You have implied that there was a profit motive behind our selection of Jim for Natalie, or vice-versa, depending on whose point of view you take. All I can say is that we take every factor into consideration, including personal, emotional, and medical issues. We want success, not failure. Now then...."

He paused to click through some files on his computer. "Yes, there he is! After much careful research and meticulous mapping of thousands of touch points, as we call them, as well as consideration of your respective genetic structures, the Medical Board has determined that you qualify for the partner match program, and we've found the ideal man for you."

"You've done what?"

Dr. Hyland turned the computer so that Sylvia could see the screen. She saw a photo of a man wearing a plaid sports jacket and a broad smile with astonishingly perfect teeth. "Meet Don Gardner. Age twenty-nine. Unmarried, no children. Born and raised in Topeka, Kansas. Worked as a sports reporter for Fact News in Kansas City. He's been a resident here for about a year. Well adjusted. Enjoys playing tennis. Have you seen the tennis courts yet? If not, I suggest you visit them. People who play tell me they're very fine. Don lives on Peachtree Way, a short drive from you." Dr. Hyland smiled and lowered his voice, as if what he was saying were confidential. "I took the liberty of showing him your photo. I must tell you, I think he's quite smitten. He's looking forward to meeting you."

Sylvia felt the old familiar pain clutch the back of her neck and jab its bony fingers into the base of her skull. A drop of sweat tickled her forehead and her lungs couldn't get enough air. Struggling to present an image of composure, she stammered, "That's very nice, but I'm not looking for someone. I have a husband."

"Oh, you mean Jason Quin. That's been taken care of. He's been granted his freedom."

"What do you mean, granted his freedom?" Now her stomach was churning and she hoped it wasn't obvious that she was gripping the arms of the chair as if she were riding a roller coaster.

"When married employees are re-assigned to the Juliette Island program," said Dr. Hyland, "their marital bonds are annulled. We've found that a clean break is much better for both partners. Jason has been sent an official letter from the Industrial Council informing him that he is free to seek another partner. I'm sure he appreciates the opportunity to start over."

"Start over? What are you talking about? I'm carrying his child!"

"But Jason is a thousand miles away," said Dr. Hyland. "He's a part of your past. And frankly, despite your feelings for him, which I'm sure are very real, from the standpoint of data he was a rather poor match for you. There were many areas of incompatibility. You are very different personality types. For example, our data shows that your personality falls under the category of extroverted-intuitive-thinking-acting, or EITA. In contrast, Jason's personality fits the profile of introverted-logical-feeling-dreaming, or ILFD. This, along with several hundred other personality touchpoints, led the Medical Board to conclude that you and Jason have a compatibility rating of two out of five, which is a poor prognosticator of marital success."

"But we love each other!"

"I understand you have those feelings," said Dr. Hyland, "but they aren't enough to sustain you through life's trials and tribulations. It may interest you to know that Don Gardner is an ELTA personality—a much closer match to you. The prognosis for a long-term relationship with Don Gardner is much better than with Jason Quin. We believe—we know—that careful analysis, coupled with a cool, detached examination of the data and the facts, results in matches that are far more long-lasting than when subjects are left to their own devices and vagaries of chance."

"I've heard enough," said Sylvia. "Not only do you poke and probe into every corner of my body, but now you assert the same authority over my heart? I'm sorry, but I reject the premise. Love cannot be quantified or put onto a spreadsheet. It cannot be summed up in a set of data points or personality types. It defies logic, which is its beauty. People who fall in love often do so despite their outward differences because they feel completed by each other. Each feels the other fills in the gaps in their own personality. If I'm an EITA personality, or whatever you call it, then why would I be attracted to someone of the same type? In your own words, wouldn't such a union be terribly inefficient, because it would perpetuate a redundancy?"

"The algorithms include the variances to which you allude," replied Dr. Hyland wearily. He glanced at the clock. Noting they were falling behind schedule, he frowned. "I must tell you," he continued, "that while you are free to say 'no,' there are penalties for declining to support the path laid out for you and Don. If you refuse, there will be subsequent reductions in your living arrangements and privileges. In contrast, if you embrace the decision of the Medical Board, which is based on sound research, you and your children will enjoy a higher level of benefits."

"Did you say 'children,' in the plural form?"

"Of course," replied Dr. Hyland. Behind his rimless glasses his eyes twinkled. "Just between you and me, Don is very anxious to start a family. He told me that he wants at least three children. Isn't that marvelous? And because of our genetic screening, it's likely these children will not suffer from the genetic conditions carried by you and Don—although you can never be certain."

"I'm sorry, but do I have any say in this? Does my opinion count?"

"As I said before, you have a choice. You can choose to live in the women's dormitory, or you can choose to live in a spacious private home with Don and your family."

"If I choose to live in the dormitory, where will my child live?"

"In foster care. We have several families on the island who would be delighted to take in a fatherless child."

Inwardly seething, Sylvia said nothing. Dr. Hyland pretended to look at some papers. The seconds ticked by. Sylvia's anger subsided enough so that she could logically consider her choices. Neither were acceptable. It wasn't that she disliked Don Gardner; she didn't even know him. The problem was that ever since she had set foot on Juliette Island—rather, ever since Carin had entered her life—her fundamental rights as a human being had been chipped away. Oh, but there was always a good reason! Giving up her rights was good for the company, or led to greater efficiency, or helped the effort in the nation's perpetually looming war against Rodinia, or was even good for Sylvia herself in some roundabout way. All of these so-called good things, and all the contracts and consent forms, added up like grains of sand until they had formed a bottomless pool of quicksand into which she felt herself sinking.

"You need not decide today," said Dr. Hyland. "Let's think about what we need to accomplish this morning."

The subject was dropped, and Sylvia worked her way through the day's portfolio of tests. The nurse reported that her baby, now at seven weeks, was developing normally. In her womb it was about the size of a blueberry, and growing rapidly, with most of the growth concentrated in the head as new brain cells were generated at the rate of one hundred per minute. At seven weeks, Sylvia might start feeling morning sickness (not yet, she replied) and food aversions (again, Sylvia reported no problems there). Then Sylvia asked the nurse why the mountains of data didn't predict how she would feel at seven weeks. The nurse smiled and said that every woman was different, and currently there were no tests to assess a woman's likelihood of having various sensations. How a person was likely to feel was still a mystery.

At home that night, with Reese still in the cooler, Sylvia made dinner with Mandy, and she revealed to Mandy Dr. Hyland's offer of a match with Don Gardner. "Dr. Hyland told me my marriage to Jason had been annulled," said Sylvia as she sautéed some onions. "Can they really do that?"

"They can erase the digital record," replied Mandy, molding some ground beef into two patties. "You could go online and search for your marriage license and record of your ceremony, and you would find nothing. If you had a paper copy, I'm sure it's been removed from your house or office. Therefore you can think or believe whatever you want, but as far as the state is concerned, you're a single woman. And you're pregnant. This will create additional problems for you. It will make life here on Juliette Island more difficult."

"Dr. Hyland told me that if I didn't hook up with Don Gardner, I'd be moved into the women's dormitory and my baby would be put up for adoption."

"He's playing hardball with you, that's for sure." She put the burgers on the skillet and went to the refrigerator for cheese. "They say that possession is nine-tenths of the law. Well, they possess both of us. They tricked us into coming to this island from which there's no escape. In my case, I've learned to accept it. Better to switch than fight. I'm at peace with myself."

"Until they do something really awful to you," said Sylvia. "Then we'll see how much inner peace you have."

At that moment, Sylvia heard the front door open. "In the kitchen," she called.

Limar entered. "How was your day today?"

"Fine, thank you," replied Mandy.

"Very pleasant," said Sylvia.

"Are either of you planning on leaving the house tonight?" asked Limar.

"No" was the answer from both.

"I see you're making dinner," said Limar. "I won't keep you. Enjoy your evening."

"Say, Limar," said Sylvia, "before you go, is there any word on when Reese's going to be released from the cooler?"

"If you mean the Re-Orientation Center," said Limar, "I do not have that information." She turned and left.

Mandy went to the window, and from behind the curtain she watched as Limar walked down the path and over to the next house. Then she turned to Sylvia. "You shouldn't ask questions like that! You'll get into trouble. You might even be sent to the cooler yourself."

"Please tell me again how happy you are to be living on Juliette Island," replied Sylvia. Mandy gave her a sour look. "Okay, we've both made our points," said Sylvia. "Let's forget about our mechanical prison guard and enjoy our dinners."

As the last rays of twilight painted the tops of the trees red, they sat down to eat. "We need to grow some tomatoes," said Sylvia, poking at the slice on her plate. "These things we buy at the market taste like cardboard. Please pass the pickles."

"We could make our own pickles, too," said Mandy. "We'd need to get some decent cucumbers and some dill. So—have you thought any more about Don Gardner? I wish they'd find a man for me. Maybe if you don't want Don Gardner, they'd let me try him."

"Mandy, really," replied Sylvia. "Is that any way to talk? Besides, it's not up to us. The matches are based on algorithms. If you match, you get the green light. No match means no green light."

"If I were you, I'd accept reality and at least give the guy a shot," said Mandy. "If the Industrial Council has really deleted your marriage, and if you're going to be living here indefinitely, why not make the best of it? It's possible that Don Gardner is a perfectly nice guy. I'm sure you could do much worse."

"But I'd feel terrible about Jason," said Sylvia. "In my heart I still love him. Nobody could ever take his place."

"Okay, I agree: no other man could take his place. But does that mean you have to become an old spinster? You've got one life to live, sister—there are no second chances."

"All right, I'll think about it."

CHAPTER TWENTY-SIX

On Wednesday morning at ten o'clock, Sylvia reported to Dr. Hyland's office.

"I hope you've brought good news regarding Don Gardner," he said when she sat down at his desk.

"Yes," she replied. "I would like to meet him for dinner."

"Splendid!" he replied. "You may call Limar on your phone. She will contact Don and make the arrangements."

"I can't call him myself?"

"We believe that in these initial stages, it's better for everyone to stick with the island protocol."

At seven o'clock that night, Sylvia met Don for dinner at the Dockside. She found him already seated at the table, and he did not stand up when she approached, offering only a bland puppy smile. He was dressed in the male equivalent of the female island uniform—a boxy blue sports jacket and white shirt that looked like they came out of an old twentieth-century Sears catalogue. His hair was longish and carefully parted on the side and plastered down with some sort of gel.

They exchanged pleasantries—how the weather was nice and the restaurant not too crowded. Then they sat in silence as they perused their menus, which took Sylvia about thirty seconds because she quickly decided she wanted the spinach ravioli; and then, for lack of anything better to do, she pretended to keep looking at the selections. With brows furrowed, Don studied his menu for a few minutes. Then, without lifting his eyes, he said, "Should I have the sirloin steak or the Statler chicken?"

"Excuse me—what?" Sylvia had been daydreaming.

He looked at her with condescending annoyance. "I said, should I have the sirloin steak or the Statler chicken?"

"Oh, I don't know. They both sound good. I haven't had either one yet— as I'm sure you know, I only arrived on the island six days ago."

"Yes—you're a newbie," he replied. "From Detroit, is that right?"

"That's right. I work in the logistics office of Sun Motors."

"Did you guys ever fix that problem with the radar system of the Comet SUV? That was a major product defect."

Sylvia cringed. The Comet radar system software had been poorly designed, had led to a recall of fifty thousand vehicles, and had cost the company tens of millions of dollars. The episode was the biggest product recall since the Global Depression and had been a major embarrassment for the company. No one who worked at Sun liked to talk about it, and especially not with a casual acquaintance.

"It was fixed," replied Sylvia. "It's in the past. I thought you would have known that, since you worked at Facts News."

"I was a sportscaster," he said without looking up from his menu.

The server came to the table and asked if they were ready to order. Without waiting for Sylvia to reply, Gardner said, "The sirloin steak—it comes with a mushroom sauce?"

The server replied, "Yes, just as it says on the menu. It hasn't changed. Always with a mushroom sauce."

He thought some more. "The salmon looks good—is that farm raised or wild?"

"Farm raised. The season for wild salmon won't start for another few weeks."

"That's no good," mused Gardner as he stroked his chin with his hand. He looked up. "Sylvia, why don't you go ahead and order."

"I'll have the tossed salad with vinaigrette dressing and the spinach ravioli," she said.

"Something to drink?" asked the server.

"Water, please."

After writing this on her pad, the server turned her attention back to Gardner.

"Let's see.... I had the roast beef last week, so that's out. Not sure if I'm in the mood for chicken. The salmon is farm raised, so I'll pass on that. You're having the spinach ravioli, so there's no point in my getting the same thing. I've had the meat loaf recently too."

"Try the steak tips," said Sylvia, trying not to show her annoyance at Gardner's indecisiveness.

"Okay, but if they're no good, I'll blame you," he said. This time he was smiling. Sylvia was not.

"Very good," said the server. "And a salad?"

"I've had the garden salad and the Caesar salad. Sylvia, do you think the coleslaw will go well with the steak tips?"

"Yes, I'm sure it will."

"And a glass of wine... let's see...."

"Sir," said the server, "we offer a choice of red or white wine. It's the same choice we've had for several years."

"I'll have the red."

"Very good."

Sylvia decided that to keep the evening moving along, she needed to be proactive in the conversation. "How did you get into sportscasting?" she asked.

Gardner explained he had been in high school and had been cut from the varsity football team—which he thought was highly unfair, even though he admitted missing key practice sessions—and so he started reporting on the team for the school newspaper. He revealed to Sylvia that for snaring girls, being associated with the team as a reporter was nearly as good as being a player, and therefore he had no shortage of girlfriends. There were lots of beer parties and wild weekends, which Gardner described in great detail.

After the salads arrived, he continued his memoirs by detailing how in college he had expanded his sports reporting platforms to include the college radio station and then the local cable access TV station. There were more beer parties and more girls.

By the time the server brought their main courses, Gardner's life story had progressed to his first full-time job as a sportscaster for a television station in Wichita. He spent two years there covering mostly high school and college games (the hottest girls were at Kansas State in Manhattan, Kansas, he reported) before joining Facts News in Kansas City.

The server cleared their plates and brought coffee.

"You've had quite a career," said Sylvia as she stirred in her sugar and cream. "Very impressive. So—if I may ask—why are you here? I don't want to pry, but we're all here for a reason."

"It was time to make a move," he said without a trace of irony. "I got caught up in a very unfair accusation from a female colleague. The station's owners were lined up against me. At around the same time, my dentin dysplasia had progressed enough to become a problem."

"Oh, I'm sorry," said Sylvia. "Since I've been here I've become something of an expert on genetic diseases—I have mitochondrial DNA-associated Leigh syndrome—but I've never heard of dentin dysplasia."

"It's also called 'rootless teeth,' replied Gardner. "It's an accurate description. Your teeth look normal, but they have stunted roots. Over time, they become loose and eventually fall out of your mouth. Just like that—pop, pop, pop. That's why I have these nice new choppers." He grinned, showing perfect white rows of teeth. "One day the station told me they were sending me on a special assignment. I got on the plane and got off here." He waved his hand, indicating the room around them. "That was one year ago. At first I was resentful, but then I figured, hey, why not make the best of it? If I could raise a family here on Juliette Island, why not?"

"Yes—why not?" replied Sylvia. In her mind's eye, she could see nothing but his toothless gums. She signaled for the server, to whom she gave her debit card. In a moment her bill was paid and the card returned. As soon as her companion had finished his coffee, Sylvia said, "Don, this has been a very pleasant evening. Thank you." She pushed back her chair and stood up.

Caught off guard, he scrambled to his feet. "Just let me get my bill—I'll go to the door with you." Sylvia waited while he paid. Outside in the parking area, Gardner turned to her. "Will you walk me to my golf cart?"

"All right," replied Sylvia, overruling the warning voice in her head. "Where is it?"

"Over there," he gestured vaguely towards the far edge of the gravel lot.

They walked together toward a stand of dark trees. Sure enough, in the shadows under the branches, outside the pool of light from the restaurant, a golf cart was parked.

"Your chariot awaits you," said Sylvia brightly.

"How about a kiss goodnight?" He moved close.

"Well, all right," she replied she offered him her cheek. "But I really must be going. I have an early day tomorrow."

Suddenly he put his arm around her waist and drew her against his body. He mashed his lips against hers and probed her mouth with his tongue.

Turning her face away and pushing against him, she struggled to twist free. His grip was strong. She felt his other hand on her breast, squeezing it. As she tried to grab his wrist and wrench it free, in a twisted tango move he kicked her feet out from under her and she toppled backward onto the grass bordering the gravel lot. He lay on top of her with his full weight pressing down. With one hand he tried to hold her head steady while he kissed her mouth. The other hand crawled down from her back to her buttocks, fingers groping, trying to hike up her dress.

Summoning all her strength, she slammed her fist into his throat. He cried out in pain and relaxed his hold on her, allowing her to break free, stand up, and run towards the light of the restaurant.

"Stupid bitch," she heard him gasp.

When she got home, she went straight for the planter on the patio. After swallowing a shot of whiskey, she went upstairs and took a shower, but the sensation of being violated wouldn't wash off. She went to bed and drifted into a troubled sleep.

The next morning, Sylvia reported to Dr. Hyland's office. Through his rimless glasses, he peered at her with an expression of disapproval.

"Don Gardner called me this morning," he said.

"Did he tell you that he sexually assaulted me in the parking lot of the Dockside?"

"He told me you punched him in the throat. He could have been seriously injured. I'd say if there was an assault, he bore the brunt of it."

"He's a predator."

"That's a strong word," said Dr. Hyland. His tone softened. "He's been here a year, without female companionship. Please try to understand how difficult it must be for him. Men have needs. Perhaps he was a little bit clumsy in his overtures. I hope you can forgive him."

"Actually," said Sylvia, "his assault on me—which back in the real world could earn him jail time—was the least of my issues with him. The bigger problem is that he's a raging bore. We spent over an hour at dinner, and during ninety percent of that time I sat and listened while he told me his life story, right down to the quantity and quality of his girlfriends. The man is both extremely dull and extremely determined that he should dominate the conversation. That's a fatal combination. His sense of entitlement is truly appalling. I urge you to re-examine your data points and find some other girl for him to victimize, both physically and emotionally."

Dr. Hyland slowly shook his head. "You may have gotten off to a rough start with Don, but I assure you he's a good man. All the data point to one conclusion: he'll be a good husband for you and a good father for your children. I'm sure that if you made an effort to see the situation from his point of view, you'd be much more empathetic. And remember that marriage to your chosen partner will bring many substantial rewards, while refusing to go along with the program will bring equal and opposite sanctions."

"Is that a threat?" asked Sylvia.

"Come now, let's not be dramatic. It's just reality. We each have a job to do here. I have mine and you have yours. Don has his. Let me ask you—did you make any effort to please him? To see the world from his point of view?"

"I made a huge effort to sit there and listen to him brag about his years as a young stud working as a sportscaster. It was one female conquest after another, interspersed with boasts about all the famous athletes he knew. He didn't let me get a word in edgewise. I'd be amazed if he even knows my name. Go ahead, call him on the phone. Ask him the name of the girl he had dinner with last night."

Dr. Hyland held up his hands in a double "stop" sign. "Sylvia, that's enough. The Medical Board has spoken. You will marry Don Gardner. You will live with him and have children with him. Perhaps you don't realize what a valuable service you will be performing for humanity. When combined, your individual genetic profiles will create in your children unique combinations we haven't seen before. And one more thing—you should also count yourself extremely lucky that Don, out of the goodness of his heart, is willing to raise your expected child as his own."

"I'm sure he's also eagerly looking forward to the fattening of his debit card balance once he's a so-called 'head of household' with a child on the way," said Sylvia.

Ignoring her comment, Dr. Hyland leaned forward and looked directly into her eyes. "Sylvia Brand, from this moment on, your happiness is in your hands. If you're determined to be miserable, then miserable you shall be. But I advise you to keep your winter of discontent to yourself. Don Gardner deserves a partner who's loving and supportive, not a shrew who cannot be tamed. Do you understand?"

Knowing she had lost this battle, Sylvia gritted her teeth and said, "Yes."

"Within the month, your marriage will be consummated. In the meantime, I encourage you to spend time with Don and get to know him." Dr. Hyland closed the file and set it aside before clicking on his computer. "Very well. Let's see what your medical examination schedule looks like today."

CHAPTER TWENTY-SEVEN

At the end of the day, Sylvia drove home, parked her golf cart in front of 15 Apple Way, and turned off the motor. She sat quietly, thinking about her life. What had she done wrong? Why did she deserve to be forcibly married to an odious clown just because the Medical Board thought his and her DNA would make an interesting and profitable combination? Was she only valuable to her fellow human beings because by some random stroke of fate she had an unusual flaw in her genetics? She felt like she had fallen into a deep, dark well from which there was no escape. What had become her reason for living? Was it to bear the baby she and Jason had conceived in love, only to have that innocent child raised by a creep allied with the Medical Board? This scenario loomed large in her heart, blocking out the light, like a vast black cloud overspreading the sky and blotting out the sun.

Sluggishly, she roused herself. Sitting like a lump in her golf cart wasn't going to help. She trudged to the front door and went inside. Entering the kitchen, she found Mandy slicing potatoes for dinner.

"I haven't seen you since before you met Don Gardner for dinner last night," Mandy said as she laid the slices on a greased pan. "How did it go?"

"Please do me a favor and don't mention that man's name," replied Sylvia. "He's a horrible boring person and he sexually assaulted me right there in the parking lot. And Dr. Hyland is just as bad. He told me I had no choice—I was to marry Don Gardner and carry his little rug rats."

"I'm so sorry," said Mandy. She put the pan in the oven. "But maybe it will all work out. After all, what else can you do? This is our life. Some higher power—call it God or fate—put us on this island. It's now our home. We need to make the best of it."

"Mandy, God did not put us here!" said Sylvia. "The Industrial Council put us here! Greedy men and women put us here! People who have power put us here and are keeping us here! We're on this island by the deliberate choice of those who are no better than us and who seek to profit from our bodies and our diseases."

"Okay, okay—I understand how you feel," said Mandy. "I didn't mean to say we have no free will. We do. Listen, I'm sure you're hungry. I'm going to make hamburgers. Do you want one?"

Sylvia took a deep breath. In a peculiar way, she wished she could be like Mandy—a carefree leaf in the wind, willing to accept whatever fate brought her. The Buddhists said that desire was the root of all unhappiness. This was true. Sylvia knew her misery was the product of her desire to control her own life in defiance of her present circumstances. She could choose to roll over and go with the flow. But that would be both morally unacceptable and physically dangerous. If her soon-to-be life partner, Don Gardner, beat her and abused her, she would find no sympathy from the Medical Board, from Dr. Hyland, or anyone else in authority. Don Gardner could even make her disappear, and as long as he wasn't stupid about it, the Medical Council would undertake nothing more than a token investigation. Her doctors could kill her. Then her body would be cremated and her name erased from the database. And her child? Knowing no other environment but Juliette Island, who could imagine what her life would be like? Would her child become an obedient sheep, making no trouble for the Medical Board and expressing gratitude for whatever tasty little scraps they tossed to her, the way a dog eagerly waits underneath the banquet table?

With a heavy heart, Sylvia ate her dinner and washed the dishes. It was hopeless. She was doomed. Without saying goodnight to Mandy she went upstairs to her room. Fully clothed, she lay down on the bed. Yes, she decided, the only solution was to end her miserable existence. To die was better than to live as a prisoner. Taking her own life meant taking that of her child, and she prayed that Jason, if he were still walking on the earth, would forgive her.

As if she were watching someone else do it, she got up from her bed and looked around her room. She had no weapon, no poison. But she had a belt, and she could hang herself. She saw herself go to her closet and take the leather belt hanging from the hook. The belt was slender but strong. She could fasten the two ends together, as if she were wearing it, and slip it around her neck. Then she could place it over the hook. How long would it take to die? Hopefully not very much time. The last thing she wanted was to be discovered not quite dead, and taken to the Medical Center and revived, and for Dr. Hyland to shake his head and tell her what a weak and pathetic woman she was.

The smooth, hard leather encircled her neck. Now was the time. She closed her eyes and relaxed her body, letting it slide down the side of the door. The belt gripped her neck. As it became tighter, she felt the blood pressure build in her face. Okay—this is it. Let your legs go. You don't need them any more.

A noise came from the hallway. A soft knock on her door.

"Sylvia—are you awake?" The voice belonged to Reese.

Damn you, Reese! Why did you have to interrupt? Sylvia struggled to her feet and the noose loosened its deadly hold. "Uh—yes, just a minute," she stammered. Feeling dizzy, she held onto the side of the door. She slipped off the belt, undid the buckle, and hung it on the hook. After talking a few breaths, Sylvia opened the door.

"My God, Reese!" she exclaimed. "What have they done to you? Please—come in."

As she entered, Reese said, "Oh, they just roughed me up. I lost a few pounds too—being fed nothing but bread and water will do that to you. But they knew they couldn't hurt me too badly because I'm too valuable. They need me for more tests." She stopped and looked at Sylvia. "Are you okay? You seem depressed." Her fingers went to Sylvia's neck. "And you've got a rash or something."

Sylvia turned and sat on her bed. Suddenly, despite her effort to hold them inside, the tears flooded from her eyes. Reese sat next to her and tenderly put her arm around her. Sobbing, Sylvia said, "I'm so sorry. I just couldn't take it anymore. I was going to—I don't know how to say this, I feel so stupid—I was trying to end it. I didn't want to live. I'm sorry."

"Sorry?" said Reese. "What on earth are you sorry for?"

"For not being strong. For complaining."

Reese took her by the shoulders. "Sylvia, you have nothing to be sorry for." She reached for a tissue from the box on the night table. "Dry your eyes. You're lucky I came upstairs when I did! A few minutes later and you might have succeeded. Now listen to me: I've had enough of this place. So have you. I'm ready to get the hell out of here."

"What are you talking about?" she said as she dabbed her tears. "Do you mean escape?"

"Sister, that's exactly what I mean. We can't continue to live like this. We live like animals in a zoo. What's the end game? I want you to think about something. Have you noticed there are very few old people living here? There's Reginald Astor. He's in his sixties. Hardly a geriatric. There are one or two elderly residents who have Alzheimer's disease, and that's why they're here. But there's no one else who's beyond middle aged. Do you know why?"

"No, I don't. Maybe they send them home when they're no longer useful medical subjects."

"Are you kidding? Send them home? So they can tell everyone about Juliette Island and all the people who are forced to live here? Get real. That's not going to happen."

"So what happens to them?"

"You mean, what will happen to us. To you and me. I'll tell you what's in store for us: I have a friend who works in the crematorium."

"Reese, you couldn't mean…"

"Yes, that's exactly what I mean. When you're no longer useful, they tell you to report for your normal medical tests. When you're on the table, they tell you they need to give you a general anesthetic. You say, go ahead, I don't care, I've gone to sleep too many times to count. They pump you full of Propofol. You drift off to slumber land and you never wake up. They slice you open, harvest your organs, take out your brain, suck out your bone marrow, and when there's nothing left but a hollow carcass they put it in a body bag, throw it into the back of a truck, take it to the crematorium, and fire it up. At two thousand degrees Fahrenheit, within two hours your pathetic cadaver has been reduced to five pounds of bone and ash. Then the remains are fed through a crusher to break up the bone fragments—although at the Juliette Island corpse roaster, they probably skip this step. They pour your ashes into a big bucket. When the bucket is full, they take it out in the boat and dump the cinders into Puget Sound. Within a few years, your fried molecules will have traveled on ocean currents all around the world."

"You're talking about the boat they keep in the boathouse next to the crematorium?" asked Sylvia. "The one they let Mandy ride in with her son's ashes?"

"That's the one. If your child dies, the Medical Board treats it like a normal death, with some vestige of dignity. They don't want the grieving parents to freak out. But when they kill you, they do it very quietly."

"I don't want to die here," said Sylvia. "And I don't want my child to grow up here. But what can we do? How can we get off this ghastly island?"

Reese leaned closer, as if the walls had ears. "I know a guy who has keys to the boathouse. He's one of the human guards at the cooler."

"Reese, how do you know this?"

"Let's just say I get around. Most of the guys who work on this godforsaken pimple of an island have two useful qualities: they aren't very loyal to the Industrial Council, and they're starved for sex."

"Reese—do you mean—just like Aldeen—?"

"It's the coin of the realm, my dear. To get what you need, you use the money God gave you. I have something guys want, and I'm ready to do business. Actually, I like Khaleed. He's cute. But the important thing for us is this: he's worried about his future. He's got an unusual genetic disorder—something called Factor X deficiency, which affects the blood's ability to clot. He told me the Medical Board has brought him in for testing, and he's scared that at any moment he'll be converted from a prison employee to an inmate. He's seen the way the inmates leave the island—in the bucket on the boat. So he's ready to jump. He'll take us with him."

"Why doesn't he just take the boat and go?"

"My dear, the Mortas weren't born yesterday. Or manufactured yesterday, as the case may be. They track every movement around the island, and if Khaleed took the boat on an unscheduled cruise, they'd be all over him. He'd never make it."

"So how can he do it?"

"By waiting until it rains. In a good hard rain, the Mortas are less efficient and the drones can't fly. We get in the boat and race away at top speed. If we're lucky, the Morta patrol boat won't catch us in time."

"And if we're unlucky?"

"They'll try to stop us, and if they can't, they'll blow us out of the water."

"Okay," said Sylvia. Looking at the flesh of her hand, she ran her fingertip over the bump in the skin above the tiny pill-shaped transponder. "What about these?"

Reese's eyes narrowed. "We've got to remove them."

"How?"

"By cutting them out."

A bolt of nausea flashed through Sylvia's body. "I don't know if I can do that."

Taking Sylvia by the hand, Reese looked into her eyes. "Trust me, the pain will be a very small price to pay for your freedom. We'll do it together. It will take only a few seconds. One quick cut and it's done. But we need to get a razor and some bandages."

Fighting back her fear, Sylvia nodded. "Okay."

Suddenly they heard Mandy's cheery voice from the bottom of the stairs. "Hey you guys," she called. "I'm making some popcorn. Want some?"

"Yeah," called Reese. "We'll be down in a second!" She turned to Sylvia. "I like Mandy, but there's no way we can tell her about this. She's a loyalist. Even if she didn't object to our escaping, she'd have a problem keeping her mouth shut. One question from Limar and she'd spill her guts, and we'd both be dead."

SYLVIA BRAND

CHAPTER TWENTY-EIGHT

The next morning at her usual appointment, Dr. Hyland asked Sylvia if she had reconsidered her attitude toward Don Gardner. She told him that although he was a bit rough around the edges, after thinking about the proposed marriage she had seen him in a new light. She had stepped back and looked at the big picture, and realized that the Medical Board had shown good judgment. She promised to do her very best to create a happy home for her husband, herself, and their children.

"I'm so very pleased to hear that," said Dr. Hyland. "I'll convey to Don the good news."

"But you must tell him one thing," said Sylvia. "I'm a woman of high moral character. While I'm looking forward to consummating our marriage and raising our children, I insist that we save our intimate relations until after we're married. This is very important to me. I'm sure that he will enjoy great piece of mind knowing that his wife takes her vows very seriously, and that an intimate relationship outside of marriage is something that will never happen with me."

"Excellent!" Dr. Hyland beamed. "Of course I will impress upon him the importance of your virtue. I can personally guarantee that he will conduct himself like a perfect gentleman—or he will have to answer to me. I'll contact the island administrator and set a date for your marriage. I know you will be very happy."

Having for the time being cleared that particular hurdle, for the rest of the day Sylvia dutifully endured the familiar rounds of tests and probing and MRIs and tubes and needles.

During the last test, an ultrasound of her fetus, the nurse received a summons and excused herself from the examination room.

Sylvia had been alone in the room before, and had never thought much of it. But today was different. She slid off the table and looked around. Bandages were easy to find—they were in plain sight, and she stuffed a fistful in her pocket. Keeping her ears attentive to the sound of the door opening, she went to a cabinet and pulled open one drawer after another. She saw lots of medical devices and sundries, but no scalpels. She went to a small table that had a single drawer. Pulling it open, she saw surgical instruments in sterile plastic bags. She took a scalpel, put it in her pocket, and closed the drawer. Then she got back up on the table.

That night, the mood at the house was relaxed and congenial. Over a dinner of grilled chicken and rice, Sylvia told Mandy that she had decided to marry Don Gardner. Mandy seemed genuinely pleased, but expressed her personal sadness that once Sylvia and Don were united, her friend and roommate would be moving to a new home. "The three of us have such a good rapport," she said. "I'm going to miss you! I'm sure Reese feels the same way."

"Oh yes, absolutely," said Reese. "Sylvia, it won't be the same without you."

There was a knock on the front door. "In the kitchen," called Reese.

Limar came in and said, "How is everyone tonight?"

Everyone agreed that they were fine. Never better.

"I understand you, Sylvia, will soon be starting your own household with Don Gardner," said Limar. "I'm sure you're very excited."

"Oh yes—very excited," replied Sylvia. Then she added, "I see that word travels quickly."

"We're all plugged into the same database," said Limar with a pointless smile. "The minute Dr. Hyland entered it into your file, all the Morta autonomous humanoid operators knew."

"All of them?" asked Sylvia. "Do you mean to say, all of them everywhere in the nation?"

Limar nodded. "Of course that particular fifty-kilobyte morsel would have been filed away with the many terabytes of other data, like one grain of sand being added to a beach; but if the data were relevant to the operator or there's query, then the information would be instantly accessed."

"Oh, I get it," said Mandy.

Sylvia was silent. She was thinking about Carin and her circle of colleagues in Detroit—and especially of Jason.

"It's Friday night—anyone going out?" asked Limar.

No, no one was going out. They were all staying in.

"If that's all," said Limar, "then I wish you a good evening."

Limar left the house. Sylvia noted the time—it was exactly twenty minutes after seven. Every night, without fail, Limar came for her inspection between seven o'clock and seven-thirty. Sylvia and Reese needed to make their escape after Limar's visit.

The weather that night was clear. Khaleed, Reese reported, had access to weather reports. He was watching the forecasts. There was nothing on the horizon. Every day when Sylvia left the house, and again when she came home in the evening, she'd scan the heavens, looking for rain clouds. All she saw were friendly white clouds.

On Sunday night, Sylvia had her second date with Don Gardner. They met at the Dockside. Perhaps Dr. Hyland had given him a stern lecture, because in Sylvia's opinion he was slightly less obnoxious than during their first meeting. He even asked Sylvia about her life at 15 Apple Way, and he lasted about thirty seconds into her answer before he started to fidget and look bored. Sylvia saw this and, with a feeling of sadness, quickly ended her story, at which point Gardner, with the spotlight again turned in his direction, launched into a detailed description of a frat party he had attended while in college, and to which the campus police had been called because too many of the boys were lewdly grabbing the girls and/or drunkenly vomiting on the lawn in front of the frat house. Of course, because the cops were from the college and not the town, the offenders suffered no consequences other than a friendly admonition to "keep it cool, okay?"

Late on Monday afternoon, when Sylvia was released from her daily medical tests she stepped outside the Juliette Island Center for Health Research and looked up to the sky. The clouds directly overhead were high and thin, but to the west she saw a dark line, and the westerly breeze felt unusually cool. She hurried home, and neither Mandy nor Reese were there. A few minutes later, as Sylvia was puttering around in the kitchen, Reese arrived.

"Have you seen the clouds?" Sylvia asked. "Looks like rain."

"Yes I did, and on the way home I stopped to see Khaleed. We're getting a storm tonight. It's supposed to start at eight o'clock and last until midnight. We need to be at the boathouse at eight-thirty."

Sylvia felt as if she had been hit by a lightning bolt. This was it! The hour was upon her. By dawn tomorrow, she'd either be dead or free. There was no middle choice. She would not allow herself to be captured. They would have to kill her.

"Are you with us?" asked Reese. Her eyes were bright and shining.

"Yes," replied Sylvia. "Absolutely. One hundred percent."

At that moment they heard Mandy's golf cart crunch on the gravel driveway.

"What are we going to do with our roommate?" whispered Sylvia.

"You'll see. Shhh—she's coming."

Mandy came into the kitchen. "Hey guys," she said cheerily. "On the way home, I picked up two frozen pizzas. Pepperoni and sausage. I thought we could have an easy dinner tonight."

"Sounds good to me," replied Sylvia.

At seven thirty, when they were eating, Sylvia got up to look out the window.

"Is there something out there?" asked Mandy as she picked a pepperoni off the last piece of pizza. "You've been up and down like a jack-in-the-box."

"Oh, nothing—sorry," she said. "I saw an unusual bird in the yard today. It looked like some kind of big hawk. Just curious to see if it were still hanging around."

A few minutes later the sky suddenly darkened. A few splats of raindrops hit the window—at first just one or two at a time, but the pace slowly increased until it became a steady drumbeat.

"Wow—we haven't had a good storm in a while," said Mandy. She went to the window and looked out. "It's really coming down."

Limar did not come to the house for the regular inspection. This was a good sign—it confirmed the Morta robots didn't like operating in the rain.

At eight o'clock, Sylvia met Reese in her room. She was carrying a length of clothesline. "It's still raining," said Reese. "We're going to go for it. Give me your scalpel."

Sylvia handed it over.

"Okay, let's go see Mandy."

They found their roommate on her bed, reading a book. "Hey guys, what's up?" she asked.

Brandishing the scalpel, Reese approached her. "Mandy, I need you to lie on your stomach with your hands behind your back."

"Why—what?"

"Just do it. Sylvia and I are leaving. We need you to stay out of the way. Believe me, it's for your own good. They must not think you were a part of this. You need to be a victim. Make a sound and I'll cut your throat."

"But why are you leaving?" said Mandy. "If they catch you they'll kill you."

"You and I have very different levels of tolerance for tyrants," said Reese. "If you want to live your life as a slave in golden chains, that's your choice. No one can make that decision for you. Sylvia and I can't do it. We can't live here. We'd rather die. That's just the way it is. Now please—turn over and put your hands behind your back. Don't make me kill you."

Dutifully—perhaps because obedience was in her blood—Mandy rolled over, face down, on the bed, and offered her hands to the rope. While Reese held the scalpel on Mandy, Sylvia quickly tied her hands and feet. "I'm sorry to do this," she said, "but we have no choice." She then cut a strip of cloth from a towel and tied it around Mandy's mouth.

With Mandy immobilized, Sylvia and Reese went to the kitchen. They sat down at the table. Reese extended her hand, palm down, on the table. She handed Sylvia the scalpel. ""Do it. Now."

"I can't," said Sylvia. "I've never—"

"Do you want to die? That's what's going to happen if we don't get out of here. Do it for your unborn child. Come on, make the cut."

"All right," said Sylvia. With one hand she pinched the flesh around the cylinder, forming a small hump. With the other hand she took the scalpel and pressed the sharp tip against the soft flesh covering the cylindrical shape.

"Breathe slowly," commanded Reese. "Steady your hand."

Sylvia pressed down and drew the blade towards her. Reese stiffened but did not cry out. Sylvia felt the tip of the blade scrape along the top of the cylinder as the blood began to ooze out.

"Okay, that's enough," gasped Reese. With her thumb and forefinger, Sylvia pinched the skin tighter. She could feel the hard cylinder, and she tried to work it upwards. Suddenly it popped free.

Reese gasped. After flicking away the cylinder, Sylvia reached for a bandage and pressed it down hard on the wound.

Reese was breathing hard. "God, that hurts!" After a moment she composed herself. "We've got to hurry. You're next. Put your hand on the table."

With fear pouring through her heart, Sylvia extended her left hand.

"Close your eyes," said Reese. "Think of a faraway happy place."

Sylvia felt Reese pinch the flesh between her thumb and forefinger. Suddenly a savage pain shot from her hand up her arm to her brain. Involuntarily she cried out. She tried jerk back her hand but Reese held it in place with a tight grip.

"One more second," she heard Reese say.

The pain obliterated every other sensation. Tears welled up in Sylvia's eyes. She gasped for air. God, when was it going to end? She felt Reese squeezing harder.

"Come on, come on," muttered Reese. Just as the agony was becoming unbearable and Sylvia was ready to yank her hand free of the grasp of her tormentor, Reese said, "Okay—good!" The pinching sensation ended and was replaced by hard pressure on a dull throbbing ache.

Sylvia opened her bleary eyes. Reese smiled as she held the bandage tight against Sylvia's hand. "Are you all right?" she asked.

"Yes—I think so," replied Sylvia, wiping away tears with the back of her hand.

"It's all over. See, you survived!" Reese removed the bloody bandage and replaced it with a fresh one, which she taped tightly to Sylvia's hand.

Sylvia looked at the clock. Eight-fifteen. "We need to get out of here. Where are the transponders?"

"Right there on the table, doing their jobs," replied Reese, pointing to the two little cylinders covered in thick, coagulating blood. "We'll leave them as little gifts."

With her hand pulsing with pain, Sylvia went to the front vestibule and took her raincoat and hat from the rack. After putting them on, she opened the door and stepped out into the downpour. Reese followed. They went to Sylvia's golf cart, got in, and set off down Apple Way.

Helpless against the mass of water droplets, the golf cart's little headlight beam refracted into an ineffectual cloud, and Sylvia could see no more than ten feet in front of her.

Within moments they were both soaked. Her left hand throbbing, Sylvia guided the golf cart to Pine Path, and then past the Juliette Island Center, which was dark. No other vehicles were on the pathways. Pine Path became Seaside Drive, and they passed the abandoned warehouse with its corrugated metal roof drumming loud in the rain, the old gas station, and the gloomy Wild Horse Bar. Rounding the hill, they came to the spot where normally you could see the causeway, but in the heavy rain they saw only darkness. They passed the sign for Tucker's Point and the food and beverage office.

"Keep going straight," said Reese, the water running off her hat.

Squinting into the deluge, Sylvia guided the golf cart along the path. They came to a chain link fence with an open gate. Sylvia drove through and a moment later the headlight revealed a door to a big industrial building. Next to the door, a utility vehicle sat in the rain. Called a "Rhino," it was made by Sun Motors, and was typically used on farms and estates for hauling tools and lightweight cargo. Here on Juliette Island, the Rhinos were used by the Morta guards and human employees.

Reese alighted from the golf cart and ran through the muddy puddles to the door, where she huddled under the small canopy. She knocked. She looked around nervously. No sign of a drone or Morta guard. Reese knocked again. The door opened and a man came out. Hunched over against the rain, he ran to the Rhino. Reese followed him, and waved to Sylvia to join them. She ran to the Rhino and climbed into the small back seat. The water poured off the canvas roof in sheets.

"Sylvia, meet Khaleed," said Reese.

Khaleed turned and quickly shook Sylvia's hand. His eyes did not linger on her and his jaw was set at a determined angle. He turned the key to the Rhino and the little two-cylinder gas engine sprang to life with a staccato roar. He flicked on the headlights and steered the Rhino further north, past the perimeter of the building that bore no markings but that Sylvia knew must be the ghastly crematorium.

They bumped along a path under dripping trees until the headlights caught a wooden boathouse. As they approached, Sylvia saw the dock, beyond which loomed vast wild darkness. Khaleed halted the Rhino by the boathouse and motioned for them to get out. Together they went to a door. Khaleed produced a key, and as the rain beat down he fumbled for the lock and, finding it, turned the key. The metal door swung open. They entered, and before them in the deep gloom a white powerboat with an open wheel rocked gently in the wavelets coming through the open entrance. Aft of the driver's seat, a red faux-leather banquette formed a U-shape around the stern, with the engine compartment acting as a sort of table. Khaleed jumped down into the boat, took the wheel, turned the key, and pressed the starter button.

Sylvia and Reese untied the lines, climbed on board, and took seats on the banquette.

Suddenly from outside a sharp light raked across the entrance to the boathouse.

"Attention—you inside!" called an amplified voice. "Come out with your hands up!"

CHAPTER TWENTY-NINE

"Damn!" muttered Khaleed. "One of the human guards on patrol. Get down! We've got to get out of here!"

Khaleed shoved the throttle forward, and with a roar from its engine the boat leaped from the narrow slip into the blinding light. As Sylvia threw herself onto the floor of the cockpit the spotlight pinned the boat in its glare. A shot rang out, then two more. Sylvia felt a bullet slam into the side of the boat inches from her head.

With the boat at full throttle, within a few seconds it had outrun the spotlight. As it raced across the waves in the pouring rain, Sylvia lifted her head.

"Oh my God," she said. In the driver's seat, Khaleed sat slumped over the wheel, his arms hanging slack by his sides. Springing to her feet, she put her hands on his shoulders. Then she saw the hole in his back, running red mixed with rainwater.

Reese was at her side. She reached over Khaleed's body and pulled back on the throttle. The boat slowed. Sylvia looked behind them. On the distant shore, the brilliant finger of the spotlight probed the darkness.

"Help me get him out of the chair,' said Sylvia. Together they lifted him from the seat and laid him on the floor. Sylvia looked at his eyes and felt for a pulse.

"He's dead," she said.

The rain lashed them. Aside from the glimmering light on the shore, deathly darkness surrounded them.

"We'll use their light to ensure we're headed in the right direction," said Sylvia. "We want to go east. We'll keep it behind us."

Suddenly the spotlight was extinguished.

"Without it, we're lost," said Reese. It was true—as Sylvia swiveled in her seat and peered into the rain, she couldn't see more than a few yards. Unless they had a landmark, they could easily head off in the wrong direction—even back to Juliette Island.

"We need to find the causeway," said Sylvia. "It's the only way we'll know where we're going. We'll follow it to the other side."

"Remember," said Reese, "the land adjacent to the causeway, and most of it along the coast, is part of the United Americas and controlled by the Industrial Union. Once you get a few miles inland, you cross into the Western Canaille Zone."

Sylvia took the wheel and pointed the boat in the direction of what she thought was south, towards the causeway. "Look at the wave patterns," she said. "They're coming from behind us. Let's make sure we maintain the same orientation."

Gingerly they crept forward through the downpour. A moment later Sylvia saw the dark shape of the concrete causeway and the phosphorescent gleam of waves breaking on the rocks.

"Okay, let's keep the causeway to our starboard," said Sylvia. She advanced the throttle and the boat's nose rose out of the water.

Through the dense rain, from the direction of the island a set of headlights appeared on the causeway and a searchlight swept the dark water. "They're looking for us," said Reese. The lights gained on them, and Sylvia increased the boat's speed. Then from the mainland side another set of headlights appeared, also with a searchlight piercing the rain-swept night.

Sylvia throttled back. "We're trapped," she said. "We have no choice but to head out into the open water." She turned the wheel and accelerated, and, with a second to spare before the searchlights caught them, the darkness of the storm enveloped the boat.

The rain poured down. Water sloshed in the bottom of the cockpit. Sylvia had long since given up any hope of staying dry—she was soaked to the skin. She looked at the body of Khaleed. Except for one handshake and greeting, she didn't know him. He looked like a boy, too young to die. His expression was peaceful. The uncaring drops of water bounced off his skin and, merging together, ran in rivulets down his motionless face. He had saved her life at the cost of his own. She wanted to cover him up. It seemed like the right thing to do. But there was no blanket, no sheet. Only the pounding rain.

She looked over the side of the boat. The water was choppy and it was hard to tell where the waves were coming from. The vessel could be slowly rotating in a current. They had no way of knowing.

"It can't be later than nine o'clock," said Sylvia. "It'll be dark for another six or seven hours. If they send out a boat, we'll see its lights. The best thing for us to do is wait for the weather to clear. If we can see the moon or the stars, we'll know which direction is east. Meanwhile, I think it's best if we put Khaleed into the ocean."

"All right," said Reese. "If they find him, they may think we've all died."

Sloshing on the deck, Sylvia took Khaleed's right arm near the shoulder, while Reese took his left arm. With a mighty effort the two women lifted the body with its water-soaked clothing so that the head and torso rested on the gunwale. While Sylvia held Khaleed by his shoulders, Reese lifted one leg and then the other. For a moment the dripping body lay balanced on the gunwale, and then both women gave it a shove and it splashed into the sea. They watched it slowly drift away into the darkness.

Sylvia and Reese sat in the boat as the rain continued its steady drumbeat. The hours passed, or so it seemed. The rain eased, then dwindled to a light drizzle. The two women talked about their previous lives and what they were going to do when they reached freedom.

"I suppose I'll just start over from scratch," said Reese. "My adoptive parents still live in Houston, but I can never set foot in the United Americas again. Visiting them will be out of the question. It makes me sad to think they'll never know what really happened to me. I'm sure the Industrial Council security people denied kidnapping me and made up some story, like I ran away with my boyfriend. Perhaps there's some way I can contact them. Maybe on social media?"

"The government blocks internet traffic from outside the country," said Sylvia.

"I guess you're right," said Reese. Then she brightened up. "Do you think there's cell phone service between the canaille and the United Americas?"

Sylvia shrugged. She didn't know.

"I hope I can find work at a women's health center," said Reese. "They must have those things, right? I mean, it's not like we're escaping to some sort of Stone Age nation, are we?"

"No, I don't think so. From what I've heard—stories, really—life in the canaille is just like life at home, only a century behind. Maybe like the Wild West was in the old days, where you had places with no law enforcement interspersed with settlements that had a sheriff. I've read about the old Gold Rush towns, where you had thousands of people living in the middle of nowhere, practically self-governing, with no legal system. People figured right and wrong out for themselves. Neighbors helped their neighbors. There was no Industrial Council that told you what you had to do. Nobody knew your business. You were judged on what you actually did, not on what some doctor though you might do in the future."

The rain was little more than a mist now, and Sylvia scanned the dark sky for a break in the clouds signified by the faint glow of the moon or a twinkle of a single star. She saw only inky blackness. The water was calm, with only the occasional soft wave lapping at the side of the boat. The boat floated lazily, in which direction they knew not.

"How about you?" asked Reese. "You're going to have a child. What are you going to do when you first set foot on free soil?"

"I need to contact my child's father. I owe that much to both my child and to Jason. That's number one. After that, I don't know. Find a job, like anyone else would. Find a place to live. At home, I have money in the bank, though I suppose that doesn't matter now." She paused. "Above all, I just want to get my body back. I don't want to be a human lab rat. I don't want some guy in his corner office on the thirtieth floor of the Bigshot Building to know more about my own body than I do. And I definitely don't want him to make decisions on my behalf! That's just crazy."

Sylvia looked directly overhead. Was there a glimmer of star? Yes, there was! There was one, and then another, and a third.

The two women huddled in the drifting boat, watching the sky. Stars became visible, only to disappear again as the clouds broke up, re-formed, and passed overhead. In the bottom of the boat, the water sloshed gently.

"Look!" said Reese as she pointed into the gloom. "Do you see that? The sky is lighter over there."

Sylvia looked, and at first she wasn't sure, but after a few minutes she had to agree the horizon was lighter there than when she looked in the opposite direction. "At last!" she said. "Now we know which direction is east. Let's go!"

Sylvia started the engine and turned the wheel to the east.

"Look!" shouted Reese. She pointed behind them, towards the island. Sylvia saw a boat with a spotlight speeding in their direction.

"A Morta patrol boat," said Sylvia grimly. She slammed the throttle down and the boat roared forward. She glanced behind. The Morta boat was gaining ground.

The sky had lightened and Sylvia peered ahead, looking for land. She saw only gloomy gray mist. The boat bounced along the waves, throwing up white curls of water from its bow.

Shots rang out, and then more. Sylvia turned. A Morta stood on the front deck of the patrol boat, holding an automatic weapon. The patrol boat was pitching in the waves, but the closer they got the more likely it was the Morta could fire accurately.

There! Up ahead Sylvia saw a dark gray line of land. A volley of bullets splashed in the water to port. Violently Sylvia jerked the wheel to starboard and the boat careened across the waves. More shots, this time falling behind in the foaming wake.

"Stop your boat!" the amplified command came across the water. "If you surrender you will live!"

The motorboat was now speeding parallel to the rocky shore. There was no place to stop, and the patrol boat was close behind. Sylvia desperately scanned the shore—too many trees, too many rocks! To run the boat onto the rocks would be fatal, and to stop the boat and get off would be equally fatal.

A volley of shots slammed into the hull of the boat, sending shards of fiberglass flying. Reese huddled on the floor. Sylvia jerked the wheel back and forth as the boat zig-zagged through the choppy seas.

"Stop!" the voice called again. "You cannot escape!"

Suddenly—up ahead—the mouth of a narrow river! Sylvia roared towards it, and in a moment the boat plunged into the shallow waters of an intertidal estuary. On each side the tall reeds swayed as the wake from her boat hit them. Ahead the river curved, and Sylvia, still at full throttle, hurtled deeper into its mouth.

The patrol boat followed, with the Morta on deck squeezing off bursts of bullets. The windshield of the speedboat shattered, crumpling the safety glass into a twisted sheet. Sylvia felt the bottom of the boat strike something and bump upward, but the propeller kept turning and the boat kept moving. Tall reeds and half-submerged rocks flew past in a blur.

Entering a straight stretch of river, she dared to glance behind her. She saw the patrol boat close behind, and the Morta on deck taking careful aim with his weapon. She was looking down the deathly barrel of the gun when suddenly the patrol boat lurched into the air and seemed to abruptly slow down. With his gun in his hands, the Morta flew off the bow of the boat and landed with a massive splash in the water.

Sylvia watched as the patrol boat came to a dead stop on the sandbar that Sylvia, in her smaller boat, had just barely made it over.

But they were not safe yet. Reducing her speed, Sylvia navigated further upstream, among the reeds and rocks, as the river narrowed and the tree-covered banks closed in. She had gone perhaps a mile up the river when she came to a shallow, rocky section where the current moved quickly. This was as far as she could go. She ran the boat up onto the marshy bank among the reeds and shut off the motor.

She turned to Reese, who was still huddled on the floor.

"Hey—we made it!" she exclaimed. "We lost them!"

Reese didn't move.

Sylvia went to her and touched her shoulder. Reese moaned and moved her head.

"Oh my God—you've been hit!" said Sylvia.

"It's nothing—I'll be fine," she whispered. She opened her eyes and looked at Sylvia. "Just hold me for a moment, would you? I feel so cold."

Sylvia reached down, put her arms around Reese, and raised her out of the water sloshing in the floor of the boat. "You're going to be all right," said Sylvia. "We'll get you to a doctor. Hang in there."

"Did we make it?" asked Reese.

"Not yet," replied Sylvia. "We need to keep moving. Let me help you up."

Reese made no reply. Her eyes lost their focus and her body went slack.

"Reese! Reese!" said Sylvia. "Don't leave me! Stay with me!" She put her ear next to Reese's mouth. Her breathing had stopped. Sylvia felt her neck for a pulse. There was nothing.

For several minutes Sylvia sat in the boat, cradling Reese in her arms. There was no doubt—she was dead.

CHAPTER THIRTY

Sylvia laid her friend on the deck of the boat. Stiff from fatigue and the cold, she stood up. She hated leaving Reese in the bottom of a waterlogged boat, but she knew that the Mortas and their drones and guns would soon come, looking for revenge, and she had to leave.

"My friend, you're beyond whatever they would do to you," she said. "Thank you for saving my life. I won't forget."

With those words she climbed out of the boat and went to the bow. Pushing with all of her strength, she moved it a few inches closer to the open water. After pausing to catch her breath, she pushed again. This time the boat broke free of the suction of the muck and floated into the current of the river. She watched as it lazily drifted downstream and out of sight.

Sylvia stepped through the mire to dry land. She looked around. The landscape was wild and desolate, without a house or road in sight. As long as the river flows from the east, she thought, I'm going to follow it. She set off, picking her way through reeds and bushes, climbing over felled logs and massive buried boulders, crossing little tributary creeks. The sun had fully risen into the eastern sky and the day was growing warmer.

She glanced behind her. The stranded patrol boat was a mile downriver, far out of sight. Soon the hijacked powerboat, carrying Reese's body, would be upon it. What was the scene there? Was the Morta guard hopelessly disabled after being immersed in water? Had others been dispatched to kill or capture Sylvia?

Suddenly in the distance, above the river, she saw a dot in the sky. It didn't fly erratically, like a bird. At an altitude of a few hundred feet it kept a straight course, coming up the river.

A drone!

Quickly Sylvia hustled to the nearest big tree and slid around behind it. Flattening herself on the ground, she brushed rain-soaked leaves and loose branches over her body.

Then she waited.

She dared not raise her head and peek—the drone's sensitive cameras could detect the slightest anomaly in the patterns of the landscape. Her heart beat fast in her chest. Her fingers gripped the muddy earth. She heard only the rustle of the wind in the trees and the cheery calls of songbirds. Then she heard another sound—a sinister whirring and the hum of motors. It approached and lingered. She held her breath and dared not even blink. Then the evil vibrations faded away.

She raised her head and listened intently. The sound was gone. She crept out of her hiding place behind the tree. She looked up and down the river. The drone was not in sight. But to stay on the banks of the river was too dangerous—if the wind picked up, shielding the sound of a drone, or if she were inattentive for even a moment, that drone, or another one, could catch her in its sights.

Clamoring through the rugged woods, keeping the river in view, she followed its banks eastward. The sun was high, and under its warm rays the trees and vegetation were drying. After crossing another tributary creek, she came to the first sign of civilization: an old barbed-wire fence, half collapsed and rusty. Made from wooden posts, it ran from the river straight into the woods and up a low hill, where it vanished in the underbrush. She crossed the fence and continued on until the woods ended and she came to a cleared field. Pausing at the edge of the woods, she surveyed the landscape. The field was about two or three acres in size, and had been recently mowed. It was dotted with trees. On the other side, the woods resumed. Clearly the field served no agricultural purpose; it was maintained by its owner simply to look nice, or perhaps as a habitat for native insect and animal species. Sylvia inhaled deeply, savoring the freshness of the damp grass and earth warming in the sun.

She turned and walked north along the edge of the field. The land rose at a gentle incline. She came to a line of blueberry bushes that marked the northern end of the field, beyond which was a green lawn, and then a house.

The house was an old wood-frame structure, painted plain pale yellow with white trim. Two stories tall it stood, topped with a peaked roof of green shingles. A big brick chimney anchored one end, and a porch closed the other.

Sylvia saw no people in or around the house. She made her way through the muddy path between the blueberry bushes and walked toward the house. Coming around the porch, she saw a car parked in the gravel driveway. It was an old Sun Motors model, called the Bluebird. The sight was startling because she hadn't seen a Sun Motors car since being kidnapped. Sylvia was particularly fond of the Bluebird, a sweet little family car with a perky profile. She hoped its presence was a good omen. She kept walking until she came to the front door of the house. It was painted blue, with a bronze pineapple for a knocker. She raised the knocker and gently tapped it against its striker. The percussive noise seemed too loud for the serene and bucolic environment.

She heard footsteps, and the door opened. An elderly man peered at her. His expression was cautious but kindly. "Yes? How may I help you?"

Sylvia took a deep breath and stood up straight. Her left hand was throbbing and her damp clothes were sticking to her. Her matted hair clung to her dirty face. She knew this man could either save her or cause her to be killed.

"I'm sorry to bother you," she heard herself say, "but I've escaped from Juliette Island."

His eyebrows furrowed and his gaze became piercing.

"When?" he asked.

"Last night, during the storm. My friend and I took a boat. They killed her. I survived." Despite her effort to put on a brave face, Sylvia felt tears well up in her eyes. "I'm sorry. I didn't mean to bother you." The tears trickled down her cheeks and she wiped them with her muddy sleeve. "I'm so sorry. I don't know where to go."

The man reached out his hand. "Quickly—come inside!" His touch was warm and comforting. Sylvia walked through the door. Her knees buckled, the room began to spin, and everything went dark.

She woke up. She was lying on a couch in a room. The ceiling overhead was white plaster with lots of little cracks. Her mouth was pasty and her hand hurt.

"Ah—there you are," said a man's voice.

She turned her head.

"Oh," she said in a faraway voice. "You're the man who opened the door. You live here."

"Yes, I do," he said, smiling. He reminded Sylvia of her grandfather, who had died long ago. "Here, have some water."

He helped her sit up, and offered her a glass of water. It was cool and refreshing.

"Thank you," she said.

"What's your name?"

"Sylvia Brand."

"Where are you from? I mean, originally."

"Detroit. I work at Sun Motors. Umm… who are you?"

"My name is Theodore Flowers. Doctor Theodore Flowers."

Sylvia recoiled. A doctor? Her brain rebelled and her soul became sickened.

"Oh, don't worry," he smiled as he reached to pat her hand. "I'm a regular doctor. No longer with the Medical Center."

"What do you mean, 'no longer with' the Medical Center?"

"I retired. I have nothing to do with them any more. I'll tell you all about it after you get cleaned up and have some breakfast. And I want to look at that hand. We don't want it to get infected. Come into the bathroom."

Sylvia stood up on stiff legs and followed Dr. Flowers. The cheery yellow walls and white tiled floor of the bathroom lifted her spirits. After he gently removed the bandage, he cleaned the open cut. Sylvia grimaced. "Sorry for the pain," he said, "but we've got to irrigate it. To properly close this wound, you need stitches. I can do it now." He left the room for a moment and returned with a medical bag. After giving her a local anesthetic, he stitched up the cut. "How did this happen?" he asked. She told him the story of the implant. He shook his head. "Barbaric. Absolutely criminal. It took quite a bit of courage to cut it out."

When he was finished stitching and applying a new bandage, he left her alone to take a shower. "My daughter comes to visit once in a while," he said at the bathroom door, "and for convenience she leaves some clothing here. You look to be the same size. Her bedroom is down the hall. Help yourself."

After Sylvia had found a pair of jeans and a sweatshirt, she went down to the kitchen, where Dr. Flowers was making scrambled eggs and toast. She sat down to eat, and with a cup of coffee he sat with her at the table.

Dr. Flowers told Sylvia that when the Industrial Council first established Juliette Island shortly after the Global Recession, he had been hired as a staff physician. The Council wanted to leverage the enormous potential of digital human data, and the idea of operating a remote island facility where scientists and their subjects could work without interruption was enormously appealing.

"At first, it was ethical and we did some good work," he said as he cradled his coffee mug. "But it wasn't long before the profit motive took over. The Medical Center began luring patients to the island under false pretenses. Then they started getting people who clearly didn't want to be there. The Industrial Council wrote legislation that President Deacon signed into law that gave them the right to enforce the fine print of their standard consent forms, which most people never read. This gave the Industrial Council the legal right to "re-assign"—that is, forcibly abduct—corporate employees who had valuable medical data, and send them to Juliette Island. I saw what was going on. It became almost like a concentration camp. And when they were done with you, suddenly you died during a routine procedure. I didn't do that— one of the other doctors did. It wasn't long before we figured out that any time an elderly patient was referred to Dr. Gladstone, they never came back. When I turned sixty-five, I put in for retirement. I had to get out."

"But you saw what was happening and you said nothing."

Dr. Flowers hung his head. He folded his hands in his lap and kneaded his fingers. "It's true. I remained silent. I let them do their dirty work. I thought, how can one person oppose their vast machine? If I protested, they would kill me. So I put a smile on my face and pretended everything was fine. It broke my heart to see what we were doing to perfectly ordinary, nice people. Surprisingly, some of the 'guests'—that's what we called them—adapted very well to their new environment. They liked being subjugated. But most people didn't like it. Some tried to escape. When they got caught they were either tossed in the cooler or, if they were deemed particularly recalcitrant, they were provided with a permanent Propofol vacation."

Sylvia looked around the comfortable living room with its patterned carpet and gold-framed paintings on the walls and marble fireplace surround. "You played your cards well," she said. "Today you are living here, in this lovely house, without a worry in the world."

"I made my choices," he said. "I have to live with them. Right now, at this moment, all that matters is that you need my help, and I'm going to give it to you." He looked at Sylvia the way a doctor looks at a patient. "You're pregnant, aren't you?"

Sylvia nodded. "Yes, I am."

He smiled. "So you and your child escaped together. After all that you've been through, there is hope. How far along are you?"

"Eight weeks, I think. I'm nervous because I was pregnant once before, and I had a miscarriage at ten weeks."

"Statistically, you're no more at risk than any other woman," smiled Dr. Flowers. He stood up. "Let's talk about your future. You cannot stay here—they will be searching for you. It is too dangerous. We need to get you to New Hudson as quickly as possible."

"New Hudson?"

Dr. Flowers laughed. "I'm amazed at how effectively the federal government and Facts News control the information doled out to our citizens. You didn't know the disorganized regions of the canaille had banded together to form New Hudson? This was a few years ago. And while President Deacon makes noise about going in there and taking over, he's never followed through. He knows a quagmire when he sees one! Now then—let's get you out of here."

Sylvia had no personal belongings other than some things belonging to Dr. Flower's daughter, so there was nothing to do except walk out to the car. Dr. Flowers opened the trunk of the Bluebird. "I'm sorry to say that until we clear the city limits of Winslow—the town you're in right now—you need to ride back here. I'm certain the Morta guards will stop me and question me. I can handle them as long as you're out of sight."

Having worked to acquire the parts from which the Sun Bluebird had been assembled, Sylvia was very familiar with the trunk of the car; but this professional familiarity did not prevent a wave of anxiety from surging through her. Dr. Flowers, seeing her stricken expression, said, "Please don't be afraid. If you feel claustrophobic, knock on the front panel. I will hear you, pull over, and pop the trunk to give you some air. Okay? Now please—we have not a moment to lose."

With her heart pounding, Sylvia climbed into the trunk. Laying on her side, she drew up her knees. "Okay," she said. "Close it."

The lid came down and Sylvia was plunged into darkness.

She heard and felt Dr. Flowers get in the car and start the engine. The car began to move. In the darkness, Sylvia tried to stay calm and comfortable, but while the trunk was carpeted the ride was rough. The car went faster and then slower, and then faster again.

Sylvia heard music. The doctor was playing a symphony. It sounded familiar—yes, it was Tchaikovsky's Swan Lake. The sweeping tones brought back memories of her childhood, when every year her mother would take her to the ballet. This was before the Global Depression, which had put the ballet company out of business. The music was soothing and allowed Sylvia to close her eyes and, at least for a while, forget her dire predicament.

The car came to a stop. The music ended. Sylvia waited in the dark. She was about to knock on the panel and implore Dr. Flowers to open the trunk when she heard talking.

"Who are you and what's your business?" said a distinctively genderless voice.

"Being a Morta autonomous humanoid operator fully plugged into the central database," replied Dr. Flowers, "you should already know who I am. But in case you can't pull up the data, my name is Dr. Theodore Flowers and I'm on my way to see a patient."

"We need to search your vehicle," said the Morta. "A fugitive is on the loose. She's considered extremely dangerous."

"I can assure you I have not seen any fugitives," said Dr. Flowers.

"We need for you to open the trunk."

Sylvia's blood ran cold. She held her breath and prepared for a bad end to her few hours of freedom.

She felt Dr. Flowers get out of the car. "Now you listen to me," he said sternly. "You know I spent twelve years working at the highest levels of the Medical Center. You should also know that despite having retired from active service, I remain personal friends with Dr. Peyton, the chair of the Medical Board. I'm sure he would be extremely displeased to learn that you have taken it upon yourself to question my loyalty and patriotism."

There was moment of silence. Inside the trunk of the car, Sylvia waited in darkness and suspense. She resolved that if the trunk were opened, she would fight back and make them kill her. To die today was better than to live as a prisoner tomorrow.

"Very well," said the Morta. "You may proceed."

She heard Dr. Flowers get back into the car, the door close, and the engine start. Then there was motion. They drove for a while—Sylvia had no idea how long—as Dr. Flowers played his classical music.

The car stopped. Dr. Flowers opened his door and got out. Then the trunk lid swung open. Sunlight flooded the cramped space as Sylvia slowly unfolded herself and unsteadily swung her legs onto the pavement. Blinking, she looked around. She saw nothing but a vast expanse of fields stretching out to a line of mountains in the distance.

"Where are we?"

"Outside the town of Chilliwack," replied Dr. Flowers. "On what used to be the old Trans-Canada Highway. This is the first place it was safe to stop, because we can see if anybody is coming long before they can see us. Stretch your legs for a minute, and then we'll get back on the road."

Sylvia stood in the afternoon brilliance and breathed deeply. High overhead in the cloudless sky, a hawk turned lazy circles. The only sound was the gentle rustle of the wind caressing endless acres of golden wheat stalks. "Where are we going?" she asked.

"The first friendly city is Banton. It's a ten-hour drive northeast of here. Crossing the border will be tricky—you'll have to get back in the trunk. But Banton is securely in the canaille. You'll be safe there."

"Do aberrants live there?"

Dr. Flowers laughed. "Aberrants? Yes, they do. I always thought that was a stupid expression. The Industrial Council invented the concept as part of its propaganda campaign. They want to make folks believe that anyone not living in the United Americas is somehow subhuman. It's just another tool of the dictatorship. Authoritarian states have been doing it since the dawn of time. You control your population by knowing everything about them, making them believe you're protecting them from a terrible enemy, and by identifying a class of people who are both 'bad' and are easy targets. President Deacon and the Industrial Council have done all three very effectively." He looked at his watch. "We'll drive for a few more hours and then stop and get something to eat. I know a safe restaurant where the patrols are rarely seen."

Dr. Flowers allowed Sylvia to ride with him in the front seat of the car. They drove through miles of farmland, seeing few other vehicles. The plains yielded to the Cascade Mountains, tall and rugged. Next to a crystal blue lake they stopped at the Timber Café, and after stepping over the threshold to make certain there were no police, Dr. Flowers signaled for Sylvia to come inside. When the bill came, Sylvia realized with horror she had no money except for her Juliette Island debit card, which was worthless.

"I think you'll do well for yourself," smiled Dr. Flowers. "This one's on me. When you can, I know you'll pay back the favor—perhaps by helping someone else in their time of need."

They drove on, winding their way through the Rocky Mountains, alongside spectacular gorges and over high bridges. The sun set, casting long purple shadows from the cold, craggy peaks. It was after dark when Dr. Flowers pulled over to the side of the road. He turned to Sylvia. "We're a few miles from the border with Banton. The police presence will intensify until we cross the last checkpoint near the river. For this final leg of our journey, I need you to get back into the trunk."

"I understand," replied Sylvia. She stepped out of the car and climbed into her familiar little prison. Dr. Flowers closed the lid. The car started up, and in the darkness Sylvia prayed the last few miles of her long journey would not be her last.

They drove for a while, and then the car slowed and came to a stop. From her hideaway, Sylvia strained to hear the conversation between Dr. Flowers and whoever was outside. Dr. Flowers said he was visiting a patient. The guard asked for the name of the patient. Dr. Flowers replied that it was confidential and a matter of doctor-patient privilege. The guard persisted. Suddenly the car accelerated, slamming her against the rear panel. She heard shouts, and then gunfire. With the force of a sledgehammer, a bullet punched a hole into the lid of the trunk inches above her head. The car careened and she felt it plunge downward. It landed with a splash. Within seconds Sylvia felt cold water trickling into the closed compartment. She screamed and pounded on the lid of the trunk. The water rose higher, soaking her clothes. Now it was encircling her head. She screamed and pounded. Suddenly the lid flew open and Dr. Flowers, standing in running water up to his chest, reached in and helped her out. Just as her legs cleared the lip of the opening, the car lurched in the shallow rapids and flipped over. In a moment it had been swept downstream. Fighting to keep her head above water, Sylvia held onto Dr. Flowers's hand as they fought to reach the opposite shore. When she thought she had no more strength and would be hurled against the rocks, her feet felt traction on the gravelly stream bed, and together they hauled themselves out of the torrent and onto dry land.

"You made it," breathed Dr. Flowers. "No more Juliette Island. You're in New Hudson. You're free."

CHAPTER THIRTY-ONE

"I'm happy, and very grateful," said Sylvia. "But what about you? You left your home! Your car is gone. What are you going to do?"

"I'm going to start over," said Dr. Flowers. "To be honest, since my wife passed away, living in that house all by myself became boring. I didn't want to leave because it seemed like too much effort. You can get into a rut, you know? The days go by, you do what you do, and suddenly you realize your life is in a holding pattern. So here I am! I cannot go back. Just like you, I need to start over. But we're not without resources. I've got some money and know a few people in New Hudson. Let's get started."

They got up and, in their wet clothes, walked up the embankment. When they reached the top they found themselves standing on the shoulder of a paved road. Dr. Flowers looked around. "That way," he pointed, "is north. About three miles from here, in a town called East Fork, there's a diner with rooms for rent on the second floor. It's been there since I was a kid. The same family has owned it for two generations. Let's go."

They started walking. The cool night air caressed Sylvia's cheek. The dark woods and fields made her feel protected, as if she belonged there. The moonless sky was ablaze with more stars than she had seen in years. Looking up in wonderment at their profusion and beauty, she thought about how far she had come, and how in the grand scheme of things her personal journey had been both miniscule and monumental, and that both descriptions were perfectly okay.

Eventually the lights of the Tip Top Diner came into view. As they approached, Sylvia looked at it with curiosity. It was not unlike any other roadside diner in the rural countryside outside of Detroit. The roof was a little bit saggy, the neon sign too bright, and the parking lot too weedy, but the place looked sturdy and inviting. She noticed the cars parked in the lot— they were older models, showing years of use, but presumably they got people where they needed to be.

"Ah—they haven't changed a thing!" said Dr. Flowers as he pulled open the front screen door. Inside, the space was divided between a bar where you could sit and a dining room with tables and booths. The customers—a mixed bunch of couples and singletons—regarded the damp newcomers with curiosity.

Dr. Flowers went to the counter. "Is Madge here?" he asked.

The girl turned her head and shouted, "Hey Madge, ya got a visitor!"

From the swinging kitchen door a woman emerged. When she saw Dr. Flowers her eyes lit up. "Teddy! This is an unexpected surprise! How are you?" She paused and looked at Dr. Flowers and Sylvia. "Have you and your friend been rolling in the mud? Of course it's none of my business, but…"

Dr. Flowers laughed. "Madge, this is Sylvia. I drove my car into the river a few miles down the road. We both got a bit waterlogged. The car's gone—swept downstream."

"How did you manage to do that?" asked Madge. "You're not drunk, are you?"

Dr. Flowers leaned closer. "No, Madge, I'm not drunk. We were escaping from the robo-cops. Sylvia is from Detroit, by way of Juliette Island. This morning she showed up at my house. I decided to drive her here."

Madge's eyes widened and she looked at Sylvia. "My child, you're from that awful island where they kill people for medical tests?"

"Yes. I was there for ten days. I couldn't take it—I had to get out. Some friends helped me escape. So did Dr. Flowers. I'm very fortunate."

"I want you both to go upstairs and get cleaned up," said Madge. She opened a drawer behind the counter, rummaged through it, and found a key. "This will let you into room number eight. Last one on the right at the top of the stairs. Then come back down and I'll give you something to eat."

Twenty minutes later, Sylvia and Dr. Flowers came downstairs and took seats at the bar.

"Now that you feel more comfortable," said Sylvia, "what can I get you? On the house. My treat."

"Madge," said Sylvia, "you're being very generous, but I don't want charity. I want to pay for what I get. I saw you have a help wanted sign in the window. I want you to hire me. I worked in restaurants all through college. I'll wash dishes, wait tables—whatever you need."

"Madge, I wouldn't argue with her," laughed Dr. Flowers. "She's a tough customer."

Madge agreed to give Sylvia a job. "You can start right now," she said. "But you can't work hungry, so you'll have your dinner first, and then I'll put you to work."

After they had eaten, Sylvia turned to Dr. Flowers. "I cannot thank you enough. You saved my life. But what are you going to do? You can't go back home."

"I own some property north of here, up in the lake country," he said. "I'll rent a car and go up there. I'm sure they could use a country doctor, and maybe I'll build a house by the water." He stood up. "Sylvia, it's been my very good fortune to meet you. I wish you the very best of luck."

She watched him walk out the door. Suddenly she felt very alone. She was a stranger in a small town, pregnant, friendless, and broke.

Madge put her arm around her. "Don't worry. You're one of us now. We take care of each other. Now let's get you started making some money."

Life at the Tip Top Diner was like going back to a world that Sylvia had forgotten once existed. The work was hard and the customers came in all shapes and sizes. Some were nice, some were brusque, and a few were just plain jerks. Madge was the same. Some days she was like a sister to Sylvia, while other days she was more like the Wicked Witch of the West. But she was relentless in taking care of her customers, and Sylvia knew at the end of the day when she counted her tips that Madge knew how to run a business. She did it without hidden cameras, GPS wristbands, or computers with screens through which your manager could talk to you. She did it without contracts and consent forms. She did it without management robots. If Sylvia had a problem, she knew she could go to Madge and at the very least get a fair hearing.

Physically, she never felt better. Despite the hard work, she never got the headaches and neck spasms to which she had become accustomed at Sun Motors. But the problem she could not solve was the fact that in just a few months her child would be born without a father. The brutal separation from Jason was a worm that ate at her heart during every waking moment. Madge knew this; every once in a while, when business was slow, she would catch Sylvia with that faraway sadness in her eyes, and come over and put her arm around her and say, "I know. I know."

One day a customer walked through the door—a middle-aged man wearing jeans and a leather jacket. He took a seat at the counter. Sylvia was in the kitchen, and she saw him through the window. As she was turning to go through the swinging doors and serve him, Madge grabbed her by the shoulders. "You stay here," she urgently whispered. "I'll take care of him. Don't go out there until he's gone."

Bewildered, Sylvia said, "Okay, I'll stay here in the kitchen and help out."

Madge pushed open the door and left the kitchen. As Sylvia went about her chores, every few minutes she glanced through the window. The man seemed perfectly ordinary. He ordered a cheeseburger, salad, and a beer. He seemed to be minding his own business. After a while, he paid his bill and left.

Madge came to the kitchen door. "The coast is clear," she said to Sylvia. "What was that all about?"

"He's a spy," said Madge, "from the Industrial Council. His job is to look for fugitives like you. Someone may have phoned in a tip, or he may have simply come here randomly."

"But isn't New Hudson a sovereign nation?"

Madge smiled. "On paper, yes. But in reality, no. The United Americas makes sure our government is very friendly to Washington. The canaille, as they call us, is a client state they use as a human dumping ground, or at least that's how they see it. It's been done before. Back in the eighteenth and nineteenth centuries, England shipped hundreds of thousands of convicts to Australia, where, despite the hardships inflicted upon them, they settled and began new lives. Today about twenty percent of the population of Australia can claim lineage from an English convict. Among the Aussies, it's become a badge of honor! The English—such nice people!—also sent fifty thousand convicts to colonial America. Many of them wound up working on tobacco plantations in Virginia, right alongside African slaves. The colony of Georgia, in the southern United Americas, was first founded by James Edward Oglethorpe as a debtor's colony populated by prisoners from English debtors' prisons. In the eighteenth century, France shipped thousands of convicts to Louisiana. And of course Russia used Siberia as a penal colony." Madge smiled and spread her arms. "Welcome to New Hudson, the land of the aberrants! We're the human jetsam thrown overboard by Washington. As for me, I'm descended from a family exiled right after the Global Depression. My parents were followers of a preacher named Isiah Gold. I'll admit he was a flaky guy—he rode around on a white horse. But by all accounts he was harmless. I have no idea what the problem was with the government—I mean, isn't the United Americas supposed to be the land of religious freedom? But they settled here and eventually opened this diner. And I'm still here today. I would never go back, even if I could. The United Americas has become a police state."

Madge took Sylvia into the back office, where there was an old computer on the desk. "I want to show you something," she said as she clicked through a series of windows. "Ah—here it is!" She swiveled the computer so Sylvia could see it.

"Oh my God—that's a photo of me!" she exclaimed. "What is this website?"

"It's called 'Counterspy.' It's our underground news service. Some smart guy figured out how to hack into Facts News, which gets local feeds by satellite from all over the country. This is the press release from Juliette Island stating you've escaped and for the good citizens of the Northwest Province to be on the lookout for you. Luckily Dr. Flowers got you across the border quickly. But you need to be careful—the UA police have long tentacles."

With her pregnancy advancing, Sylvia needed to find a prenatal healthcare provider. Madge asked her if she needed help in locating one, but Sylvia, beset by anxiety about doctors, kept putting it off. The last thing she wanted was to be re-immersed in the oppressive world of the Sun Motors Employee

Wellness Plan, not to mention the horrors of Juliette Island.

Madge came to her one day and said, "Sylvia, you're off duty the rest of the afternoon. Come with me. I'm going to take you to a doctor."

Despite Sylvia's protests, Madge got Sylvia into her car and drove her to the next town, where there was a clinic. Madge walked with Sylvia into the simple one-story building, where they were met by the receptionist, who gave Sylvia one of those ubiquitous clipboards with a sheaf of medical forms attached, and a pen on a string.

"No! I'm not doing this," said Sylvia as she turned to leave.

"These papers are different from what you're used to," said Marge, firmly taking her by the arm. "Here, let's review them together." They sat down in the waiting area and examined the forms one by one. The first page was an insurance from.

Sylvia went to the receptionist. "Does the Sun Motors Employee Wellness Plan work here?"

"No," she smiled, "but there's no need to worry. We'll get you signed up for New Hudson universal health care. It's free for everyone."

"What do you mean, free? Nothing's free."

"Corporate and personal taxes pay for it."

"Isn't that called socialism?"

The receptionist smiled at her. "Down in the UA they use that outdated term. That's because each person has been taught to believe the other guy is getting a better deal or is cheating the system. Therefore you need to screw him before he screws you. Up here in New Hudson, we call it 'neighbors taking care of neighbors.' Our system is built on trust, not suspicion."

Sylvia returned to her seat. There was a liability form. Lastly was a form that Sylvia didn't recognize. Attached to her medical history form was something called a Personal Health Data Release.

"This says," explained Madge, "that in regard to your health data, you have a choice. You may elect to keep all of your health data as your own personal property, not to be shared or sold at any price to any third party. In this case, your relationship to your doctor is the same as your relationship with your lawyer, who must take an oath to keep the details of your client-lawyer conversations absolutely confidential. This is a right only you can forfeit. No one can take it from you.

"Or, you may choose to lease your data for a price. If you choose this, you're placing your data on the market the same way you'd put your car or house on the market. From a reputable broker, you'll receive a fair price for your data. The system is tightly controlled and supported by blockchain technology."

"Blockchain?" said Sylvia. "I thought New Hudson was some sort of technological backwater."

Madge shook her head. "That's another myth spewed out by the United

Americas propaganda machine. Blockchain technology is the foundation of all of our contracts, both personal (like marriage) and business." She pointed to an apple in a bowl on the receptionist's desk. "We use blockchain to track and verify the journey of that apple from the orchard to the store. The beauty of blockchain contracts is that they require a low level of trust. Since every transaction is verified by the blockchain's public record, it's both safe and reliable. At this moment, you have a fair choice: you can keep your medical data private, or you can be paid what it's worth while a reputable company uses it for a clearly defined purpose."

"After what I've been through, I'd rather keep it private," said Sylvia as she signed the form.

"No problem," replied Madge. "If you ever change your mind, you can file a new form. The records of your choices will all be right there on the blockchain."

Sylvia met her new doctor, who examined her and said that she and her baby were both healthy. She left the clinic feeling as though a new day had dawned. No longer would she be a victim of an oppressive medical establishment that used her as a human research subject. She was in control now, and her self-image as a strong, independent woman began to blossom again.

Later that day, as Sylvia was cleaning tables at the diner, a man entered and sat down at the counter. She fetched a menu and was walking towards him when she stopped in her tracks.

The man was Randolph Meekin. He looked the same as the last time she had seen him on his final Friday afternoon at Sun Motors—well-fed and smug.

Taking a deep breath, Sylvia approached him. "Mr. Meekin, this is an unexpected pleasure," she said as she handed him the menu.

He looked at her and said, "Sylvia? Sylvia Brand? What the hell are you doing here?"

"It's a long story," she replied. "But here I am. What can I get for you?"

His eyes gave her the painfully familiar crude once-over. "Let me think about that for a minute. I gotta say, Sylvia, you are looking good! Better than ever. I'm amazed our paths have crossed out here in the middle of nowhere. I think it means something. Damn! We definitely need to get together. And you know what? It's going to be a lot easier for us now that we don't work together. Those rules about fraternization at Sun Motors were a nuisance." He broke out into a grin from ear to ear. "I swear, this is my lucky day! So tell me, where are you staying? You got a place around here? I live over in Red Hook. I work as a driver for a bread company. Make good money, too. Of course my wife lives there too, but we can figure out that little problem, right?" He winked at her and then stared at her with his greedy eyes.

At these words, Sylvia felt a volcano of anger rise up inside her. When she had worked under Meekin at Sun Motors she had suppressed her rage by sheer force of will, but now it was forcing its way into her consciousness, implacable and unstoppable.

She leaned close to Meekin and, parting her lips seductively, said, "Randy, this is your lucky day. I've got something special for you. Meet me behind the diner. I'll be waiting."

With those words and a warm smile she disappeared behind the door to the kitchen.

Sure enough, within a minute Meekin came around the corner of the building. With a lascivious grin he said, "I always thought you were playing hard to get! Maybe we were just in the wrong place at the wrong time." He put his arms around her and drew her close. She went along with the game.

"Say," she said, putting her hand on his chest, "I heard you were getting it on with Judy Loring. I don't know if I like that."

"Judy Loring? Are you kidding? I wouldn't go near her. She's crazy."

"Have you seen her?"

"Just once. She and that loser husband of hers live down in Rocky Falls. She works at an insurance company. But who cares? Right now I have you. C'mon, give me a kiss."

"I'm going to give you something I've wanted to give you for a long time," she whispered.

Randolph Meekin was bigger and stronger than Sylvia. She knew she had just one shot at him. It had to be right on target, or else she'd have a serious problem.

One shot.

With as much force and speed as she could muster, she slammed her right knee up into his crotch.

Meekin howled in pain. Eyes went glassy. Doubled over and fell to the grass. Legs twitching. Gasping for air.

Sylvia took a knife she had concealed in her pocket and held it in front of his nose. "If you show your face here again, I'm going to turn you from a bull into a steer. Then you can explain to your wife why you have a headache every night. Now get out of here."

Pocketing the knife, she went inside the restaurant.

Meekin did not return to his stool at the counter. She never saw him again.

The next day, Sylvia went into town and rented a car. She drove to Rocky Falls. It was a small town with a couple of gas stations, churches, and convenience stores. It didn't take her long to find an insurance office—John Quimbly Associates. She parked and went inside.

She found herself in one large room. Behind the service counter were a dozen desks. Seated at one of the desks, peering at a computer, was Judy Loring.

"Hey old friend," called Sylvia.

Judy looked up and gave a cry of joy. She ran to Sylvia and they embraced. "I can't believe it's you!" exclaimed Judy. "Did they exile you too? How long have you been here?"

Sylvia briefly told her story.

"Oh my God," said Judy, "we've all heard about Juliette Island. Horrible things! They say people who go there never come back. They use you and then they kill you. And you escaped! I cannot tell you how overjoyed I am to see you! Listen—you absolutely must come to our house for dinner. Tim and the kids would be thrilled to see you." Sylvia tried to demur, but Judy insisted, and Sylvia relented.

The Lorings lived in a small cabin next to a big apple orchard. At the dinner table, Judy said, "When they exile you, they literally drop you off on the sidewalk, give you a hundred dollars, and tell you to fend for yourself. So there we were, the four of us, wondering what we were going to do. We were hundreds of miles from home, we had next to nothing, and we didn't know a soul. But you know what? Throughout New Hudson there are networks of volunteers. They keep their eyes open for new arrivals. You can spot the exiles—they're the bewildered people standing by the side of the road, looking as if they've just dropped out of the sky. We were standing there when a woman approached us. Her name was Yvette. She befriended us, and put us in touch with Mr. Madrid, who owns this farm. This cabin was empty, and he let us have it."

"I'm so happy that you've managed to rebuild your lives," said Sylvia. "But you must dream of going back, right?"

Tim shrugged. "We're getting used to being here. The people are friendly, and while our life is not as glitzy as it used to be, in many ways it's better. We've seen just how much the UA government lies to its citizens. President Deacon acts like he's the savior of the nation, and the supposedly impending war with Rodinia is used to justify any number of abuses. The Industrial Council is driven by nothing but the profit motive, and they teach the people to be suspicious of each other. Technology is used to disenfranchise people, not uplift them. Here in New Hudson, we all have a shared set of values— simple things like honesty and fair play. And there are some very smart people here! When you create an environment where smart, educated people are viewed as the enemy, guess what? Eventually they leave. The woman who lives down the road from us is a computer scientist. She was so sickened by what the Industrial Council wanted her to do that she emigrated here."

"People come to New Hudson willingly?" asked Sylvia.

"The UA government will never admit it, but yes, they do," replied Judy. "They decide the United Americas isn't what it used to be, and all hope is lost, so they pack up and slip over the border."

Sylvia left their house that night resolved to contact Jason and urge him to emigrate to New Hudson. But how?

When she returned to the Tip Top Diner she asked Madge, "Who's the smart guy who runs Counterspy News and who hacked the Facts News satellite feed?"

The next day, Sylvia drove two hundred miles to the city of Hopewell. She went to an address Madge had found, and rang the bell on the door marked Lakelands LLC. A bearded man wearing glasses opened the door.

"Are you Neil Gormley?" she asked.

The man looked at her suspiciously, and then his expression changed to surprise and he said, "Wait a minute—I recognize you! You're the woman who escaped from Juliette Island." He glanced up and down the street. "Please—come in."

The office was small and crammed with computers. Sylvia sat on a metal folding chair.

After telling Gormley her story, she said, "I have a great favor to ask of you."

"I'll do my best to oblige," he replied as he pushed his glasses higher on his nose.

"Can you send an email to an address in Detroit?"

Gormley thought for a moment. "The firewalls set up by the UA government are extremely effective," he said. "But because many Two Hundred K companies are engaged in trade with firms in New Hudson, a limited amount of business-to-business communication is allowed. Is your email address at a company?"

"Yes. It's called Hilltop Financial. The person I need to contact is an employee named Jason Quin."

Gormley nodded and began to work at his computer keyboard. As he peered and pecked, the minutes ticked by. Sylvia began to lose hope. It was a stupid idea! Suddenly Gormley swiveled the computer on its base and showed Sylvia the screen. To her astonishment, she saw Jason, sitting at his desk!

Tears flooded her eyes. "I can't believe it," she said. "There he is! How did you do that?"

"Many companies have computer networks with old operating systems," shrugged Gormley. "They spend millions on perks for the firm's partners and brag about their cutting edge technology, and yet the computers sitting on their desks have operating systems that date back to before the Global Depression. I hacked into your husband's computer and took over the built-in camera. A fifth-grader could have done it."

"Can I talk to him?"

"No, but you can send him an email. Do not reference yourself directly, because his work account is being monitored by his Morta boss. Among the Two Hundred K companies, nearly all have blanket monitoring of employee communications. Nothing escapes their scrutiny. In addition, they may be watching him very closely because they know he's your husband. You must be extremely careful."

"Okay," she said. She typed an email:

"Dear Mr. Quin,

"I have heard about your company, and I would like to inquire about your financial services. Let me tell you a little bit about myself. Until recently I lived in Mexicantown, but two weeks ago I was relocated to the West Coast. I didn't like it there and have since taken up residence in the Northwest. I'm eight weeks pregnant, but unfortunately my husband, who is the child's father, has been separated from us. I confess I have very few assets: I suppose the most valuable is the diamond ring my husband gave me when he proposed. It was evening, and we were in a park, seated on a bench under a willow tree. He got down on one knee, just like in the movies. At that moment I knew I'd love him forever.

"Unfortunately I cannot travel to meet with you in person. I hope you make client visits. I live in a lovely apartment above a restaurant. If you ask around, you'll find me.

"Sincerely,

"Winifred Pearson."

"My mother's maiden name," said Sylvia as she clicked the "send" button. With the email on its way, they both watched Jason's face as he continued to work at his computer.

Minutes passed. Five, then ten. After fifteen minutes, Gormley said, "He's checking his email."

For a few seconds Jason showed no response. Then he suddenly peered intently at the screen. He seemed to be reading something intently. He looked around at the office before returning his gaze to the screen. A disbelieving smile flickered across his face. He typed.

His email response arrived:

"Dear Client,

"Thank you for contacting me. I'd be delighted to arrange a meeting so that we can discuss your future. While it's unfortunate that your husband was separated from you and your unborn child, I'm sure this terrible situation can, and will, be rectified as soon as possible.

"Sincerely, Jason Quin."

Then he put his palm flat against the screen of his computer. He held it there.

Sylvia did the same, and for a moment they stayed like that, electronically united over the miles.

SYLVIA BRAND

@richieetwaru

ABOUT THE AUTHOR

Richie Etwaru is the eldest of two brothers born in a rural farming village in Guyana, South America in the late 1970s to parents who were both schoolteachers. He was raised to believe that the most important ingredient of life is courage. Courage not mistaken with risk but consistent with the bravery required to embark upon something never attempted.

He has been quoted in NPR, The Wall Street Journal, The New York Times, The Financial Times, The Washington Post, Computer World, Forbes, VentureBeat, WIRED, and has appeared on dozens of television stations and media outlets globally. Richie is most known for founding the 31st Human Right: "everyone has the right to legal ownership of their inherent human data as property." He is driven to reshape the world by creating a new data economy, where inherent human data is legally human property.

Richie currently lives with his wife and two sons in the Northern mountains of New Jersey USA, where this novel was written during the summer of 2019.

Made in the
USA
Middletown, DE